The Identifying Fictions of Toni Morrison

The Identifying Fictions
of Toni Morrison

Modernist Authenticity and
Postmodern Blackness

John N. Duvall

palgrave

First published 2000 by
PALGRAVE™
175 Fifth Avenue, New York, N.Y. 10010 and
Houndmills, Basingstoke, Hampshire, England RG21 6XS.
Companies and representatives throughout the world.

PALGRAVE™ is the new global publishing imprint of St. Martin's Press LLC Scholarly and Reference Division and Palgrave Publishers Ltd (formerly Macmillan Press Ltd).

ISBN 0–312–23402–3 hardback

Library of Congress Cataloging-in-Publication Data
Duvall, John N. (John Noel), 1956-
The identifying fictions of Toni Morrison : modernist authenticity and postmodern blackness / John N. Duvall.
    p.   cm.
  Includes bibliographical references and index.
  ISBN 0–312–23402–3
  1. Morrison, Toni—Criticism and interpretation.   2. Afro-American women in literature.   3. Afro-Americans in literature.   4. Race in literature.   5. Modernism (Literature)—United States.   6. Postmodernism (Literature)—United States.   7. Women and literature—United States—History—20th century.   I. Title.
PS3563.O8749 Z616   2000
813'.54—dc21

00–055682

A catalogue record for this book is available from the British Library.

Design by Letra Libre, Inc.

First edition: December, 2000
10 9 8 7 6 5 4 3 2 1

Printed in the United States of America.

In memory of Noel H. Duvall (1908–1982)
With thanks to Jeannette B. Duvall

Contents

Acknowledgments

Anyone who writes knows that the largest fiction one operates under is the notion of the single-authored book. First and foremost I wish to thank the students from the three undergraduate sections of a course I developed on Toni Morrison at the University of Memphis from 1995 to 1997. These students' willingness to engage Morrison's ethically complex and aesthetically challenging fiction often had me furiously scribbling notes when I returned to my office after class. My deep appreciation goes out to my former colleagues at the University of Memphis—Theron Britt, Paul Naylor, Susan Scheckel, Jennifer Wagner-Lawlor, and Jeff Williams—who listened to me more than I deserved as I obsessively outlined and revised this project. Thanks also to my colleagues at Purdue, particularly Thomas Adler, William J. Palmer, Nancy Peterson, and Anne Fernald for their insights and support.

So much depends on the good will and interest of those who read and discuss one's work as it develops. A number of people valuably commented on portions of the manuscript at various stages of its production. Philip Weinstein read an early draft of chapter 1 and usefully reminded me about the inescapability of one's subject position. Patrick M. Murphy, Katherine Gunther Kodat, Theresa Towner, and Jerry Ward, Jr., also read portions of my manuscript and pointed out matters that allowed me to refine my thinking. Others, through their questions about or responses to my work, often led to significant revision. Most notable among that group are Carolyn Denard, Martin Kreiswirth, Barbara Williams Lewis, Richard Moreland, and Philip Page. Whatever the reader may find illuminating in what follows is in many instances undoubtedly due to the intelligence and good sense of the above-mentioned people. Any limitations or errors that remain are, of course, my sole responsibility.

A special thanks to John ("Chip") Elam, an attorney and my long-time friend from Columbus, Ohio, who provided valuable information about the location and status of Ohio birth certificates. To Kathy Schroth, my wife and most conscientious editor, thank you for forgiving me those days when the pleasures and pains of my text made me less than the ideal partner. Patrick, Margaret, and John S. often reminded me that there is more to my identity than being an English professor.

The Identifying Fictions of Toni Morrison grows out of my thinking about Morrison during the 1990s. Ideas from my contribution ("Toni Morrison and the Anxiety of Faulknerian Influence") to *Unflinching Gaze: Morrison and Faulkner Revisited* (University Press of Mississippi, 1997) edited by Carol Kolmerten, Stephen Ross, and Judith Wittenberg manifest themselves at various moments in this study. A note-length version of chapter 2 appeared in *Studies in American Fiction* 25.2 (1997). A portion of chapter 4 appeared as "Doe Hunting and Masculinity: *Go Down Moses* and *Song of Solomon*" in *Arizona Quarterly* 47.1 (1991). A slightly modified version of chapter 5 was published in *Contemporary Literature* 38.2 (1997). My thanks to all these editors for the opportunity to present my work and for permission to use this material here.

Chapter 1

Introductory Identifications:
Making It Up or Finding It?

I'm interested in characters who are lawless. [. . .] They make up
their lives, or they find out who they are.

—*Toni Morrison*

Insensitive white people cannot deal with black writing, but then
they cannot deal with their own literature either.

—*Toni Morrison*

As Kwame Anthony Appiah has noted, although contemporary scientific thinking largely disavows cultural notions of essential racial difference, race still matters because "races are like witches: however unreal witches are, *belief* in witches, like belief in races, has had—and in many communities continues to have profound consequences for human social life" (277). Having lived and taught for eleven years in Memphis, Tennessee, a city deeply divided by racial tensions, I am acquainted with the ways in which culturally scripted notions of racial essence still cast a palpable spell over the daily lives of individuals. So when on the first day of the semester I walked into my courses on Toni Morrison, there were immediate identifications. For a number of students, I was—because of my whiteness—the visible man.

This racial identification points to a difference between my students' and my own expectations and desires. Although composing nearly one-fifth of the student body at the University of Memphis, African-American students were scarce in the upper-division literature courses not specifically designated "African-American." When I taught one of the American literature surveys (despite a syllabus with a significant representation of African-American writers), I might have no black students—and never more than three—in a class of thirty-five. But in the Toni Morrison class, close to two-thirds of the students I addressed were black. For me, the difference represented an opportunity to help build a nascent African-American concentration in the English major.[1] But what was a welcome change for me—this racial mix—was not, at least in the initial moment of our meeting, as congenial to some of the African-American students, who hoped their professor would be black too.

I am aware that some of my study's biographically informed observations about Morrison's fiction will not be acceptable to all. There are those who believe that a white man is a double category mistake—as a white and as a man—and therefore can or should have nothing to say about a relationship between a black woman's life and her art. Such readers are, of course, free (like the one or two students who dropped my Morrison course) simply to set this book aside. Yet some of the personal connections that may discomfit certain readers were in fact precisely the material that legitimized me for the African-American students to whom I taught the fictions of Toni Morrison. By representing a Morrison who herself had experienced an uncertain sense of self and who was not always the empowered figure who appears on *60 Minutes* and the cover of *Time,* I was able to teach an author who was not a remote and unapproachable genius but someone whose youthful identity was a bit more like their own—fragile at times and definitely still under construction. Perhaps only by speaking of Morrison's life did I have the opportunity to question students about the construction of their inner eyes and become visible to them as not just a white man but as someone who cared deeply about the texts and their understanding of them.

What I attempt to do in this study is to see Morrison not only as a novelist who has written about history, but also as a historical figure in her own right. From this perspective, I argue that it does matter to her work that she grew up in pre-civil rights America, just as it matters that she became a writer in post-civil rights America. In locating Morrison historically, I turn to her personal history that manifests itself in all of her writing—her literary and social criticism, as well as her fiction. What results is a reflexive intertextual space: between her nonfictional self-representations (both in her criticism and in her interviews) and her novels that represent identity formation, there emerge curious traces of Morrison's own complicated becoming.

Part of that becoming resides in the names by which African Americans have been known. In the seventy years of her life, Morrison has been identified—whether by legal document or social custom—as "Negro," "colored," "Black," "Afro-American," and "African American." If public black identity has been fashioned and refashioned in each of the decades in which Morrison has written, it is hardly surprising that this phenomenon would manifest itself privately in an author intensely concerned with individual identity formation. Morrison's self-making manifests itself in a variety of forms: as a light-complexioned former black beauty pageant contestant who critiques hegemonic formulations of beauty; as a young woman who changed her name, yet whose fiction repeatedly explores the relation between naming and authenticity in the African-American community; as an avowed Catholic whose fiction questions the Word and posits the legitimacy of a variety of female (West African, Gnostic) spiritual possibilities; as an author who urges critics to read her work only within the context of the African-American aesthetic past, but whose thinking about the role of the novelist ranges over such white writers as Herman Melville, Mark Twain, Willa Cather, Virginia Woolf, Ernest Hemingway, and William Faulkner. By noting these things, I am not simplemindedly claiming that Morrison at times falls short of the ideals espoused in her writing or that her words are sometimes contradictory.[2] Rather, in all these areas of identity, one can trace Morrison's personal and professional implication in the things she critiques. Examining this implicated critique helps bring into focus the very cultural scripts of identity. A just and ethical critique of Morrison, I believe, should do no less than attempt to read these scripts, for it is what both her fiction and her literary and social criticism urge us to do by constantly reminding us that there is never a position outside of implication—including, of course, my own.

Although race neither can nor should disappear from my reflections on personal implication, my perceived need to explain my motives in these opening remarks at times may have less to do with race than with another delicate matter—reading for links between life and art in the work of a living author. I vividly recall a moment during a discussion session at the 1996 American Literature Association Conference titled "New Directions in Morrison Studies." A woman from the audience asked if anyone knew whether any biographically informed criticism was being done on Morrison. The response from the discussion leader was immediate and unequivocal—that, no, this was not the time for work that attempted to look for Morrison in her fiction. The reason given was simple and final: Toni Morrison is a private person and would not want such work published.

Yet this position leads to an odd situation vis-à-vis the quick and the dead. With an author conveniently dead, certain ethical considerations apparently drop out. For example, if one wishes to identify Herman Melville as, say, a wife beater, such analysis is welcomed by the best journals.[3] Certainly, being dead, Melville cannot be personally embarrassed or angered by such identifications. Yet neither can Melville answer to these representations. This makes me wonder if it is not perhaps at least as ethical to make certain speculative readings while the author is alive as it is to perform such speculation when the author will never have another (let alone the final) word on the matter. Taking the former tack at least allows the author—should she or he wish—the opportunity to intervene and tell a different story.

There are boundaries, I believe, to a biographically informed criticism of a living writer. For example, it would be inappropriate at present to posit the source of Morrison's depictions of black male-female relations as her failed marriage to Harold Morrison. Such speculation would likely produce reductive readings of Morrison's texts and would undoubtedly be personally hurtful to the author. And yet it is surely possible to imagine a critical landscape fifty years hence—when Morrison, I, and perhaps you also, gentle reader, are all dead—in which such analyses will proceed unabated.

The conference session on the future of Morrison studies noted above is just one of many instances in which I have experienced an uncanny sense of simultaneous similarity and difference—of being at home and not at home in Morrison studies. To explain what I mean, I would like to draw upon my earlier thinking about Faulkner and his emergence as a canonical figure. For me, then, the uncanny resides in certain resemblances between the study of Morrison in the 1990s and the study of Faulkner in the late 1950s and early 1960s, the historical instances when these two writers experienced their respective moments of canonization. Because this resemblance hinges on the issue of disciplinary boundaries within American literature, I believe the comparison to Faulkner studies will prove illuminating. What happened to Faulkner earlier is oddly mirrored in what is happening to Morrison now.

During the crucial period of Faulkner's canonization, roughly from his receiving the Nobel prize in 1950 through the early 1960s, certain borders were felt to be under siege by those working in the subdiscipline of Southern literature. Without gainsaying the work of the New York critics on Faulkner, many of the practices of academic Faulkner studies originated in a specifically Southern context, such as the work of Cleanth Brooks, an intellectual descendant of Southern Agrarianism. Another Southern critic who certainly was involved in the institutional mechanisms of disciplining Faulkner is James B. Meriwether. His essay, "Faulkner and the South," serves as an instance of what today we might call identity politics. This piece is particularly relevant to developing a parallel between Faulkner and Morrison studies, since it appeared in 1961 when Faulkner was still alive. Meriwether could argue against certain kinds of thinking about Faulkner on the grounds of "propriety"; Faulkner was a private person and critics should respect that privacy. But the reason this essay functions as an instance of identity politics is Meriwether's argument that Northern critics are not really capable of understanding Faulkner. The essay concludes by directing us to the aesthetic as the "proper perspective" to view Faulkner, which certainly relegates to marginality sociological, political, and psychological readings of Faulkner (160–61). All cultural contexts for examining Faulkner would drop out, all save the context of the South and Southern literature, which Meriwether, as a Southerner, was in the authoritative position to adjudicate. Essentially Brooks and Meriwether (as well as others like them) wanted to have their cake and eat it too; that is, they wanted Faulkner to be a fully canonical figure of American literature, but they also wanted to retain disciplinary control over what could be said about his fiction, using their position within Southern literature as a strategy of containment. In the long run, this strategy failed, and the Faulkner taught today bears fewer traces of such identity politics.

The current status of Morrison studies echoes that of Faulkner studies in the 1960s. It has been several years since she won the Nobel prize, and criticism on her work currently outpaces that of the Faulkner industry. Morrison's fiction appears not only in the *Norton Anthology of African American Literature* but also in the *Norton Anthology of American Literature,* surely a clear institutional sign of her work's canonical status. Once again, disciplinary boundaries are becoming unstable. Certainly much good work has been done placing Morrison in African-American contexts, emphasizing her fiction's relation to African-American folk tales or tracing her novel's refiguration of a black novelistic tradition. But when such work becomes prescriptive and argues that these are the only appropriate contexts for thinking about Morrison's work, then the situation recalls certain rhetorical gestures of Southern literary critics of the 1960s who wanted to retain exclusive possession of the meaning of William Faulkner's texts. But while I could feel virtuous in my Faulkner criticism (after all, I was trying to eradicate all traces of reactionary, segregationist Southern identity politics from my writing), when I try to take what I learned in Faulkner studies to the study of Morrison, something happens—the homey side of the uncanny suddenly turns unhomey and puts me outdoors, much as Cholly Breedlove puts his family outdoors.

Let me carry the parallel just a bit further. Faulkner made some appalling statements about race during the 1950s, statements that seem to run counter to his complex fictional representations of race from the 1930s. I in no way feel the need to be an apologist for Faulkner or to reproduce his racism in my criticism. In fact, I assume that my cultural function is to use Faulkner's racialized statements as an opportunity to think the issue of race further. But what can my stance be when Morrison says things about gender politics in the 1990s that seem at odds with her portrayal of gender issues in her fiction of the 1970s? For example, when she suggests in 1997 that women who appear publicly in sexually revealing ways are guilty of contributory negligence if they are raped ("Official" xxiii), am I permitted to note any disjunction between criticism and fiction?[4] To be a (white male) Morrison scholar, do I need to turn off my critical faculties? Must I embrace Morrison's implication that all young women should be impregnated by age sixteen so that they will have "no chance of getting any cancer of any of [their] reproductive organs" (Morales) in order to validate my membership in the Toni Morrison Society?[5] As a white man, my choice seems to be either to fully celebrate her words or to politely not mention them when they seem problematic. It's a dilemma because there is so very much I want to celebrate in her texts, but there are moments when celebration needs to give way to critical engagement, and that's when things get mighty uncomfortable.

Michael Awkward, whose book on intertextuality in African-American texts has been valuable to my study, has pointed out elsewhere that the investment white critics have in writing about black literature can never be the same as that of African-American critics. And so I attempt to interrogate my subject position as one not the object of racial oppression, yet this move itself turns out to be highly suspect: "Even in self-reflective white critical acts, racial privilege may create interpretive obstacles or, more importantly, points of resistance that color, in racially motivated ways—perhaps even hegemony-maintaining ways—the effects of an exploration of blackness. In other words, white reading can mean the adoption of a posture antithetical to Afro-Americanist interests" ("Negotiations" 583). I admit Awkward's point about the irreducible difference of my reading of Morrison but wonder whether he can ever imagine, with his implied distinction here, a discourse in which "different" does not equate with "antithetical." Am I doomed merely to ventriloquize the voice of the hegemony? Certainly the only authority to adjudicate the meaning of my difference—at least within the language game thus constituted—is Awkward or another African-American critic. But perhaps there may not be consensus on what constitutes reading that is antithetical to "Afro-Americanist interests."

In *Playing in the Dark: Whiteness and the Literary Imagination,* Morrison has pointed out the unfortunate consequences for literary criticism when critics, through "scholarly moeurs" and a mistaken "liberal gesture," fail to notice race, and so I ask to be allowed to risk the "adult discourse" she calls for (10). When I write about Morrison, I am unlikely to seek my own truest self reflected back to me from the pages of her text, which is in fact what many African-American Morrison critics do. Yet when Morrison critics seek to discover their own identity within the name "Toni Morrison," far from discovering personal authenticity, they occlude the very possibility for understanding the cultural authority that the novelist has constructed for herself.

The problem with identity politics as it emerges in Morrison studies (or the study of any writer for that matter, as I hope my comments on Faulkner studies have suggested) is that it creates an absolute hierarchy that determines the authority of a critic's interpretation in advance of the actual interpretation. A woman critic can tell me that she is better prepared to understand Morrison's oppression by patriarchal culture. An African-American man can say I know nothing of what it means to experience racism. But then the black woman can trump either of the previous two to claim that her experience more closely parallels that of the author and so she is better able to give voice to the meaning of Morrison's text. However, a black woman born into the working class can overtrump the African-American woman raised in the middle class and so on. To push such thinking might lead one to say that the best critic of Morrison would be an African-American woman born some time in the early 1930s in a working-class industrial town located somewhere on the Great Lakes. In fact, the absolute horizon of such a perspective must posit that the only critic who can truly understand Toni Morrison is Toni Morrison. Whatever is political in identity politics would dissolve into the literalized and tautological moment of identity. But we live too much in the age informed by Freud and Marx (not to mention their poststructuralist interpreters) to think that the author has an absolute understanding of her work. We admit that there are inevitably social and psychological blind spots that make the author an unreliable arbiter of the meaning of her texts. Moving back outward from the author to a larger set of readers, it is equally possible to say that there are also blind spots in other kinds of interpreters, no matter how many elements of their subject position that they share with the author. In other words, identity politics runs into a kind of can't-see-the-forest-for-the-trees folk logic. Being an African-American woman critic of Morrison may create obstacles as well as advantages to a reading of Morrison and does not ensure correct interpretation. One's ability to adequately unpack the ideological baggage of a text may be limited if the contexts allowed by one's subject position fail to recognize problematic aspects of that text.

The irony, then, is that while Morrison herself in her criticism has written of the dangers of fetishizing blackness, the critical commentary on her fiction frequently becomes complicit with that very fetishization. That such criticism does so, however, is not entirely without warrant, since there is a current in Morrison's work that encourages such reading. Early in her career, Morrison herself articulated this element when speaking about her characters, a description I use as the first epigraph of the chapter. In describing her focus on lawless characters she calls them the ones who "make up their lives" or "find out who they are" (Stepto 20). In this characterization, Morrison points to the productive tension that drives her work. In short, the latter notion—finding out who you are—suggests modernist authenticity, while the former—making up your identity—points us toward postmodern constructed blackness. Critics have been better at hearing the "finding out" strain than heeding the "making it up" side of the Morrison equation.[6]

Morrison's fiction can be read in two distinct phases. Phase one runs from her first novel, *The Bluest Eye,* through *Sula* and *Song of Solomon,* and culminates in *Tar Baby;* the second phase to date consists of her historical trilogy consisting of *Beloved, Jazz,* and *Paradise.* What characterizes the former is Morrison's construction of a useable identity as an African-American woman novelist; what characterizes the latter is the author's working out the implications that follow from the recognition that identity may be more a construction than a biological essence. I am not sure that the Morrison who wrote the first four novels would have used the phrase "construction of a useable identity" to describe her fictional project; in fact, if I were to substitute language more appropriate to that first phase, I might have written instead "discovery of an authentic identity."[7] But her work in the second phase suggests a more postmodern articulation of identity as a process plural and fluid. With the trilogy, she turns from the transfiguration of biographical material toward a new African-American historiography. While this formulation seems to chart a shift in Morrison's fiction from modern to postmodern representations of identity, the early novels' crucial self-reflexive work—the creation of a subject position from which Morrison can confidently speak—means that these fictions, even as they thematize authenticity, also can be read through the lens of postmodern identity formation.

Identifying Fictions focuses largely on the earlier phase of Morrison's fiction, though I will draw upon the later novels when they may be related to the earlier, self-reflexive stage of her writing. Because I see Morrison's early fiction involved in the process, at times conscious and at times perhaps unconscious, of creating useable identity, I will turn frequently to interviews she has given and to various published biographical sketches of the author for evidence. In some instances, this material allows me to speculate about links between her fiction and the characterizations she has made of herself; however, it is not my intention to privilege any particular assertion that she has made in these "nonfictional" moments. My quotation marks around the word "nonfictional" are purposeful. With Morrison's celebrity has come ever-increasing requests for self-representations, and she has been generous over the years with many interviewers. Although from interview to interview one can recognize certain familiar riffs, when Morrison is asked once again the same question that she has been asked numerous times before, the answers are not always identical. Invariably the subtext of an interviewer's question is "Who are you?" And so Morrison is asked five, and then fifteen, and then twenty-five years after the moment of her production, "What were you driving at in this character or this relationship or that novel's ending?" The process inevitably creates revision that cannot always be fully conscious. How could it be, given the spontaneous flow occasioned by the nature of interviews? How could there be an absolute identity between all her responses? And given this inevitable space of difference, how could the interviews, taken collectively, not in some sense be both autobiographical and fictional, a fiction of self-representation? To say this is not to single out Morrison for contradicting herself, since any famous person subjected to seemingly endless interviews will similarly produce such fictions of self. It's what the interviewer calls for. It's what the reader wants.

Philip Page recently has urged us to take deconstruction as an important context for reading Morrison's fiction.[8] Calling specifically on Jacques Derrida's concept of *différance,* Page sees an apt vocabulary for describing the work Morrison's fiction performs in deconstruction's inversions of hierarchies that are unstably based on the supposed temporal privilege of one term of an opposition over the other (4–6). Page further justifies his reading practice by noting the improvisational nature of Morrison's fiction, which allows him to draw parallels between jazz as a specifically African-American cultural expression and deconstructive strategies: "Like deconstruction, African-American musical forms challenge traditional notions of transcendent universals and bipolar oppositions" (16). I would only add that we might also take Page's deconstructive perspective to what Morrison says in interviews and in her literary and cultural criticism. Doing so may point us to Morrison's more complex relation to notions of transcendence. While her writing at times most definitely challenges certain "bipolar oppositions," those same oppositions may return to drive her fictional engines. As I have already suggested, the tension between identity as a biological essence and identity as a social construction is perhaps the central motivating opposition in her work. Following Roland Barthes's handwritten epigraph prefacing his autobiographical *Roland Barthes* that we should read what follows "as if spoken by a character in a novel," I suggest that Morrison's comments, both on herself and on her own and others' fictions, may be read as a series of suggestive pieces of character delineation that work intertextually to enable one to ask certain kinds of questions.[9]

My title, *Identifying Fictions,* resonates then with Barthes's directions to the reader. On the one hand, I mean that Morrison's first four novels, which overtly represent identity formation, serve as the writer's reflections on the fictions of identity. On the other hand, if we take the term "fiction" in its broader sense, there is also the critic's work of identifying the impersonal social fictions regarding race, gender, and class that produce subjectivity, even that of a brilliant and internationally famous novelist. This second order of fiction, what Louis Althusser termed ideology, may provide contexts for a better understanding of Morrison's novels as her own various acts of writerly self-creation. In this doubled space of fiction, there are numerous hints about the author's personal and private battle to move from consciousness to self-consciousness in order to get some purchase on culture's profoundly unconscious systems of representation that mediate the individual's existence. Through interviews, Morrison has provided a valuable record in the stories she has told about herself, including her memories of the processes of composition and the struggle she experienced in order to feel legitimate in claiming the designation "writer." To see Morrison's early fiction participating in her fashioning of a useable identity as an African-American woman novelist allows one to emphasize any one of the terms—"African-American," "woman," or "novelist"—so that one may think of this construction along racial, gendered, or aesthetic lines. But even this three-term formulation falls short of identifying the coordinates of Morrison's subjectivity inasmuch as the less visible dialectic of class almost always serves as a strong undercurrent informing her characters what they should think about the authenticity (or inauthenticity) of their racial identity.[10]

Even the most cursory outlines of Morrison biography suggest that class identity was at least as important as racial identity in the first quarter-century of her life. But noting this perhaps only draws attention to another kind of invisibility, since middle-class white America tends to conflate race and class, equating blackness, poverty, and crime. Morrison's characters frequently struggle in this space of collapsed race-class thinking, and her novels tell, in coded form, something about her simultaneous interrogation and construction of such multiple identities. In the opening chapter of *The Souls of Black Folk,* W. E. B. Du Bois early in the last century argued the case of African-American double-consciousness; black Americans, rather than experiencing themselves and the world as an "identity" (with its implications of wholeness, unity, and oneness), could only view the world in a doubled fashion since their sense of themselves as Americans was constantly undermined by the fact of being black. What I hope to suggest is that Morrison's dilemma, a very productive one, may be a tripled or quadrupled consciousness in which class and gender also significantly figure.

Morrison comes of age as a writer drafting *The Bluest Eye* from 1965 to 1969. In terms of racial identity, this means that she is squarely in the period of the "black is beautiful" movement (as Morrison herself has noted in the afterword of the Plume paperback edition of *The Bluest Eye*) that called on African Americans to rethink their relation to white culture. In terms of gendered identity, Morrison is clearly aware of the feminist challenge to masculinist culture, even though some of that awareness is expressed as a disavowal. And in terms of aesthetic identity, she comes of age during a period when high modernist fiction had become fully canonical and the 1960s' Black Aesthetic movement called for a distinctively black voice and a black nationalist identity. Whether acknowledged or not, these historical conditions necessarily must have marked an aspiring black woman novelist. Morrison in fact does at times acknowledge some of these conditions regarding her fictional foregrounding of the processes of identity formation. In order to examine these processes, I draw explicitly on Stephen Greenblatt's term from *Renaissance Self-Fashioning: From More to Shakespeare*. Greenblatt uses the term "self-fashioning" to describe "the power to impose a shape upon oneself" as "an aspect of the more general power to control identity" (1). He speaks of the homologous ways literature functions as a concrete historical embodiment—"as a manifestation of the concrete behavior of its particular author, as itself the expression of the codes by which behavior is shaped, and as a reflection upon those codes" (4). Self-fashioning, then, helps describe the development of Morrison's identity as she attempts to wrest a portion of freedom from necessity through her self-reflexive fictions of racialized thinking.

In certain instances I will speculate about the extent of self-portraiture one might see in Morrison's characters. To suggest that characters in an author's fiction represent aspects of that author is not to say anything new or startling. To write is to write the self. When one writes, one always tells, consciously or unconsciously, one's intellectual autobiography, and in novels, autobiography emerges most clearly through character, though certainly writers play themselves out through several characters. For a long time critics have acknowledged that in F. Scott Fitzgerald's *The Great Gatsby*, the portraits of James Gatz/Jay Gatsby and Nick Carraway depict different aspects of the author. Similarly, William Faulkner's art can be read as the transfiguration of biography. As Judith Wittenberg has argued: "Faulkner knew that his fiction was all about Faulkner. Like so many other writers, he 'was,' in one way or another, many of his characters, from Julian Lowe to Bayard Sartoris, Quentin Compson, and Lucius Priest. Their narratives told the continuing story of his life providing, as it were, a sounding board for his official biography, and even a kind of supplement to it" (5). And just as Wittenberg is able to point to statements Faulkner made that show his awareness of the autobiographical element in his fiction, one can find evidence from Morrison herself that supports a similar line of inquiry.

Morrison has commented explicitly on the role of African-American autobiography and the role it once played in constructing community. In "Rootedness: The Ancestor as Foundation," she is critical of the emphasis on the individual in contemporary African-American autobiography, but notes that "[t]he autobiographical form is classic in Black American or Afro-American literature because it provided an instance in which a writer could be representative, could say 'My single solitary and individual life is like the lives of the tribe; it differs in these specific ways, but it is a balanced life because it is both solitary and representative'" (339). She goes on to explain her decision to write novels in terms of what this expressive form does "for the class or group that wrote it" (340). Emphasizing the didactic and the informational role of the novel, Morrison argues that now is a crucial moment of need for the African-American novel, an expressive form that can do the cultural work of constituting the tribe previously done by African-American oral tales, music, and autobiography. Emphasizing the political purpose of the novel, Morrison concludes by saying, "I am not interested in indulging myself in some private closed exercise of my imagination that fulfills only the obligation of my personal dreams [. . .]" (344). The point again is that Morrison's novel writing does what good African-American autobiography previously did. In 1983 however, a year prior to the publication of "Rootedness," Morrison seems to foreclose any possibility of considering her life as a context for reading her work when she says flatly, "I don't use much autobiography in my writing. My life is uneventful. Writing has to do with the imagination" (Tate 166). Strikingly, in order to deny autobiography, Morrison valorizes the very exercise of imagination that she condemns in "Rootedness."

A third instance provides another perspective, one less extreme in what it avows and disavows. In 1981, Bessie W. Jones opens an interview by asking Morrison if her novels have "autobiographical elements." Morrison responds:

> It is difficult always for me and probably any writer to select those qualities that are genuinely autobiographical because part of what you are doing is re-doing the past as well as throwing it into relief, and what makes one write anyway is something in the past that is haunting, that is not explained or wasn't clear so that you are almost constantly rediscovering the past. (Jones and Vinson 171)

Morrison continues at some length to consider specific instances in *The Bluest Eye* and *Sula* that might be "genuinely autobiographical," but the implied distinction here is what I am interested in. Beyond the *genuinely autobiographical*—what she says about a specific detail, such as having heard of a woman named Hannah Peace as a child—seems to lie a broader category of how the author addresses those things from the past that haunt. This is, of course, an interesting characterization of writing from the author who would go on to write so compellingly about Sethe's haunting in *Beloved,* but here the comment linking the motivation for writing to being haunted by one's past points in another direction. Morrison appears to limit the autobiographical to exact correspondences of specific details, yet at the same time the author's obsession with revisiting the past suggests another realm of the writing of self. Supplementing the *genuinely autobiographical* is the *symbolically autobiographical,* since "what makes one write anyway" is the need to confront self. But here the supplement dwarfs that which is supplemented. Since Morrison casts this haunting past as the central rationale for writing, it would be difficult to mark anything in a fictional world that is not inflected in some way by this autobiographical reclamation.

Still, to read Morrison's work with an eye toward its autobiographical gestures may raise some objections because of the implied relation such interpretation has to a psychological approach and the notion of the unconscious. Traditionally, there has been reluctance among African-American critics to work with psychoanalytic frames of reference. Arnold Rampersad's essay, as well as the responses that follow it, in *Afro-American Literary Study in the 1990s,* rehearses some of the issues with which I am concerned. Rampersad, himself the author of a psychoanalytically informed biography of Langston Hughes, in a carefully worded piece acknowledges the dangers of deploying a eurocentric model for examining African-American texts. Still he calls for more psychoanalytically inflected biographical work on African-American authors. In an important sense, Claudia Tate in her recent study, *Psychoanalysis and Black Novels: Desire and the Protocols of Race,* has begun to answer Rampersad's call. Her psychoanalytically informed work, although focusing on African-American novelists who are less acknowledged in the canon of American literature than Morrison, points the way toward the work this study attempts.

Morrison grew up in Lorain, Ohio, during the 1930s and 40s. In these years, the primary coordinates of her identity were working class. Her father, George Wofford, was a blue-collar worker in the shipyards of this steel town. If we credit Morrison's 1992 account, the Lorain of her youth did not have a cohesive African-American community; growing up in this working-class town, Morrison experienced a youth and adolescence largely free of race consciousness. "I never absorbed racism," Morrison says, "I never took it in. That's why I wrote *The Bluest Eye,* to find out how it felt" (Bigsby 28). Morrison's account of her relation to *The Bluest Eye* invites speculation on how not only her first novel but also her subsequent fiction figures in a project of racial self-fashioning.[11]

Douglas Century's brief biography, although aimed at adolescent readers, is nevertheless interesting because of the photographs he reproduces from Morrison's high school yearbook. One repeatedly finds—among the white girls in plaid skirts and bobby socks—an attractive, light-skinned young woman, the only non-Caucasian involved in such activities as the yearbook staff and the student council. These images seem to underscore the characterization of Lorain quoted above and to reveal a youthful Morrison who was much closer in appearance to Maurine Peal than Pecola Breedlove. At the same time, in terms of class position, Morrison was closer to Pecola than Maureen.

When Morrison leaves Lorain for Washington, D.C., to attend Howard University, the working-class coordinates of her identity are confronted by the very different possibilities represented by an institution of the black middle class. Morrison has indicated that she did not like much of Howard's social life, which turned on skin color, and recalls a friend who was not asked out because of her dark coloration:

> She was the straight man to the pretty girls. I liked her a lot, but she had no dates, and wasn't popular. She didn't care, she had a boy back home whom she liked and eventually married. But during her senior year, her parents came to visit her. They turned out to be very wealthy, and, good God, she was overwhelmed. Suddenly all the dudes on campus, in their white jackets with their stethoscopes dangling out of their pockets, started coming around. They had a rush on that poor girl for the last six months. (De Witt C3)

This critique of Howard's colorism and classism is striking inasmuch as it underscores the examination of such prejudices within the black community that one repeatedly finds in Morrison's work. Yet her mature reflection on this situation in college elides the possible contradictions Morrison's younger self may have experienced. Whatever sense of injustice she might have felt (and clearly feels now), she was one of the light-complexioned "pretty girls," belonged to Alpha Kappa Alpha sorority, and at one time participated in a beauty pageant (Strouse 52). I do not wish to be mistaken here as criticizing Morrison, since people during their young adulthood often participate in activities that they later find suspect. What my discussion points to is that whatever cultural authority Morrison has achieved is not some discovered essence but rather a discursive production linked to her acts of writing.

As my subtitle, *Modernist Authenticity and Postmodern Blackness,* suggests, I am interested in identifying how critics might categorize Morrison's contemporary fiction, especially given the variety of ways that postmodernism has been defined. For me, Morrison's treatment of an individual's identity formation, especially as it occurs within a community, points to what is both modernist and postmodernist about her work. In terms of content, what she writes about, Morrison has a modernist concern for authenticity, similar to the concern for authenticity we see, for example, in Ernest Hemingway's *The Sun Also Rises.* Hemingway seeks a community that would authentically enact masculine identity for his wounded Jake Barnes; for Hemingway, Pamplona, Spain, is that site of authenticity. Similarly, Morrison's recurring explorations of alienated and wounded characters (such as Milkman Dead, Jadine Childs, and Sethe Garner) take place in the context of their search for a community that enacts authentic black identity. So that Morrison, like the modernists, holds out hope that somewhere out there, there's still a place where the alienated individual might discover authenticity.

In her critical work, such as "Unspeakable Things Unspoken" and *Playing in the Dark,* Morrison is committed to a thorough exploration of the construction of white identity. In particular, she takes canonical white writers' figuration of black otherness as crucial evidence for seeing whiteness as culturally constructed. In other words, there is no biological essence that makes an individual white. The message of Morrison's cultural constructionist position on whiteness is clear. When it comes to white identity, the very notion of authenticity is inauthentic. But although she demystifies whiteness, her relation to blackness is more complex and seems at times to hold out hope for both authenticity and essence, as her comments on the difference between white evil and African-American evil in a 1974 interview indicate: "I know instinctively that we [African-Americans] do not regard evil the same way as white people do. We have never done that. White people's reaction to something that is alien to them is to destroy it."("Conversation" 8). Morrison's "instinctive knowledge" (or a knowledge unmediated by culture) fairly directly essentializes race, and says, in effect, that by nature, white people's evil is worse—more evil—than that of blacks. My reader might object that it is unfair to look at something Morrison said fifteen years prior to her fully worked-through position on the construction of whiteness, so that it might be helpful to look also at what her 1985 comments on African-American irony suggest:

I can't really explain what makes the irony of Black people different from anybody else's, and maybe there isn't any, but in trying to write what I call Black literature which is not merely having Black people in or being Black

myself, there seems to be something distinctive and I can't put it into critical terms. I can simply recognize it as authentic. (Jones and Vinson 175)

But in claiming a distinctive black difference, essence in this instance
once again creeps into Morrison's thinking about race. And it does so in
a particularly modernist fashion. African-American authenticity is
something, this comment maintains, that exceeds the medium of language, and to attempt to speak of it in critical terms is to register the
epistemological limit of thinking race; one simply intuits authentic
African-American irony and literature, overleaping the epistemological
wall. In short, whiteness may be a construction, but blackness is at least
possibly an essence. This tension in thinking the category of race seems
almost to reintroduce an inverted version of "the fatal drop of black
blood," a concept long used in the United States (and particularly the
South) to enforce notions of white racial purity and to designate the
impurity of black blood. But while black blood may have been viewed
as impure, it certainly was powerful, since any trace of it could over-
whelm all other genetic material. Morrison's comments on evil and
irony seem to play on (and perhaps reverse) the implications of the fatal
drop by suggesting that access to black authenticity is potentially available to the individual no matter how much or how little African genetic
material a particular African American has. In effect, the fatal drop of
black blood becomes the sacred drop. This notion of the sacred drop of
black blood is something Morrison's fiction does not thoroughly over-
turn until her most recent novel, *Paradise,* where black racial purity becomes as problem-ridden as dreams of white racial purity.

Conservative critics of identity politics tend to overlook that much of
white culture itself is already a powerful form of identity politics, so that
for someone, such as Morrison, to assert a black essence as something positive serves as a useful moment of reversal that disrupts the way white culture positively marks its sense of its whiteness while stigmatizing black
difference.[12] But this kind of epistemological affirmative action has its limits.[13] Statements that postulate the essential difference between white and
black evil or white and black irony still privilege nature over culture; such
statements therefore exist in a continuum with essentializing racist statements that say that "blacks naturally have rhythm," which is a metonymy
for the racist notion that African-Americans have body but not intellect. I
do not think that Morrison's work ultimately confirms a racial essentialism, but such essentialism at times comes into play, particularly in her earlier novels. It is perhaps Morrison's enactment of a dialogue between
identity as essence and identity as construction that makes her fiction as
powerful and poignant as it is.

If Morrison's content recalls modernist concern with authenticity, her techniques, particularly in her more recent novels, suggest certain postmodern fictional practices. To invoke the postmodern, however, is problematic because of the various ways it is defined. Through the 1980s, a standard view on postmodern fiction saw it as the work of white, male experimental writers, primarily from the 1960s and 70s, a definition that confined the category "postmodern fiction" to a set of highly aestheticized novels that produced very limited political engagement. A broader and potentially more political view of postmodern fiction, and one closer to what I mean by Morrison's postmodernism, can be found in Linda Hutcheon's work. In Hutcheon's poetics, the postmodern novel is "historiographic metafiction" (*Poetics* 5). This term blends the reflexivity of metafiction—fiction that calls attention to its own production as fiction—with a post-stucturalist historiography that recognizes that all attempts to construe the past are interpretive. For Hutcheon, the techniques of historiographic metafiction function in the service of a poststructuralist critique of hierarchy, which in turn drives poststructuralism's questioning of unified subjectivity and identity.

Thus, in Hutcheon's scheme, Morrison is a postmodernist.[14] The novelist's use of history, however, does not unambiguously embrace a postmodern questioning of subjectivity. That is to say, her fiction does not detail the disintegration of identity and subjectivity that occurs in characters such as Todd Andrews in John Barth's *The Floating Opera,* or Oedipa Maas in Thomas Pynchon's *The Crying of Lot 49,* or Jack Gladney in Don DeLillo's *White Noise.* Rather, Morrison's modernist concern for authenticity complicates Hutcheon's postmodern poetics of fiction. So that despite the formal experimentation in her work (indeed a number of these experiments resonate more fully with a modernist poetics), Morrison is hard to classify as a mainstream postmodernist. If, however, we modify Hutcheon's postmodern poetics with bell hooks's thinking on the problematic relation between African-American writing and postmodernism from her 1990 essay, "Postmodern Blackness," we may begin to articulate what is postmodern about Morrison's fiction. Although hooks acknowledges a value in engaging the anti-essentialist impulse of postmodernism on matters of subjectivity and identity, she nevertheless takes seriously the African-American wariness toward postmodernism. Writing from a marginalized position means that it is more difficult to embrace the denial of hierarchies that is the basis of the postmodern critique of subjectivity and identity. There is something disturbing, hooks notes, for African Americans to work from premises that seem to deny the validity of identity politics: "Yeah," her imaginary black critic says to the white one: "it's easy to give up identity when you got one" (28).

What hooks finally advocates is a cautious deployment of postmodern suspicion. In Morrison, then, we have a modernism partially postmodernized in terms very similar to the cautious engagement that hooks has mapped as the way for African-American writers to think about the postmodern challenge to essence. Morrison works in the space between a modernist desire for authentic identity and a postmodern understanding of the constructedness of all identity. My sense of Morrison's work is that, precisely because her project of establishing a useable identity in her first four novels is so successful, in her more recent work she is able to entertain the possibility of, if not exactly giving up that identity, at least interrogating it more thoroughly. And the way she does this is through a writing practice that may have as much to do with postcolonialism as it does with postmodernism. This is another reason why, whatever questions one may have about Hutcheon's insistence upon an identity between postmodern aesthetics and politics, her multicultural and gender-balanced version of postmodern fiction allows for a bridge between the "posts" of postmodernism and postcolonialism, and certainly helps describe a trend in Morrison's work from *Beloved* to the present.[15]

Morrison herself signals that postcolonialism may be one lens through which to view her work. In her 1988 lecture "Unspeakable Things Unspoken," she refers to a foundational text of postcolonial studies, Edward Said's *Orientalism*. Her reading of Herman Melville's *Moby-Dick,* which sees Melville—through Ahab—as a traitor to the cultural construction of whiteness, clearly points the way to her thinking in *Playing in the Dark*. Following Said, who sees the British construction of "oriental" colonial identity as revealing more about British conceptions of self and nation than about colonial identity, Morrison reads for the Africanist presence in canonical American literature to argue that the figuration of blackness is really about the construction of white identity.[16]

A major impetus for what this study attempts in fact derives from the criticial project Morrison articulates in *Playing in the Dark,* a project that lends support to an autobiographically informed criticism. The central authorizing claim she makes for her critical voice is that, from the perspective of "a writer reading,"

the subject of the dream is the dreamer. The fabrication of an Africanist persona is reflexive; an extraordinary meditation on the self; a powerful exploration of the fears and desires that reside in the writerly conscious. It is an astonishing revelation of longing, or terror, of perplexity, of shame, of magnanimity. It requires hard work *not* to see this" (*Playing* 17).

Morrison figures the relation between novelist and novel in decidedly psychoanalytic terms—"the subject of the dream [the narrative] is the
dreamer [the narrative's producer]." If Morrison's own protocol for interpretation rests in the belief that novel writing is inevitably a record of the
novelist's "fears and desires," how does Morrison's fiction look if we use
her insight reflexively as a way to think about her own novelistic dreaming? Might not her fiction also record these figuratively coded moments of
longing and terror, perplexity and shame? The reason that reading Morrison the novelist through Morrison the critic is a compelling strategy is
suggested by her own fictional representation of difference within the
African-American community. In this representational space, colorism—
prejudice within the black community that is based on skin color—mirrors the destructive power of white racism. In *The Bluest Eye,* the
light-complexioned Geraldine teaches her son this difference within difference: "his mother did not like him to play with niggers. She had explained to him the difference between colored people and niggers. They
were easily identifiable. Colored people were neat and quiet; niggers were
loud and dirty" (87). And by the end of her son's encounter with Pecola,
Geraldine on the basis of her racial thinking has identified the child as a
"nasty little black bitch" (92). To be an American for Morrison is to talk
and write about oneself "through and within a sometime allegorical,
sometimes metaphorical, but always choked representation of an Africanist presence" (*Playing* 17). As her fiction repeatedly demonstrates, African-
American subjectivity is shaped by the dominant American ideology. If
Morrison powerfully reads the figuration of blackness in the work of
canonical American novelists, how might this canonical African-American
novelist use blackness in the construction of her own identity? I argue in
the following chapters that blackness is as much a figurative space in Morrison's writing as it is in Cather's, Hemingway's, or Poe's. This does not
mean that the ends of their uses of blackness is identical, since Morrison
struggles always to move from consciousness to self-consciousness, while
white writers in their representations of race largely remain innocent of
this motivation.

If we read reflexively Morrison's understanding of the way the dominant culture colonizes African-American identity, then a striking instance
of such discursively produced identity becomes Morrison's decision to
change her name from "Chloe" to "Toni." Although Morrison has said that
she made the change because people at Howard University found "Chloe"
too difficult to pronounce, the question of motive, as I scrutinize in my discussion of *The Bluest Eye,* seems more fraught than this explanation admits.
Whatever the exact motivation for Morrison's decision to become Toni,

one thing is clear: the question of identity is not a given for Morrison because she rejects her given name. Moreover, she repeatedly refers to this act of self-naming in coded, yet fairly overt ways, creating the paradox of the thing that wants simultaneously to be concealed and revealed.

Chapter 2 reads Morrison's self-naming through the connections she herself makes in her first novel to Ralph Ellison. In addition to coded references to *Invisible Man, The Bluest Eye* activates Ellison's 1964 essay, "Hidden Name and Complex Fate," as a more covert intertext, suggesting the complex relation Morrison has to Ellison's literary project. This link between Morrison and Ellison suggests a bridge between the autobiographical impulse and intertextuality. If to write is to write the self, then another aspect of fiction as intellectual autobiography may be found in the explicit intertexts that a novel engages. Although intertextuality in its broadest, poststructuralist form makes it legitimate to hold any cultural text against another, I am particularly interested in the intertexts that Morrison seems consciously to deploy for deliberate effect. If, for example, there are unmistakable allusions in her titles *Song of Solomon* and *Tar Baby,* then her novels in other more coded ways always direct the reader to the fictions of previous novelists. To say that other writers obliquely speak through Morrison's novels is not simply to seek sources or to privilege the model of influence; rather, what I hope to suggest is the way Morrison's novels engage in a critical dialogue with modernism that participates in her fashioning of an artistic identity.

The subject of Morrison's aesthetic self-creation continues in chapter 3, where I take up *Sula* and its title character as an exploration of the artist manqué. Although not signaled as directly as Ellison is in Morrison's first novel (where *Invisible Man* is at one moment quoted without quotation marks), Virginia Woolf functions as the textual unconscious of *Sula.* The same-sex friendship of Sula and Nel, as well as the relation between two pariahs—Sula, the artist who lacks a form, and Shadrack, who substitutes ritual for art—serves as a variation on the relation between Pecola, Soaphead, and Claudia, one that points to the collapsing space of textual and sexual desire.

Contextualizing the Claudia-Chloe-Church matrix through the self-fashioning represented by the masculine-feminine poles of the artists manqué, Shadrack and Sula allows us to see the twinned relationship between the protagonists of Morrison's next two novels, *Song of Solomon* and *Tar Baby.* Milkman Dead and Jadine Childs, although operating in these two different novels, are similarly twinned and mirroring figurations of authorial self-fashioning.

In chapter 4, I examine *Song of Solomon* as Morrison's further meditation on both the racial and the artistic self. On the one hand, the novel fairly directly draws on Morrison's maternal family history of their migration from the South, so that Milkman's quest for authentic identity points to the author's. This is heavily underscored by Morrison's beginning *Song of Solomon* on her date of birth, February 18, 1931. On the other hand, Morrison's third novel also suggests her engagement with another modernist figure. In *The Bluest Eye,* Morrison reclaims Ellison's modernism; in *Song of Solomon,* she begins a sustained fictive critique of William Faulkner's major fiction. Against the overtly signaled biblical intertext, Faulkner's *Go Down, Moses* serves as the more coded intertext, providing a different purchase on her portrait of the artist as a young man. Indeed, Milkman Dead continues a kind of masculine figuration of artistic potential previously embodied by Soaphead Church and Shadrack. The two artist figures from Morrison's earlier novels have already made minimal gestures toward a writing of self, but Milkman's act of interpretation—his ability to read correctly his family's genealogy in the song the children of Shalimar sing—also prepares the ground for self-knowledge.

Chapter 5 turns to *Tar Baby,* a novel that largely completes even as it begins to problematize Morrison's construction of a useable identity. Had her career ended in 1977 with *Song of Solomon* and Milkman Dead's triumphant discovery of an all-black agrarian community, Shalimar, Virginia, then the existentialist implications of "authentic" identity would be correct. That novel suggests that Milkman is able to slough off his inauthentic self—urban (or perhaps "suburban") and identified with the white middle class—for an authentic enactment of self with the men of Shalimar. It is as if the black community, lost in *Sula,* has been recovered in *Song of Solomon.* But *Tar Baby,* even as it completes the first phase, already points the way to the second phase in one important regard; namely, it shows that Morrison's fiction dialectically overturns the syntheses of her previous fiction. One way the novel does so is by rethinking the relation between race and class to entertain the notion that black identity need not be linked to black poverty. In her first three novels, the possibilities of black authenticity lie squarely in economically distressed African-American communities. In *The Bluest Eye,* the light-skinned, middle-class Maureen and Geraldine are demonized, and if the Breedloves fall victim to a culturally scripted racial self-loathing, the working-class MacTeer family nevertheless embodies the African-American ideal. In *Sula,* once again the middle-class pretensions of Helene Wright are marked as inauthentic; moreover the novel concludes on a decidedly nostalgic note, suggesting that what has been lost in the pre-civil rights community of the Bottom cannot be compensated for by new economic opportunities available to African-Americans in 1965. And *Song of Solomon* unwaveringly locates black authenticity in the racially pure, impoverished rural community of Shalimar, Virginia. In this regard, *Tar Baby's* Eloe,

Florida, comments critically on Shalimar as the site of authentic identity. By doing so, Eloe points the way toward Morrison's consideration of black communities in post–Civil War Cincinnati, in 1920s Harlem, and in Ruby, Oklahoma, of the 1950s through the 1970s. In addition to its critique of agrarian community, *Tar Baby* also may be thought of as participating in Morrison's intertextual engagements with both black and white modernism, which I stress in the earlier chapters. If her earlier fiction refigures Ellison, Woolf, and Faulkner, then Morrison in *Tar Baby* refashions her earlier self, the modernist Morrison of *Song of Solomon*.[17]

In her more recent trilogy, Morrison has attempted a kind of revisionist African-American historiography, and so seems not to be as interested in allegorizing her struggle to become an author. A reason for this is that by the time she has written *Tar Baby*, Morrison has authorized herself. But even though such coded self-representation no longer dominates her later fiction, my final chapter examines various moments in *Beloved, Jazz,* and *Paradise* that nevertheless revisit the metafictional, reflexive, and autobiographical turn. Morrison's work of self-fashioning, though more of a background matter, continues in her delineation of Baby Suggs, the narrator of *Jazz,* and Patricia Best, characters that figure the possibilities of artistic production—both its joys and its discontents.

My introductory identifications are largely done, now that the chapters that follow have been mapped. Yet I spoke earlier of my own personal and professional implication and feel compelled to move, however awkwardly, toward the personal, at least as I know it. If you are the kind of reader—black or white—with little patience for a white male critic's attempt to finesse his subject position in order to constitute some authority to speak about the work of an African-American writer, you may jump ahead now to my reading of Morrison's fiction that begins in chapter 2. I promise to be brief, but Morrison's assertion, which I used as the second epigraph to this chapter, "[i]nsensitive white people cannot deal with black writing" (Tate 160), seems to call for some comment from the white critic. Although sensitivity itself may be simply a necessary but insufficient quality for the white reader of African-American writing, what might constitute my potential to listen to Morrison's texts?

If I speculate, as I have done in previous work, on the gender trouble figured forth by Faulkner's interest in the aesthetics of homosexual artists such as Oscar Wilde and Aubrey Beardsley, or wonder whether Faulkner's fictional representations of masculine identity (such as his fictional claim to have been an RAF pilot shot down in France during WWI) serve as a cover for what he feared might be perceived as the feminine vocation of writing, don't these very topics immediately work reflexively? If I wonder about Faulkner's fascination with Wilde, is not my identity in part shaped by my fascination with Faulkner's fascination? I recall a time that my mother drove several hundred miles to visit me while I was writing my dissertation. One morning she emerged from my combination study/bedroom holding a picture of William Faulkner. "What," she demanded, "is this picture of a man doing in your bedroom?" I assured her that she had not discovered a new aspect of my identity and that, at any rate, the man was dead. Despite the humor of the misunderstanding, her question perhaps gets at a certain kind of truth regarding textual pleasure: (my interest in) Faulkner, as well as (in) Morrison, speaks my difference. Spending countless hours reading and rereading the texts of these authors is simply not what "normal" people do. And I admit that my very act of noting the implicating reflexivity in Morrison's writing (that her criticism's examination of figurative blackness provides a context for reading her fiction) inevitability implicates me. I too am playing in the dark, using figurations of Morrison's relation to blackness to construct my identity as a writer of literary criticism. How could I not be? But does this admission mean simply that I am inauthentic to the task of examining Morrison?

One generation removed from the farm, the first in my family to graduate from college, I'd have to say that I seldom experienced identity as a given. Although we lived in an upper-middle-class suburb of Columbus, Ohio, we did not exactly dovetail in terms of class. We had the "economic" but not the "socio" to fit the socioeconomic profile. For the 40-some years that she lived in that neighborhood, my mother held a grudge against our next-door neighbor for a statement that came to her in the gossip chain: "The Duvalls don't have the education to live on this street." You may imagine that I have heard my mother recall the statement more than once. And what's in a name? I know I didn't like mine very much as a child, being a Duvall in an age long before anyone had ever heard of the actors Robert or Shelley. It didn't seem like a name anyone else—other than family—had. What is for me the primal scene of the name occurred when I entered first grade. The teacher went through the roster, reading names and asking the children to say something about themselves. When she got to me, she asked me how to pronounce "Duvall." I paused . . . and had to admit that I wasn't sure. And for a reason that I could not have articulated then, but that seems clear now. My relatives from the country all pronounced the name with the accent very decidedly on the first syllable, but those living in town had shifted the accent to the second syllable. I can still hear my country-bred father, a car insurance salesman, answering the phone, "DU-vall talking," but my mother identified us as "Du-VALL." And what of the child left unable to identify the correct pronunciation of his name? Let's just say that humiliating laughter is not the ideal way to enter the scene of instruction. In case you're wondering, I now accent the second syllable. So if I turn in this study to the fragility of identity that resides in names, wonder ye then at the fiery hunt?

Let me hasten to add that invoking my own sense of difference arising from my name does not mean I am trying to essentialize all forms of difference in order to claim some universal and transcendent access to Morrison's representation of black difference. I don't for a minute think that my personal sense or memories of ex-centricity are equal to the oppression of African Americans who struggle under the representational weight of a massive ideological apparatus that continues to relegate them to second-class status. But just as Morrison has commented that she could read Tolstoy and Joyce even though they were not written for "a little colored girl in Lorain, Ohio" (LeClair 124), I want to ask the reader to imagine that, even though I know that I am not a member of the audience for whom she writes, the fictions of Toni Morrison might nevertheless speak to a big white guy from Columbus, Ohio.

Chapter 2

Invisible Name and Complex
Authority in *The Bluest Eye:*
Morrison's Covert Letter to Ralph Ellison

Well, as you must suspect, all of this speculation on the matter of
names has a purpose, and now, because it is tied up so ironically with
my own experiences as a writer, I must turn to my own name.

—*Ralph Ellison, "Hidden Name and Complex Fate"*

I am really Chloe Anthony Wofford. That's who I am. I have been
writing under this other person's name.

—*Toni Morrison*

In a 1981 interview, Charles Ruas, in questioning Toni Morrison about
The Bluest Eye, asked her to comment on her relation to "the great
black novelists of the past." She responded:

I was preoccupied with books by black people that approached the subject
[the African-American girl], but I always missed some intimacy, some direction, some voice. Ralph Ellison and Richard Wright—all of whose books I
admire enormously—I didn't feel were telling *me* something. I thought they
were saying something about *it* or *us* that revealed something about *us* to
you, to others, to white people, to men. (96)

Although Morrison downplays the impact of Wright and Ellison on her
conception of *The Bluest Eye,* I wish to excavate the hidden and complex

ways her first novel creates—even as it challenges—Ellison as a precursor.[1] In addition to working as an intertextual critique of Ellison's masculine perspective, *The Bluest Eye* also participates in Morrison's fashioning of herself as an African-American woman novelist, a function perhaps not surprising given her characterization of herself during the time she was writing her first novel. Her various comments about this time of production constructs a paradox suggesting that *The Bluest Eye* was written but had no writer. Part of this story of becoming a writer is straightforward enough. When she first put pen to page, writing was the supplemental activity she engaged in only after performing her paid daytime role as an editor and her evening role as a single parent. Morrison has told this story in many forms, but the version she generates in 1985 seems a good place to begin because it succinctly represents a particular identity issue:

> I took forever to write that first book: almost five years for just a little book. Because I liked doing it so much, I would just do a little bit, you know, and think about that. I was a textbook editor at that time. I was not even trying to be a writer, and I didn't let anybody know that I was writing this book because I thought they would fire me, which they would have. [. . .] But that's why I was very quiet about writing. I don't know what made me write it. I think I just wanted to finish the story so that I could have a good time reading it. But the process was what made me think that I should do it again, and I knew that that was the way I wanted to live. I felt very coherent when I was writing that book. But I still didn't call myself a writer. And it was only after my third book, *Song of Solomon,* that I finally said [. . .] "this is what I do." ("Faulkner" 301)

A couple of things seem worth highlighting here. First is the issue of the coherence, which refers to her sense of self and identity; coherence resides solely in the writing process and is not prior to or outside of writing. The other issue is that, even after becoming a published author, Morrison claims to be unable to identify herself as a writer. This self-representation, then, tells of a before and an after, of a self constituted by writing (before *The Bluest Eye* exists as published artifact) and of a self unable to fully identify itself as an author (after the novel's publication). Her story of the novelist who was almost a novelist perhaps owes something to Morrison's engagement with Ellison in her first book. Ellison models the possibility that the experience of being a writer may not be reproducible; despite the recent posthumous publication of *Juneteenth,* Ellison published but one novel in his lifetime.

Despite Morrison's apparent desire to distance herself from Ellison through her claim that his writing did not help her find her voice, the very subject matter of both *Invisible Man* and *The Bluest Eye* would be sufficient to argue for reading them intertextually. Several of Ellison's crucial issues are suggested by the way Morrison approaches racial self-loathing in Pecola and the entire Breedlove family:

> Although their poverty was traditional and stultifying, it was not unique. But their ugliness was unique. No one could have convinced them that they were not relentlessly and aggressively ugly. [. . .] You looked at them and wondered why they were so ugly; you looked closely and could not find the source. Then you realized that it came from conviction, their conviction. It was as though some mysterious all-knowing master had given each one a cloak of ugliness to wear, and they had each accepted it without question. (*Bluest* 38–39)

Self-loathing motivates Pecola's desire for blue eyes, since this wish is re-vealed in relation to an earlier desire to make herself literally invisible, as her first prayer indicates: "Please, God, [. . .] Please make me disappear" (45), and closing her eyes, she imagines what it would feel like to make each part of her body disappear. What she cannot imagine, however, is how to "get her eyes to disappear." Pecola's desire only turns to blue eyes when she re-alizes that, even if she achieved invisibility, she would still see through her African eyes that "held the pictures, and knew the sights" of the violence and ugliness within her family's life. Both lighter-skinned blacks and whites cannot see her but instead recognize only a category. She is in Ellison's terms already the invisible girl, and her prayer for new eyes symbolizes a de-sire for perception outside the culturally iterated messages of white superi-ority. Pecola's obsession first with invisibility and then with literal blue eyes points directly to the ocular metaphor that Ellison introduces in the pro-logue of his novel. The prologue opens famously with the narrator's claim to be invisible despite being a creature of "flesh and bone" (3). One of the most striking images the narrator introduces is of a "beautiful girl" and her "recurring nightmare in which she lay in the center of a large dark room and felt her face expand until it filled the whole room, becoming a form-less mass while her eyes ran in bilious jelly up the chimney" (6–7). This fig-uration of blindness prefaces his discussion of his discovery of his invisibility after twenty years of denial. People (most often white people) do not see him but rather see a stereotype—whether the threatening or the happy-go-lucky black male. If invisibility is a metaphysical condition for Ellison, it is one structured by subliminal messages, such as the one found in his adver-tising slogan for Liberty Paints' premium brand: "If it's Optic White, It's the Right White" (213). The white-is-right subtext of this advertisement re-minds us that, like *Invisible Man*, *The Bluest Eye* is about the construction of what Ellison calls the "*inner* eyes" (3), those internalized cultural images that unconsciously shape racialized perception of world and self. The world Pecola lives in is also highly commodified, and consumer desire is always represented by a white face in Morrison's novel.

In a specific and compelling manner, Michael Awkward already has linked Morrison and Ellison, suggesting that "*The Bluest Eye* serves as a revisionary reading of the [Jim] Trueblood episode of *Invisible Man.*" Noting the similarities between the Trueblood and the Breedloves, Awkward argues that a crucial difference allows Morrison to enter "the Afro-American literary tradition"; by giving voice to what Ellison silences, the female victim of father-daughter incest, Morrison "seems to be taking Ellison to task for the phallocentric nature of his representation"(*Inspiriting* 87). Building on this line of reasoning, I would add, however, that the intertextual relation between these two writers becomes more vexed and complicated if we look at Ellison material other than the Trueblood episode. To approach what I mean, one needs to examine Morrison's first novel through its most metafictional moment, one that calls attention to the production of a personal fiction, Soaphead Church's entry into authorship.

Church and his letter to God have occasioned a variety of critical responses, though the consensus is that the letter is relatively minor.[2] A fact generally overlooked in the commentary on *The Bluest Eye,* even in articles specifically on narration, is that Soaphead, precisely because of his letter, is a narrator too.[3] His narration is coterminous with his act of authorship. Since authorship is what Morrison herself stakes a claim to in her first novel, I wish to argue that Church stands as a significant early figure in her attempt to fashion a useable racialized authorial identity. Morrison herself gives an oblique endorsement to this kind of thinking about her life and novel when she talks to Gloria Naylor about why *The Bluest Eye* is and is not autobiographical; to the extent that the novel is a reclamation of her past, Morrison says, "And all those people were me. I was Pecola, Claudia. . . . I was everybody" (199). It is the space of Morrison's ellipses—those characters not named, yet still part of "everybody"—that I wish to explore. As I discussed in my preface, Morrison has at times claimed that her youth and adolescence were largely free of race consciousness. "I never absorbed racism," Morrison says in a 1992 interview, "I never took it in. That's why I wrote *The Bluest Eye,* to find out how it felt" (Bigsby 28).[4] Whatever the truth of this claim, it nevertheless invites speculation on how her first novel figures in a process of racial self-discovery that is indistinguishable from the act of writing.

Taken as an instance of self-fashioning, Church's letter to God reveals itself as a metafictional gesture that encodes Morrison's own ambitions and anxieties regarding her authorial identity. In part, Church's urge to address

God's transcendent spiritual authority symbolically represents Morrison's desire to address and contest the cultural authority of Ralph Ellison. Church's letter, as we shall see, provides further evidence for Awkward's argument regarding the way the central plot situation of *The Bluest Eye*— Pecola Breedlove's rape by her father—rewrites the Jim Trueblood episode in chapter 2 of *Invisible Man*. But because the letter directly quotes from a different chapter of Ellison's novel, Church's text points to Morrison's intimate acquaintance with the whole of *Invisible Man*, not just the Trueblood episode. Moreover, Church's letter allows Ellison's 1964 essay, "Hidden Name and Complex Fate," to emerge as the less direct intertext in Morrison's initial writing of self.

To argue that Soaphead Church should be read as an instance of self-fashioning might seem to perversely overlook the more obvious authorial figuration, Claudia MacTeer, who rather straightforwardly seems a portrait of the artist as a young woman. Like Morrison, Claudia is in 1941 a ten-year-old girl living in Lorain, Ohio. Although Morrison has at times said that *The Bluest Eye* cannot be called autobiographical, she does admit in a 1976 interview that in terms of setting "I was clearly pulling straight out of what autobiographical information I had" (Stepto 10). Her autobiographical impulse becomes even more apparent when one examines her character's name. Morrison was born "Chloe," and "MacTeer" is a family name. Beginning the novel speaking from the child's perspective, Claudia/Chloe nevertheless concludes the novel speaking from an older and wiser adult perspective. From this adult perspective, she speaks a theory of radical implication, one that refuses to blame Cholly entirely for Pecola's fate and sees rather the entire community's role in what befalls Pecola. Nor does Claudia excuse herself in her communal/self-critique:

> [. . .] we were not strong, only aggressive; we were not free, merely licensed; we were not compassionate, we were polite; not good, but well behaved. We courted death in order to call ourselves brave, and hid like thieves from life. We substituted good grammar for intellect; we switched habits to simulate maturity; we rearranged lies and called it truth, seeing in the new pattern of an old idea the Revelation and the Word. (205–206)

This moment of self-critique by one author-figure leads back to Soaphead Church in two ways. First, there is his letter's content. Church makes his living through false revelation by marketing himself as the medium of God's Word, but his letter contains a strong element of self-critique even as it overtly criticizes God for flaws in his design. Second and perhaps more significant, a rhetorical pattern in Church's letter directly echoes the rhetorical strategy Claudia/Chloe deploys at the end of the novel. Speaking of his

Caribbean genealogy and its relation to the white ruling class, Church maintains:

> In retaining the identity of our race, we held fast to those characteristics most gratifying to sustain and least troublesome to maintain. Consequently we were not royal but snobbish, not aristocratic but class-conscious; we believed authority was cruelty to our inferiors, and education was being at school. We mistook violence for passion, indolence for leisure, and thought recklessness was freedom. (177)

In this rhetorical doubling, the metonymic chain of displaced author-figures becomes clearer. Church, by repeating the content and form of the novel's communal critique, approximately substitutes for the adult Claudia who in turn approximately substitutes for Morrison. This chain of substitutions suggests that there are some issues constellated around the cultural authority of names and naming, as they relate to identity, that Morrison perhaps can only address through the deeper cover of Church. As we shall see, the changes that transform Elihue Whitcomb into Soaphead Church obversely reflect Chloe Wofford's construction of Toni Morrison as her authorial identity.

One of course might reasonably object that Church could not be authorial self-representation because Morrison, as a Midwestern woman, is nothing like Church, a West Indian man. Moreover, Morrison has explicitly distanced herself from the ideological blindness of Church, even as she claims to have needed a character like him to provide Pecola her revelation; she sees him as someone who "would be wholly convinced that if black people were more like white people they would be better off. And I tried to explain that in terms of his own Western Indian background—a kind of English, colonial, Victorian thing drilled into his head which he could not escape" (Stepto 22). But by analogy, neither is the respectable Nathaniel Hawthorne overtly like his tortured artist figures, such as Roger Chillingworth, who delve into the human heart. "Ethan Brand" is perhaps the best example of Hawthorne's authorial anxiety. Ethan's life-long search for the unpardonable sin constructs him as that unpardonable sinner—precisely because of his consciously willed artistic detachment from other people in order to study human motives.[5] Again, Ethan is not like Hawthorne, yet the character surely figures the author's sense of the implications of authorship. In the self-exiled Soaphead Church, Morrison also seems to intuit the problematic that Hawthorne repeatedly represents in his artist figures—the eccentricity, marginality, and even the misanthropy of those who pursue their art.

In Soaphead Church, then, Morrison, who has stated that "the impetus for writing *The Bluest Eye*" was to construct a fiction about a group of people "never taken seriously by anybody—all those peripheral little girls" (88), has created a character who is equally, albeit pervertedly, serious about peripheral little girls. In a conversation with Robert Stepto, Morrison recalls that she needed someone who could give Pecola blue eyes—"that kind of figure who dealt with fortune-telling, dream-telling and so on" (Stepto 22). And indeed *The Bluest Eye* identifies Soaphead's own construction of self as a "Reader, Advisor, and Interpreter of Dreams," a calling "that brought him freedom and satisfaction" because it affords the misanthropic Church with "numerous opportunities to witness human stupidity without sharing it or being compromised by it" (165). Church's satisfaction with the nature of his chosen work begins to create a series of parallels to the conditions Morrison deems necessary to writing. Morrison has said that although the writing of her first novel followed a period of depression, "the words 'lonely, depressed, melancholy'" inadequately describe her state of mind while working; rather, she says, writing comes during "an unbusy state, when I am more aware of myself than of others" (Tate 167). Church deliberately creates the "unbusy state," which Morrison identifies as the precondition to artistic creation, by removing himself to the monastic existence of the backroom apartment he rents. In fact, Church's solitude suggests Morrison's own isolation while writing her first novel. She tells Kathy Neustadt that what may have been conducive to writing was the absence of social contact: "I didn't have any friends and didn't make any, didn't want any because I was on my way somewhere else" (89).[6]

The solitary act of writing, then, constructs authorial identity, as Morrison's comment to Gloria Naylor indicates; writing *The Bluest Eye*, "I fell in love with myself. I reclaimed myself and the world—a real revelation. I named it. I described it. I listed it. I identified it" (198). As Morrison describes it here, *The Bluest Eye* serves as a writing of self for self and suggests a trope for authorship as old as the novel—the author as God of the fictional world—though with a twist. Morrison's description of the ex nihilo construction of identity through language would make her the metaphorical equal to God or to any other writer who similarly appropriated the role of self-creation and self-revelation through the word. Because Morrison experiences writing *The Bluest Eye* as a revelation, special consideration ought to be given to Church, who—after witnessing what he takes to be Pecola's moment of revelation—turns to the act of writing. Again, Morrison claims to have needed a character like Church who could provide Pecola her revelation, even though that revelation is fraudulent.

It is, therefore, in his role as dream teller and reader that Church's identity most clearly figures Morrison's own, if we credit another of her accounts about the composition of her first novel: "I was writing for some clear, single person—I would say myself, because I was quite content to be the only reader. [. . .] I am not being facetious when I say I wrote *The Bluest Eye* in order to read it. And I think that is what makes the difference, because I could look at it as a reader, really as a reader, and not as my own work" (Neustadt 89). This emphasis on herself as audience for her novel collapses the space between reader and writer, consumer and producer. For Church to be a reader of dreams means necessarily that he tells others what their dreams mean. In this regard, Morrison herself is a dream-teller, for in constructing the climactic moment of her narrative, she deploys the symbolic logic of the dream work; her plot's climax is not one moment but two moments that speak together.

The letter to God occurs immediately after the novel's central moment of symbolic doubling, one with clear psychoanalytic implications. In Cholly's rape of Pecola, Morrison explicitly invokes the psychoanalytic notion of repressed memory. Pecola passes out and does not recognize what has happened to her. Her descent into madness occurs only when she unwittingly participates in Church's plan to kill old dog Bob by giving the animal poisoned meat. The death of the dog presents to Pecola something akin to a symbolic dreamscape that represents the rape through a distorted lens that blurs the clarity of victim and victimizer. Although itself a victim of a plot, dog Bob becomes a symbolic substitute for Cholly, who from the outset is troped as "old Dog Breedlove" (16–17); the dog's spasmodic death symbolically repeats Cholly's orgasm. Prior to raping his daughter, the drunken Cholly approaches her "crawling on all fours" and, like the dog, which eats the meat prior to his spasm, Cholly nibbles on the back of Pecola's leg (162). Unlike the moment when her father rapes her, Pecola is fully conscious of what is happening to the dog:

> Choking, stumbling, he moved like a broken toy around the yard. The girl's mouth was open, a little petal of tongue showing. She made a wild, pointless gesture with one hand and then covered her mouth with both hands. She was trying not to vomit. The dog fell again, a spasm jerking his body. Then he was quiet. The girl's hands covering her mouth, she backed away a few feet, then turned, ran out of the yard and down the walk. (176)

Pecola's nausea, of course, could be read as having little significance, since any child could become ill seeing a dog in its death throes. But in the specific context of Pecola's violation, something more seems to be at stake. Pecola's dawning equation of her father's orgasm with the dog's death spasm helps explain her nausea, since the dog's death, according to Church's deception, is the sign that God will grant her blue eyes. Given her intense desire to possess blue eyes, one might almost expect the favorable sign would allow Pecola to ignore the dog's pain and to actually experience joy at learning that she will receive the gift she has so wished for. Pecola's subsequent belief that she now indeed has blue eyes, therefore, represents another form of repression. Her unconscious effectively forecloses the recognition of her violation that begins to happen in old dog Bob's death.

Church's letter, then, completes while complicating the symbolic repetition of Pecola's violation represented by the dog's death. On the one hand, by revealing the intimate details of his molestation of little girls, Church presents an unflattering self-portrait of himself as Cholly's double. But on the other hand, Church's passionate critique of God for allowing the pain of the Pecolas of the world introduces an oddly sympathetic note. This element of sympathy in the portrait of Church perhaps results from his symbolic kinship through authorship to Morrison. However arrogant and unbalanced he may be, in the act of writing, Church has made a minimal movement from consciousness to self-consciousness; witnessing Pecola's felt revelation serves as Church's own revelatory moment inasmuch as it takes him from a position of nonimplication (his belief that his life allows him to be a witness to "human stupidity without sharing it or being compromised by it" [165]) to one that recognizes his implication. In his self-reflexive letter is the beginning of self-critique, a situation that parallels the revelation Morrison claims writing her first novel provided her. Significantly, Church's identity as a writer—the one capable of self-critique—occurs precisely in the moment of his composition and is not prior to his act of writing.

Here Michael Awkward's reading of *The Bluest Eye* as a rewriting of the Jim Trueblood episode of *Invisible Man* helps prepare the ground for understanding Church's letter to God as Morrison's letter to Ellison. For Awkward, Morrison's plot serves as a feminist revision of Ellison's representation of Trueblood's violation of his daughter. Ellison's portrayal is problematic, as Awkward notes (*Inspiriting* 83–84), for the way it silences the women and constantly makes the father-daughter incest a voyeuristic site for the male gaze. What I would add to this argument regarding Morrison's rewriting of incestuous rape is the presence of another silenced female who, although very minor in Ellison's novel, underscores the metafictional nature of Morrison's revision of Ellison. There is a midwife whom Jim Trueblood fears will abort the fetuses of his daughter and wife and whom he threatens to kill if she comes near his house. Her name is Aunt Cloe. *The Bluest Eye,* then, also functions as an act of literary criticism in which Cloe/Chloe finally does succeed in acting as midwife, helping birth a story that serves as a woman-centered counterpoint to Ellison's masculinist presumption in representing the father's violation of the daughter as the father's problem exclusively.

Church's letter is crucial because it reveals that not only has Morrison revised Ellison's novel, she also has commented covertly on her revision in a way that is nevertheless unmistakably signaled, so that the criticism of God becomes simultaneously a criticism of Ellison. The letter's opening suggests its coded intent: "The Purpose of this letter is to familiarize you with facts which either have escaped your notice, or which you have chosen to ignore" (176). It is precisely the violated daughter's perspective about which Morrison (through Church) is speaking, a fact made clear later in the letter: "Tell me, Lord, how could you leave a lass so long so lone that she could find her way to me? How could You? I weep for you, Lord. And it is because I weep for You that I had to do your work for You" (180). Here Morrison suggests why it was necessary for her to revise Ellison. It is as if Matty Lou Trueblood had wandered lost for nearly twenty years only to be transformed into Pecola Breedlove:

> Do you know what she came for? Blue eyes. New, blue eyes, she said. [. . .] She must have asked you for them for a very long time, and you hadn't replied. [. . .] She came to *me* for them. She had one of my cards. (Card enclosed.) By the way, I added the Micah—Elihue Micah Whitcomb. But I am called Soaphead Church. I cannot remember how or why I got the name. What makes one name more a person than another? Is the name the real thing, then? And the person only what his name says? Is that why to the simplest and friendliest of questions: "What is your name?" put to you by Moses, You would not say, and said instead *"I am who I am." Like Popeye? I Yam What I Yam?* Afraid you were, weren't you, to give out your name? Afraid they would know the name and then know you? Then they wouldn't fear you? It's quite all right. Don't be vexed. I mean no offense. I understand. (180, emphasis added)

Although beginning with Pecola's troubled identity, as the passage progresses, the focus shifts to the equally troubled identity of the writer, Church. In framing questions regarding the relation of one's name to one's identity, Morrison alludes specifically to a key moment of identification in chapter 13 of *Invisible Man*. Prior to his speech to the crowd at the eviction of the old couple, Ellison's young man has a moment of self-reflection occasioned when he buys a yam from a street vendor. While eating the yam, anger rises in him about the discomfit that surrounds his attempts to enjoy aspects of African-American culture: "This is all very wild and childish, I thought, but to hell with being ashamed of what you liked. No more of that for me. *I am what I am!*" (259, emphasis added). When the invisible man orders two more yams, the old African-American vendor says, "I can see you one of these old-fashioned yam eaters," to which the protagonist replies, "They're my birthmark. [. . .] *I yam what I yam*" (260, emphasis added). What the invisible man's declaration reveals is that Morrison has quoted Ellison's text in her own. First and foremost it makes clear that Morrison has read and is recasting *Invisible Man,* a fact that helps clarify the relation of Church's God to Morrison's Ellison. But the passage also reflexively turns the question of names and identity back on Morrison as she now claims authorship in her first novel.

This moment in *Invisible Man* to which Morrison alludes resonates with one of her recurring thematics—the dilemma of characters caught in conflict between a desire to assimilate to the values of the white middle class and the voices that urge them to acknowledge a black racial identity. Immediately prior to seeing the street vendor selling yams, the invisible man notices a window advertisement for skin-lightening cream. This instance of the overdetermined cultural messages that value white over black is of course precisely Morrison's subject matter in *The Bluest Eye,* a fiction that interrogates why even the black community prefers the light-skinned Maureen Peal to the dark-skinned Pecola Breedlove.

Having recognized Morrison's address to Ellison in Church's letter to God, one can now hear the end of the letter resonate in a new way:

> I did what You did not, could not, would not do: I looked at that ugly little black girl, and I loved her. I played You. And it was a very good show! [. . .]
>
> Now you are jealous. You are jealous of me.
>
> You see? I, too, have created. Not aboriginally, like you, but creation is a heady wine, more for the taster than the brewer. (182)

In particular, Church's observation that the work of creation is more for the consumer than the producer recalls Morrison's claim, quoted earlier, that in writing her first novel she was "quite content to be the only reader."

Church then signs his name—Elihue Micah Whitcomb—choosing his birth name rather than the name he is known by in the community. This seems a particularly pertinent detail given what Morrison said in 1992 about her true identity: "I am really Chloe Anthony Wofford. That's who I am. I have been writing under this other person's name. I write some things now as Chloe Wofford, private things. I regret having called myself Toni Morrison when I published my first novel, *The Bluest Eye*" (Bigsby 28). Morrison reiterates in 1994 how upset she was to see "Toni Morrison" on the cover of *The Bluest Eye,* adding "I write all the time about being misnamed. How you got your name is very special. My mother, my sister, all my family call me Chloe. It was Chloe, by the way, who went to

Stockholm last year to get the Nobel Prize" (Dreifus 74). But is Morrison really Chloe Anthony Wofford? The answer to this question is hinted at by Soaphead Church's admission that he is not actually Elihue Micah Whitcomb, since the middle name is his invention. And it is an invention that is quite reflexive inasmuch as the one who addresses God is "Micah," a name that means, as Karen Carmean has pointed out, "he who is like God" (26).

Morrison's relation to her own name encompasses the apparent anxiety that Ellison's protagonist manifests by remaining unnamed and that we see Ellison articulate in his 1964 essay, "Hidden Name and Complex Fate," in which he comments on his own uneasiness growing up with the name Ralph Waldo Ellison: "all of this speculation on the matter of names has a purpose, and now, because it is tied up so ironically with my own experiences as a writer, I must turn to my own name" (150). Ellison hides his parents' self-consciously literary act of giving him Emerson's middle name, a decision that resonates with Morrison's relation to her middle name and to her experiences as a writer.

The reason Church/Morrison can sympathize—indeed almost condescend to God/Ellison—is that Morrison takes an alternative yet parallel path to the invisible man's in order to create a foundation for an authorizing voice: she is not the unnamed (Ellison's protagonist) but rather the self-named.[7] Morrison's act of self-fashioning is figured in Church's presentation of his card to God (again, the one who, like Ellison's protagonist, prefers to remain unnamed). In this moment of presentation, Church confides "By the way, I added the Micah—Elihue Micah Whitcomb."[8] In order to understand the issue of identity that is at stake with this detail of the invented middle name, it is necessary to consider the transformation of Chloe Wofford into Toni Morrison. While the designation "Soaphead Church" manifests a communal act of naming that reclaims his African-Americanness from his white, ruling-class-inspired name (Elihue Whitcomb), Morrison's individual act of self-naming seems to move in the opposite direction.

Wofford becomes Morrison when she marries Jamaican architect Harold Morrison in 1958, but more interesting is Morrison's decision to become known as "Toni." In a conversation with Colette Dowling in 1979, Morrison claims to have made the change in college "[b]ecause the people at Howard seemed to have difficulty pronouncing" Chloe (50).[9] What makes Morrison's coded reference to her own name change in Soaphead Church's letter so striking is the way her fiction repeatedly examines the possibility for African Americans to forge an authentic identity for themselves. Often she ties this quest for identity to African-American names and the act of naming. Responding to a question about the significance of naming in *Song of Solomon,* Morrison argues that for African Americans "[t]he best thing you can do is take another name which is yours because it reflects something about you or your own choice" (LeClair 126). In *Song of Solomon,* Guitar Banes, responding to Milkman's complaint that he does not like his name, says, "'Let me tell you somthin, baby. Niggers get their names the way they get everything else—the best way they can'" (88). It is difficult not to hear in Milkman's complaint about his name some echo of Morrison's relation to her own name.

Although not directly signaled as one of *The Bluest Eye*'s intertexts as *Invisible Man* is, Ellison's "Hidden Name and Complex Fate" strongly resonates with Morrison's discussion of names, particularly when he suggests:

> We must learn to wear our names within all the noise and confusion of the environment in which we find ourselves; make them the center of all of our associations with the world, with man and with nature. We must charge them with all our emotions, our hopes, hates, loves, aspirations. They must become our masks and our shields and the containers of all those values and traditions which we learn and/or imagine as being the meaning of our familial past. (148)

This apparent need for African Americans to embrace their names, Ellison acknowledges, can be problematic for "potential writers," who may "be more than ordinarily concerned with the veiled and mysterious events [of slavery], the fusions of blood, the furtive couplings, the business transactions, the violations of faith and loyalty, the assaults; yes, and the unrecognized and unrecognizable loves through which our names were handed down unto us" (148). Such potential writers, Ellison goes on to say, may discard "their original names in rejection of the bloodstained, the brutal, the sinful images of the past. Thus they would declare new identities, would clarify a new program of intention and destroy the verbal evidence of a willed and ritualized discontinuity of blood and human intercourse" (148). This moment in Ellison's essay seems to provide one frame for understanding Morrison's relation to her name and to the significance of naming throughout her fiction.

Morrison denies "Chloe" and chooses "Toni," but why? It is hard, perhaps, to register why such a change might have been useful, especially since recently "Chloe" has gained a certain cachet, as evidenced by the white female characters who bear this name in two recent television dramas, *ER* and *Malibu Shores.* But in the 1950s, to a bright young black woman with career aspirations, "Chloe" strongly signaled a form of racialized identity from which Morrison may have wished to distance herself. Quite simply, this name often signals a particularly hated form of racial oppression and servility in the agrarian South. In her undergraduate and graduate literary studies, Morrison certainly could find unflattering Chloes in American literature besides the one in Ellison's novel, whose role as a rural midwife is marked as backward and folksy. For example, in Harriet Beecher Stowe's *Uncle Tom's Cabin* (1852), Uncle Tom's wife, the prized cook of the Shelby family who loves her master's son better than her own children, is named Aunt Chloe. Taken together, both Stowe's and Ellison's Aunt Chloes participate in a racial stereotype that suggests something akin to Aunt Jemima. In refashioning herself as Toni, Morrison distances herself from black rural connotations, creating a self-consciously hip, modern name for the 1950s. The newness of the name "Toni" is lessened for those who have experienced the subsequent decades and the emergence of names such as "Lori" and "Brandi," but for the early 1950s, Morrison's name ending in "i" might almost be seen as exotic. "Toni" falls short of the exotic, however, because her choice reproduces the brand name of a popular post–World War II beauty aid, the home permanent in a box.[10] Given Morrison's new middle-class surroundings in Washington, D.C., so far removed from her working-class home, her apparent desire to identify with the contemporary suggests a meaning latent in the brand name Toni that is explicit in the identically pronounced adjective, "tony," meaning elegant or exclusive. Over and above the connotations of elegance and newness, the name "Toni," as a product, depended on the notion of the double, as Gillette's long running "Which Twin Has the Toni?" advertising campaign illustrates.[11] (See figure 2.1) And as we shall see, in her early novels Morrison encodes a fictive double of herself and the Chloe-Toni name issue. This is not to say that the future author was in complete control of the meanings constellated around the signifier "Toni" when she chose it as her name; she may, in fact, have been unconscious of some or all of these possibilities. Still, whatever the exact motivation for Morrison's decision to become Toni, one thing is clear: the matter of identity was not a given for Toni Morrison because she rejected her given name. (See figure 2.2)

One might object that I am placing too much emphasis on this name change. After all, the published biographical information on Morrison agrees that her full name was Chloe Anthony Wofford, so that the adoption of "Toni" as a substitute for "Chloe" still honors her given name, if somewhat obliquely.[12] Morrison's middle name, however, was not Anthony; her birth certificate (See figure 2.3) indicates her full name as Chloe Ardelia Wofford, which reveals that Ramah and George Wofford named their daughter for her maternal grandmother, Ardelia Willis.[13] While the origin of "Toni" is now obscure, the example of Milkman Dead illustrates that names in the African-American community do not come exclusively from birth certificates. Moreover, the naming of Milkman's grandfather, the original Macon Dead, through a gesture of casual racism by a drunken Union soldier, is but one example in Morrison's fiction that should remind the reader not to place too much faith in legal documents. But Morrison's name change seems fundamentally different than those suggested by Milkman and Macon Dead because there is no apparent need to subvert a white authority to name, since "Ardelia" comes from her parents.

Why, then, has Morrison constructed "Anthony" as the fictional origin of "Toni"? Perhaps by 1979 (when she tells Dowling that "Toni" is derived from "Anthony") Morrison was uncomfortable with a first name that might be perceived as masking familial identity. Perhaps, though, one might read the fictional Anthony/Toni as a gesture of authorial self-fashioning, akin to Willa Cather's employment of "William" when she enters the University of Nebraska or to William Faulkner's insertion of the "u" in his family name. (Indeed, the young Faulkner's fashioning of self is highly theatrical: after World War I he walks the streets of Oxford, Mississippi, in uniform and uses a cane to support his fictional claim that he was injured as a result of having been shot down in aerial combat over France.) What Morrison seems to have done is to have created an authorial identity that can only be true insofar as it is fictional, as the examples from *Tar Baby* and *Song of Solomon* suggest through their recurring hints about the author's name. Both possibilities—uneasiness over disguised identity and an authorial self-fashioning—converge in her claim to be "really Chloe Anthony Wofford." In a sense, however, only by denying Chloe (as well as Ardelia) as her public name can Morrison become Chloe in her private discursive creation of herself as novelist. By creating a space between the private and familial name (Chloe) and the public name (Toni), Morrison maintains a zone of safety around what is truly the most personal. But Chloe refuses to remain silent, as her subsequent fiction demonstrates, so that in a sense one might see these fictions as collaborative—the ongoing dialogues of Chloe and Toni. Like Cather's and Faulkner's gestures of self-creation, Morrison's first major work of fiction, psychologically speaking, is herself.

In 1998, Morrison tells an interviewer, "When I was a little girl, I was walking down the street in Ohio. A man came up and said, 'Are you a Willis?'—referring to my mother's maiden name—'I thought so, by the way you walk.' And I knew he knew my family. It was a comfort to be identified as a Willis" (Morales). But in the 1950s, such identification was apparently not a comfort. Despite Morrison's substitution of "Anthony" for "Ardelia," she nevertheless identifies with her maternal grandmother in an essay on the black experience in America that appeared in *The New York Times Magazine* on July 4, 1976, our nation's Bicentennial. The essay, "A

Which Twin has the Toni?

Lucille and Lois Barnes of Los Angeles. The Toni Twin says, "Toni always gives me a wave that's soft and natural-looking." Can you tell which is the Toni Twin? See answer below.

Hair styles in this picture by Don Rita, famous Hollywood hair stylist.

Toni _looks_ as lovely as a $20* permanent — _feels_ as soft as naturally curly hair

Now—*any day, any time*—for only one dollar you can get a wave that's caress-ably soft—like naturally curly hair . . . that's long lasting, easy to manage, looks just as lovely as a beauty shop perma-nent costing $20. (*Including shampoo and set.)

What's Toni's secret? It's the lotion. Toni waving lotion is an exclusive creme formula developed through years of research. This gentle-action formula was especially created to give you a wave that's free of harsh frizziness from the very first day—a wave that *feels* and *behaves* like naturally curly hair. But re-member, *only* with Toni Home Perma-nent do you get this superb waving lotion.

Wonderful results—again and again! What better proof of Toni quality? Toni is the only permanent that has given over 67 million lovely, long-lasting waves. Some women have used Toni ten times or more and say their waves are always soft, natural-looking, easy to manage. Letters of praise come from women with every type of hair—even gray, bleached and baby-fine hair. So whether you are buying your first Toni or your tenth, you can be sure of getting a wave that looks as lovely as a $20 permanent—feels as soft as naturally curly hair. Lois, the twin on the right, has the Toni.

For complete hair care get Toni Creme Shampoo and Toni Creme Rinse, too.

"I'm not a twin, but I am a Toni fan" says Carol Maurer, student at North-western University. "Toni is the only permanent that seems just right for my baby-fine hair . . . never leaves it frizzy, but always soft and natural-looking."

TONI SPIN CURLERS
twice as easy · twice as fast

All plastic. No rubber bands. They grip the hair . . . spin up the curls . . . and lock with a flick of the finger.
Available in combination with Toni Refill . . . only $2.29

197

Figure 2.1 Advertisement from *Good Housekeeping*, March 1950. Photo courtesy The Gillette Company. Reprinted by permission.

CHLOE WOFFORD

Figure 2.2 From Chloe to Toni: A Permanent Change? Photo above from 1949 Lorain High School yearbook (courtesy of the Black River Historical Society); photo at bottom from 1953 Howard Bison yearbook (by permission of the Moorland-Spingarn Research Center, Howard University Archives).

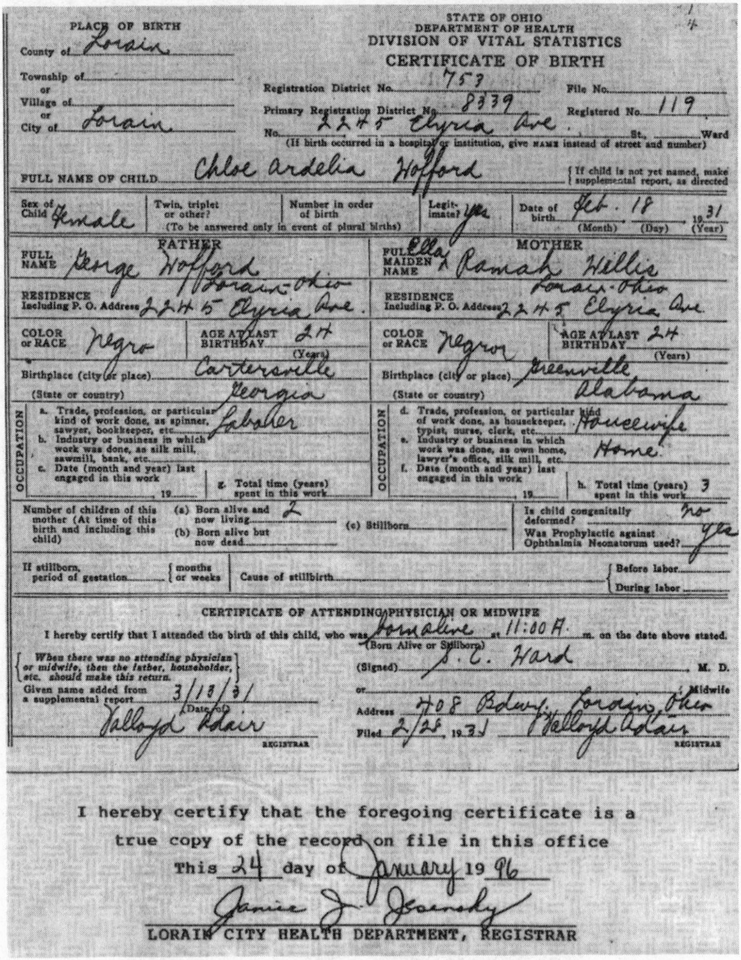

STATE OF OHIO
DEPARTMENT OF HEALTH
DIVISION OF VITAL STATISTICS
CERTIFICATE OF BIRTH

PLACE OF BIRTH
County of Lorain
Township of
or
Village of
or
City of Lorain

Registration District No. 753
File No.
Primary Registration District No. 8339
Registered No. 119
No. 2245 Elyria Ave. St., Ward
(If birth occurred in a hospital or institution, give NAME instead of street and number)

FULL NAME OF CHILD Chloe Ardelia Wofford
{If child is not yet named, make supplemental report, as directed

Sex of Child Female
Twin, triplet or other?
Number in order of birth
(To be answered only in event of plural births)
Legitimate? yes
Date of birth Feb. 18 1931 (Month) (Day) (Year)

FATHER	MOTHER
FULL NAME George Wofford	FULL MAIDEN NAME Ella Ramah Willis
RESIDENCE Including P. O. Address 2245 Elyria Ave. Lorain-Ohio	RESIDENCE Including P. O. Address 2245 Elyria Ave Lorain-Ohio
COLOR or RACE Negro; AGE AT LAST BIRTHDAY 24 (Years)	COLOR or RACE Negro; AGE AT LAST BIRTHDAY 24 (Years)
Birthplace (city or place) Cartersville (State or country) Georgia	Birthplace (city or place) Greenville (State or country) Alabama
OCCUPATION a. Trade, profession, or particular kind of work done, as spinner, sawyer, bookkeeper, etc. Laborer	OCCUPATION d. Trade, profession, or particular kind of work done, as housekeeper, typist, nurse, clerk, etc. Housewife
b. Industry or business in which work was done, as silk mill, sawmill, bank, etc.	e. Industry or business in which work was done, as own home, lawyer's office, silk mill, etc. Home
c. Date (month and year) last engaged in this work 19 ; g. Total time (years) spent in this work	f. Date (month and year) last engaged in this work 19 ; h. Total time (years) spent in this work 3

Number of children of this mother (At time of this birth and including this child) (a) Born alive and now living 2 (b) Born alive but now dead (c) Stillborn
Is child congenitally deformed? no
Was Prophylactic against Ophthalmia Neonatorum used? yes

If stillborn, period of gestation { months or weeks } Cause of stillbirth { Before labor / During labor

CERTIFICATE OF ATTENDING PHYSICIAN OR MIDWIFE
I hereby certify that I attended the birth of this child, who was Born alive at 11:00 A. m. on the date above stated.
(Born Alive or Stillborn)
{When there was no attending physician or midwife, then the father, householder, etc. should make this return.}
(Signed) S. C. Ward M. D.
or Midwife
Given name added from a supplemental report 3/13/31 (Date of)
Address 708 Bdwy. Lorain, Ohio
Valloyd Adair REGISTRAR
Filed 2/28, 1931 Valloyd Adair REGISTRAR

I hereby certify that the foregoing certificate is a true copy of the record on file in this office
This 24 day of January 1996
Janice J. Kennedy
LORAIN CITY HEALTH DEPARTMENT, REGISTRAR

Figure 2.3 Toni Morrison's Birth Certificate.

Slow Walk of Trees (as Grandmother Would Say) Hopeless (As Grandfather Would Say)," meditates on the status of African Americans and begins with a comparison of how Morrison's grandparents, Ardelia and John Solomon Willis, had viewed the prospects for racial progress. The essay contrasts her grandfather's pessimism with her grandmother's optimism:

> And [Ardelia] would pay attention to the music [her husband played on the violin] but not to the sadness in her husband's eyes, for she would see what

she expected to see—not the occasional historical repetition, but, like the slow walk of certain species of trees from the flatlands up into the mountains, she would see the signs of irrevocable and permanent change. (104, 150)

The essay catalogues problems Morrison sees in America's treatment of blacks, but at the midpoint she returns to her grandmother: "Maybe Ardelia Willis had the best idea. One sees signs of her vision and the fruits of her prophecy in spite of the dread-lock statistics" (Morrison "A Slow Walk" 160). Morrison herself finishes the essay on a note of cautious optimism. Both *Song of Solomon* and *Tar Baby,* concerned as they are with the possibilities of authentic identity, seem anticipated by Morrison's personal reminiscence, which serves, in effect, as her declaration of identity, particularly as the granddaughter of Ardelia Willis.

Soaphead Church's letter to God, with its oblique reference to the necessity of an authorial self-fashioning distinct from that generated by a birth name, encodes many of the issues of identity that Morrison clearly struggled with, not just in *The Bluest Eye,* but—as my subsequent chapters hope to make clear—throughout her next three novels, where the matter of naming and authentic racial identity are central. At the same time, her covert address to Ralph Ellison indicates the scope of her writerly aspiration, which even with her first novel seems to be to question Ellison as a cultural authority on the African-American experience, even as she acknowledges him as a significant precursor. Church's letter, as well as his perversion, serves as Morrison's metafictional reminder to herself that the author can never escape implication in what she critiques.

If Church points to the constructedness of Morrison's authorial identity, *The Bluest Eye* nevertheless yearns for authenticity, and given the character referred to by the title, that yearning is particularly for a black female authenticity. The novel explores authenticity by explicitly marking what is inauthentic. And there is nothing so inauthentic as the thin sugar-brown girls who have left behind their Southern roots and unconsciously have sold out to the dominant culture: if these women "go to land-grant colleges, normal schools, and learn how to do the white man's work with refinement," it is part of a larger process of acculturation and learning "how to behave. The careful development of thrift, patience, high morals, and good manners" (83). Key in this description of these women's inauthentic behavior is their repression. But what is it that they repress by denying "the dreadful funkiness of passion, the funkiness of nature, the funkiness of the wide range of human emotions" (83)? Is it black cultural identity—by their internalizing white culture's judgment and stereotyping of their blackness (such as the white racist notion that "blacks smell funny")? Or is it a repression of their true essence—the funkiness of nature? The implication in this particular phrase is that, indeed, white culture creates a surface, one psychologically masking an essential biological nature. So by worrying about the "laugh that is a little too loud; the enunciation a little too round; the gesture a little too generous [. . .]" (83)—any body language that could be read as a sign of their sexuality—these light-complexioned women, the text suggests, far from simply failing to enact a black cultural identity, in fact live an inauthentic relation to their bodies.

Where, then, does authenticity reside? Although the novel suggests that beneath the tough exterior, Mrs. MacTeer is loving and maternal, the MacTeer household is not the site of true funk. The MacTeers are too implicated—they give white dolls to the girls at Christmas and laugh at Mr. Henry's joking identification of Claudia and Frieda as Greta Garbo and Ginger Rogers. Home is precisely what Claudia, as we have seen, learns to critique by the novel's end. In fact the location of funkiness is restricted to one particular site, a building "on the southeast corner of Broadway and Thirty-fifth Street in Lorain, Ohio" (33), where both the Breedloves and the three prostitutes—China, Poland, and Miss Marie—live.

Life in the Breedlove household is anything but restrained. The ritualized violence of Cholly and Mrs. Breedlove's relation emotionally scars their children, who repeatedly witness parental fights that possess "a darkly brutal formalism [. . .] paralleled only by their lovemaking" (43). But the source of this family's absence of repression is hardly marked as positive. Accepting fully the negative valuation of their blackness, the Breedloves have given up any pretense or attempt to act "colored." They see themselves not only as whites but also as the light-complexioned Geraldines and Maureens see them—as niggers. And yet there was a time early in Cholly and Pauline's relationship when their unrepressed passion represented something more fully authentic. It is in this fashion that *The Bluest Eye* marks the absent site of authenticity as the African-American agrarian community. Until the death of his Aunt Jimmy, Cholly is nurtured by his rural Georgia community, just as Pauline is the product of a black agrarian community in Kentucky. Morrison's mother and father, from Alabama and Georgia respectively, seem coded in the novel's invocation of the rural as the surest site of authentic black identity. The small black community becomes the setting that Morrison uses to meditate on authenticity in her next three novels—first the Bottom in *Sula,* then Shalimar, Virginia, in *Song of Solomon,* and finally and more problematically Eloe, Florida, in *Tar Baby.* What spells the beginning of the end of the Breedlove's happier moment—when their unrepressed life was not merely a sign of modernist alienation—is Cholly's decision to move his bride north for the economic opportunities represented by industrial jobs. Seen in this light, it is perhaps possible to understand Claudia's assessment—one always difficult to bring up with students—that Cholly, despite his rape of his daughter, loved Pecola "enough to touch her, envelop her, give something of himself to her" (206). At the instance before the rape, his thoughts are clearly with his initial intimacy with Pauline and suggest that what he—as best his drunkness can conceive—wants to give Pecola is a sense of authentic identity that he recalls from his time in the rural South. Still, living on the lower floor of this building at the corner of Broadway and Thirty-fifth, the Breedloves represent the underside of funk.

The three man-hating prostitutes who live above the Breedloves, however, are a metonymy for the cult of true black womanhood in *The Bluest Eye*. These women, unlike the sugar-brown girls, are not guilty of thrift, patience, high morals, or manners. This structural opposition in the text does not mean that the novel's cultural function is to recruit African-American women to become prostitutes. What the text does, however, by juxtaposing the prostitutes to the sugar-brown girls is to imagine a way to inhabit the African-American female body: "Three merry gargoyles. Three merry harridans. Amused by a long-ago time of ignorance" (55). Morrison's whores, socially marginal, are able to pierce through all pretense of their community, both men's and women's. Their conversation is a running critique of the sexual politics of middle-class convention, even as they recognize their own foibles and implication. And their identity clearly does not depend upon men, whom these women hate "without shame, apology, or discrimination" (56). At the conclusion of the "Autumn" section of the novel, Pecola looks at these women and wonders "Were they real?" As if in response to the child's unspoken question, "Marie belched, softly, purringly, lovingly" (58). Here, the novel proclaims, is a truly lived relation to the body. Outside of the absent agrarian past, one that exists only as memory, China, Poland, and Miss Marie are as authentic as it gets in *The Bluest Eye*.

In the chapter that follows, I take up *Sula,* a novel that amplifies *The Bluest Eye*'s anxiety about authorship. Whatever thinking about authorship that Claudia and Soaphead allow Morrison, Sula and Shadrack complicate the issue in their doubled role as the artist manqué. In the figure of the college-educated Sula, Morrison begins her examination of a question that will need to wait until *Tar Baby* to find a useable answer: although the funk may erupt, can the funk rise? In other words, can the authentic black woman succeed in ways that challenge her position within an economically impoverished community?

Chapter 3

Engendering Sexual/Textual Identity:
Sula and the Artistic Gaze

[. . .] the very next words I read were these—"Chloe liked Olivia . . ." Do not start. Do not blush. Let us admit in the privacy of our own society that these things sometimes happen. Sometimes women do like women.

—*Virginia Woolf,* A Room of One's Own

I n its overt content, *Sula* is certainly much less involved than is *The Bluest Eye* in what Morrison terms the "genuinely autobiographical" (Jones and Vinson 171). After all, *Sula* is not set in Lorain, Ohio, and does not have a narrator such as Claudia who so directly serves as the author's exact fictive contemporary. And although Morrison does speak at some length about a woman named Hannah Peace, whom her mother in fact knew, these remarks work to police the border between autobiography and fiction. Prefacing her discussion of the Hannah Peace who lived in Lorain, Morrison identifies her comments as an "autobiographical fact that I thought might interest you" but then adds:

I don't know much about her, except I remember how she looked, not a lot, just the color of her skin, so dark, rose in it, and the lids of her eyes were very deep. Now I was little, so she seemed tall to me. And my mother and her friends, whenever they mentioned her name, and called her Hannah Peace, it seemed to me in the way they called her name there was some mixture of awe and approbation, some quality of both in it. Now I've never asked my mother about that lady, and I don't remember seeing her more

than two or four times, but it made an impression on me. There was a quality about that, I thought they sort of liked her and—not disliked her—they
liked and admired her and disapproved of her. [. . .] Whenever something
was up, they didn't say her name like you say other people's names. So when
I was writing Sula [*sic*], I used the name because I couldn't not use it. It was
all caught up with the sound of "Hannah Peace." (Koenen 79–80)

Although she points to a real-life Peace woman, Morrison at the same time
undercuts the notion that this individual serves as any kind of literal presence in the text since the author asserts not only a very slight knowledge
of this Hannah, but even a reluctance to find out more about the woman.
Thus the genuinely autobiographical element of *Sula* reduces to two
words, "Hannah Peace," a fleeting visual impression, and a certain tone of
voice; everything else, Morrison's discussion implicitly claims, is fictional.
But once again I want to insist on fiction as a form of symbolic autobiography, a supplement that challenges and complements the author's very
limiting sense of how her writing might represent issues of her identity.

Elsewhere Morrison makes clear that Medallion and the Bottom are
not figurations of Lorain, Ohio. However, the representation of Medallion
points to a transfiguration of personal experience similar to what Morrison does with the name "Hannah Peace." As the author notes, the setting
of her second novel, which at the outset opposes valley and hills, is based
on her parents' time in Pittsburgh: "I used something that my mother had
said to me when I was young, about her living in Pittsburgh when she was
first married—how all the Black people lived in the hills and all the white
people lived in the valley because the land was rich" (Bakerman 39). Morrison's discussion of both character and setting in *Sula* tend to deflect potential readings of her fiction that would seek autobiographical resonances;
her comments effectively say, "There's little in my fiction, other than minor
details, that reveals anything about my life." Yet her anti-autobiographical
characterization of *Sula* may recall Henry James's critique of the advice
often given to beginning writers—namely, that they should write from
personal experience. In "The Art of Fiction," James illustrates how the notion of "personal experience" can be much broader than commonly supposed given the talented writer's ability to synthesize disparate elements of
her life experiences. The leap from speaking about personal experience to
encoded autobiographical figurations is not, I believe, very great, so that for
"personal experience" one might substitute "unacknowledged autobiography" in order to ask with James, "where does it begin and end?" (56).

In order to address that question, I want to explore two areas that
emerge as sites of anxiety both in *Sula* and in Morrison's comments on her
second novel—1) the relation between artistic identity and ethics and 2)

the gendered identity of the artist. Although I might ideally like to keep these discussions distinct, the novel resists giving me such a straightforward rhetorical strategy inasmuch as the identity of the novel's most artistic consciousness, Sula, is constituted through her attempts to manipulate (as well as her manipulation by) the social codes that prescribe and proscribe her sexual pleasure; her sex is a text that she only incompletely authors. Moreover, the intertextual resonances in *Sula,* which suggest Morrison's reading of Virginia Woolf, urge a kind of reading of *Sula*'s figurative language. Such a reading challenges the presumptive heterosexuality of various relationships in Morrison's second novel.[1]

Moving from the author's narrow category of the genuinely autobiographical to the broader notion of the symbolically autobiographical, *Sula* emerges as an allegory of identity. One of Morrison's most interesting recurring self-representations continually defers the moment when she identifies herself as a writer. In 1983, when asked when she knew she was a writer, Morrison responded: "When I'd written *Sula*" (Tate 167). If, as we saw in the previous chapter, Morrison felt that she could not claim the designation "writer" while she was producing *The Bluest Eye,* then these doubts persist through the writing of her second novel. *Sula* paradoxically stands as another written text without a writer. Morrison's assertion that her sense of herself as a writer emerged only after completing her second novel invites a reading that looks for traces of her doubt, not only about her ability to become a writer but also about the questionable virtue of wanting to be a writer. Such a line of inquiry seems authorized, as it were, by the title character of Morrison's second novel. Sula is an individual who should have but did not become an artist. *The Bluest Eye* represents characters just crossing the threshold into writerly interpretation—Church as author and Claudia as narrator; *Sula* explores the painful consequences for those whose voices do not find their appropriate expression. In this regard, Sula stands as a distorted figuration of Morrison's own subject position, for Sula, like Morrison, leaves her small-town poverty and goes to college. Unlike Morrison, Sula returns to her hometown after college, so at one level Morrison's second novel allows the author to think what her life might have been like had she also returned home. If this is the case, to be the artist manqué is to wind up dead. *Sula,* from this perspective, serves as the novelist's justification for artistic expression by way of negative example. Morrison has also spoken of the time of composing *Sula* as an inability not to write: "If all the publishers had disappeared in one night, I would have written anyway. [. . .] But writing was a thing that I could *not* not do at that point—it was a way of thinking for me" (Neustadt 90). *Sula,* then, expresses why Morrison could not not become an author; in other words, if authorship suggests pariahhood and the risk of becoming Soaphead

Church, Sula serves as a different delineation of Morrison's choice of textual outsider status, a choice that doubles her character's decision to become a sexual outsider.

Her second novel, then, continues Morrison's coded meditation on what it means to write as an African-American woman novelist, working through the simultaneous desire to become an artist and the fear of the consequence of what such a desire entails. Becoming a writer, as the example of Soaphead Church suggests, is not a wholly unambiguous good. Yet the possibilities of aesthetic perception, a necessary precondition to writerly production, are crucial to *Sula*. To say this is not to deny that this novel has a content that overtly stages issues of moral and ethical behavior. Recently Axel Nissen has usefully summarized much of the previous discussion about the ethical content of the novel:

> In the implicit debate in the novel between those favoring a personal ethic based on perception through dialogue and those holding firm to principle and universal ethical laws, the Peace women—Eva and Sula and to a certain extent Hannah—would seem to stand on the side of ethical improvisation and the Wright women—Helene and Nel—on the side of convention. To some extent, the conflict is whether the mind or the emotions should have preeminence in our ethical deliberations. (279–80)[2]

While I do not wish to gainsay this characterization, Nissen's description of the way Sula's "egocentric individualism" prevents her from being "the ethical center of the work" (275) nevertheless deflects attention from what I would say is this character's function as the aesthetic "center" of this remarkably reflexive novel.[3] In a richly suggestive piece, Barbara Johnson points to two apparently random words—"aesthetic" and "rapport"—which Sula has introduced to the Bottom; Nel apparently arbitrarily thinks of these words after seeing her husband and Sula making love: "I waited for Sula to look up at me any minute and say one of those lovely college words like *aesthetic* or *rapport*, which I never understood but which I loved because they sounded so comfortable and firm" (105). For Johnson, "the very arbitrariness" of the words offers them "as keys to the preoccupations of the novel as a whole" (169):

> The novel presents us with a series of horrible images, painful truths, excruciating losses. Do we just sit back and watch? What is the nature of our pleasure in contemplating trauma? What would be a response that would embody rapport rather then aesthetics? Is this what Toni Morrison is challenging us to consider? Or is she merely trying to make us less innocent in our contemplation, our analysis, our "interest"? (171)

These queries are all pertinent; however, I will insist on the reflexivity of the questions Johnson asks. In my reading, Morrison, in the very act of inscription, uses her writing to map her own difficult relation to aesthetics. So we might turn Johnson's questions to ask: is the ethical problem of aesthetic distance what Morrison is challenging herself to consider? Or is she merely trying to make herself less innocent in her contemplation, her analysis, her "interest"? To be an artist, or even an artist manqué, may mean that one is beyond good and evil, and this link between amorality and artistic production provides one way to think about why Morrison hesitates to embrace fully the role of the writer-artist.

In pursuit of my larger claim that her first four novels encode the construction of a useable identity as an African-American woman novelist, I wish now to bring gender—and how such identity might impinge on Morrison's sense of authorship—into sharper focus. In Morrison's fashioning of "Toni" as a new name for a new identity, one cannot fail to be struck by her drawing that name from a play on an invented middle name: the "A" of feminine Ardelia becomes the "A" of masculine Anthony, "origin" of Toni. This act of self-naming performs a gender shifting that recalls Willa Cather's fashioning of identity through self-naming, such as her inscribing her personal library books with "William" or her masculine nickname, "Willie." As for Cather, authorship for Morrison seems to be in part a masculine activity.

My epigraph for this chapter, taken from chapter 6 of Virginia Woolf's *A Room of One's Own,* underscores the issues of gender and authorship in several ways. Barbara Christian asks "what about Woolf?" (22), in order to speculate on how this British modernist came into Morrison's field of vision in the early 1950s. Unable to narrate a definitive answer to that question, Christian goes on to delineate thematic connections between the two novelists, including the "relationship between the inner life of [their] characters and the world within which [these characters] find themselves" (28) and the way "inner time is always transforming outer time through memory" (32) in their fiction. Whatever the specifics are regarding this discovery of Woolf, Morrison in 1955 completed her master's thesis titled "Virginia Woolf's and William Faulkner's Treatment of the Alienated." Morrison's chapter on Woolf exemplifies 1950s New Critical practice. It is a close reading of *Mrs. Dalloway,* selected because it "is sufficiently representative of Virginia Woolf's use of isolation as a theme to serve [the thesis] as an example of her approach" ("Virginia" 3). Morrison focuses on two characters, Clarissa Dalloway, the middle-aged wife of a government official whose most passionate memory involves a kiss from another woman (Sally Seton), and Septimus Warren Smith, the traumatized war veteran who commits suicide. But even to briefly name these characters is to have an odd sense of déjà vu: Clarissa/Sula, a woman for whom a man can never be as fully intimate a companion as the woman from her youth; Septimus/Shadrack, the veteran obsessed with death and suicide.[4]

I would like to name a series of relations that may imply further relations: Clarissa likes Sally, Chloe likes Virginia (who imagines a Chloe liking Olivia), and Sula likes Nel. Chapter 2 of *Identifying Fictions* attempts to imagine the discomfiture Morrison may have developed during her undergraduate literary studies toward her birth name in light of the American "Chloes" found in Harriet Beecher Stowe's *Uncle Tom's Cabin* and Ralph Ellison's *Invisible Man*. Over and above these Chloes, she would have been familiar with Woolf's discussion of this other Chloe, since, as Chloe Wofford, Morrison read, thought, and wrote about this British modernist. And while the reference to Chloe found in *A Room of One's Own* does not have the potential to wound racial identity in the way Stowe's and Ellison's Chloes could, Woolf's use of "Chloe" to refer to women's same-sex friendship nevertheless seems to point to issues central not only to *Sula* but also to Morrison's intervention in the academic discussion of the novel.[5] If Morrison consciously directs us to Ellison as an intertext of *The Bluest Eye,* using the African-American male modernist to record her aspirations as a writer, she seems to trope more subtly upon this British female modernist. Chloe's liking Virginia in the 1950s and Morrison's refiguration of Clarissa's passion and Septimus's suicide may mean that Woolf's lesbian discursive practice functions as the textual unconscious of *Sula,* one that complicates the space of Morrison's relation to the gender of authorial identity.[6]

Woolf scholars, well before the Woolf revival of the 1970s, have been aware of the lesbian subtext of *Mrs. Dalloway.*[7] But the issue of passionate female friendship in *Sula* needs to be approached carefully, especially in light of Morrison's insistence on the heterosexuality of her novel. Eve Kosofsky Sedgwick's discussion of what is at stake in same-sex friendship speaks fairly directly to what I wish to pursue. In her work on the way homoerotic figuration mediates the poles of male homosociality and homosexuality, language often becomes the site of fraught identifications. Barbara Smith's reading of *Sula* begins to articulate a portion of the problematic space of same-sex liking that Sedgwick theorizes. Smith's essay, originally published in 1974, is reprinted as a separate, unpaginated pamphlet—*Toward a Black Feminist Criticism*—in 1980. For Smith, despite the overt focus on women's heterosexual acts, *Sula* "works as a lesbian novel not only because of the passionate friendship between Sula and Nel, but because of Morrison's consistently critical stance towards the heterosexual institutions of male/female relationships, marriage, and the family." Smith's reading of the novel hints at an underlying eroticism in the relationship between these two women characters. In 1980, Anne Koenen asks Morrison about readings of her work by "Black feminist critics" (67). Morrison's response, which distances her from certain forms of feminism, appears to speak indirectly to Smith's reading:

> Contemporary hostility to men is bothersome to me. Not that they are not deserving of criticism and contempt, but I don't want a freedom that depends largely on somebody else being on his knees. I also think that part of the women's complaint has to do with enormous expectations. The women like to say they are not dependent on love—as we said before—but there's so little left to love anyway—otherwise why make the man into opera, they make them into opera. What I'm trying to say is there was a time when you could love god, or your race, or your brother, or your sister, or your mother, but all those things have been taken from us in a way, because if you love god they think you are backward, if you love your mother they think you got some Freudian thing. . . . And you could have a friend that you loved. Now if you have a friend that you love somebody will think that you are lesbian or homosexual. (73)

Morrison's expresses concern that contemporary thinking has rendered problematic certain objects of love (notably, god, race, and family). And the problem is that another person can read the things one loves as symptoms of one's psychopathologies. Race seems an odd member of the series since so often Morrison's fiction wants to transform racial self-loathing into racial self-love. But what occasions her most anxious discussion comes in relation to having a same-sex friend and the possibility of being identified as "lesbian or homosexual"—with the implication that to be so identified is distasteful.

What is implicit in Morrison's comments to Koenen becomes explicit in her remarks to Claudia Tate, remarks that oddly circle back to Woolf's speculations on the fictional representation of women's same-sex affection in *A Room of One's Own*. For Jane Marcus, the Chloe-Olivia passage, which I cite as this chapter's epigraph, is central to the sapphistry and rhetorical seduction of a woman author addressing women effected by *Room*'s use of ellipses and question marks (169). Yet even as Morrison's words recall Woolf's passage, they effectively serve to repudiate Smith's lesbian reading:

> Friendship between women is special, different, and has never been depicted as the major focus of a novel before *Sula*. Nobody ever talked about friendship between women unless it was homosexual, and there is no homosexuality in *Sula*. Relationships between women were always written about as though they were subordinate to some other roles they're playing (Tate 157).

Morrison's categorical denial of homosexuality in her novel would certainly seem consistent with a characterization the narrator makes that "those Peace women loved all men. It was manlove that Eva bequeathed to her daughters. [. . .] The Peace women simply loved maleness, for its own sake" (41).[8] Yet despite this unambiguous declaration, the figurative language of *Sula* repeatedly questions the exclusivity of heterosexual affect in the novel. There may be no homosexuality in *Sula,* but there very definitely is a representation of female homosociality in the friendship of Sula and Nel, a bond apparently broken by Nel's marriage to Jude. Between men, homosocial relations are dispersed throughout culture, often in positively marked ways, through friendships and mentoring (Sedgwick, *Epistemology* 186). For Sedgwick, such homosocial relations are constantly shadowed by the possibility of homoerotic desire.[9] In other words, homoerotic figuration in language serves as the hinge between homosocial relations and queer possibilities regarding identity.[10]

In *The Bluest Eye,* Morrison addresses the matter of authorship through a male character, Soaphead Church, but in *Sula* she underscores the difficulty of the woman writer's finding a voice by making her title character an artist manqué. The distance between feminine and masculine identity collapses in a textually bisexual space not simply in Morrison's invented name but also in *Sula.* The plural identities of (feminine) Chloe and (masculine) Anthony/(androgynous) Toni seem to find a fictive embodiment in Sula and Shadrack as the twinned artist manqué figures in Morrison's second novel, figures that explicitly encode Morrison's anxiety about identifying herself as a writer. To see Sula and Shadrack as doubles is to read *Sula* as Morrison reads the relationship between Clarissa and Septimus in *Mrs. Dalloway.* Morrison notes that in draft, Woolf had considered leaving the veteran out of the book but "later decided to make Septimus Clarissa's 'double' [. . . and] the parallel between the two is striking" ("Virginia" 19). What makes them doubles is their relation to alienation; Septimus's "insanity is an extreme of Clarissa's detachment" ("Virginia" 19), a comment that could be refigured to say that Shadrack's insanity is an extreme of Sula's aesthetic detachment. Although Sula and Nel's relation is the most crucial in the novel, Shadrack's mediating function between the two women is more crucial than that of the other male third, Jude Greene. What argues for a relation of twinning between Sula and Shadrack is that both are delineated through negation and lack. The reader knows them by what they are not and do not have. At the same time, Sula's female double, Nel, crucially participates in the construction of Sula's artistic stance toward the community. By revealing to Sula the gaze of disinterested interest, Nel may be the novel's most displaced embodiment of the artist manqué.

In one important sense, Sula is similar to Pecola Breedlove, perhaps Morrison's most famous character defined by lack. What Pecola lacks most decidedly is a sense of self. And the function the two characters serve in relation to their respective communities is nearly identical. As we saw in Claudia's moment of self-critique at the end of *The Bluest Eye,* Pecola's abjection from the body social serves as a crucial way for individuals in the black community to find both personal and communal identity. Individuals know themselves by what they are not, and they are the not-Pecola. So too does Sula, upon her return to the Bottom, come to constitute the identity of the rest of the community. The community quickly learns to define its virtue by Sula's difference, which it reads as a malign supernatural force. Even Teapot's drunken mother becomes "sober, clean and industrious" (114), thus claiming the role of motherhood she had previously avoided, in order to combat what Sula represents. Despite Pecola's and Sula's similar role, there is a crucial difference between the two characters. Sula becomes an empowered Pecola, as it were. In other words, while Pecola acquiesces to her marginalization (in a fashion that is marked as a form of unconscious complicity), Sula takes her lack and attempts to construct identity out of her very marginality and absence of self.

In the section titled "1939," Morrison provides an extended piece of character delineation that identifies Sula by specific lacks. Speaking of the two crucial moments of her childhood—her accidental killing of Chicken Little and overhearing her mother remark that she did not like her—the narrator says:

> The first experience taught her there was no other that you could count on; the second that there was *no self* to count on either. She had no center, no speck around which to grow. . . . She was completely free of ambition, with no affection for money, property or things, no greed, no desire to command attention or compliments—no ego. For that reason she felt no compulsion to verify herself—be consistent with herself. (118–19, emphasis added)

What is striking about this passage is how much of it could be taken with very little modification as a description of Pilate Dead in *Song of Solomon* at the moment of her recognition that she cannot have a full life within the community because she lacks a naval. Sula is not weighed down by egotistic self-love, which as Milkman learns in *Song of Solomon,* prevents one from loving others. Like Pilate, whose missing navel forces her into intense self-examination, cast in almost exactly Thoreauvian terms ("tack[ling] the problem of trying to decide how she wanted to live and what was valuable to her" [149]), Sula similarly constructs identity through the tradition of American transcendentalism, enacting a self that disavows the need to be consistent. But unlike the respected Pilate, Sula is demonized by her community as the embodiment of evil; this might be explained in part by Pilate's renunciation of a sexual role contrasted with the sexual threat Sula represents to women of the Bottom. Whatever the precise reason, the possibilities for fashioning a self from a position of marginality remain limited in *Sula* and must wait until *Song of Solomon* for further development.

The above description of Sula in "1939" resonates uncannily with a particular characterization Morrison made of herself in 1979. In an autobiographical sketch that she wrote for *Contemporary Biography,* she comments on the time leading up to her divorce and the pressures that propelled her to join a writers' group: "It was as though I had nothing left but my imagination. I had no will, no judgment, no perspective, no power, no authority, no self—just this brutal sense of irony, melancholy, and a trembling respect for words. I wrote like someone with a dirty habit. Secretly. Compulsively. Slyly" ("Morrison, Toni" 265). This mirrored articulation of lack that joins Morrison's description of herself with her delineation of Sula is particularly underscored by author's and character's shared absence—"no self." But what author and character do with that condition differs. Morrison has a way to address the issue of the absence of authority and self, namely, the compulsive turn to writing and authorship, which—as I have been arguing—becomes a writing of self. At age twenty-nine, Sula, however, has no access to a compulsive expressive form:

> In a way, her strangeness, her naïveté, her craving for the other half of her equation was the consequence of an idle imagination. Had she paints, or clay, or knew the discipline of the dance, or strings; had she anything to engage her tremendous curiosity and her gift for metaphor, she might have exchanged the restlessness and preoccupation with whim for an activity that provided her with all she yearned for. And like any artist with no art form, she became dangerous. (121)

Sula may not have a form of expression but she does have an aspect of artistic consciousness that Morrison elsewhere speaks of positively. Although my subsequent chapter will address in greater detail Morrison's reading of William Faulkner, I would like to point to a comment she made in 1985 about his writing: "there was something else about Faulkner which I can only call 'gaze.' He had a gaze that was different. It appeared, at that time, to be similar to a look, even a sort of staring, a refusal-to-look-away approach in his writing that I found admirable" ("Faulkner" 297). It is this artistic detachment, very little removed from voyeurism, that characterizes Sula's relation to life. One scene particularly illustrates this. As the stunned community gathers around the horribly burnt body of Hannah Peace, "a young girl finally broke the profound silence" (76) by vomiting, which then seems to allow people to talk to God and call on Jesus. While in the hospital recovering from injuries sustained in attempting to save her daughter, Eva reflects on her granddaughter:

> [. . .] she knew that as she lay on the ground trying to drag herself through the sweet peas and clover to get to Hannah, she had seen Sula standing on the back porch just looking. When Eva [. . .] mentioned what she thought she'd seen to a few friends, they said it was natural. Sula was probably struck dumb, as anybody would be who saw her own mamma burn up. Eva said yes, but inside she disagreed and remained convinced that Sula had watched Hannah burn not because she was paralyzed, but because she was interested. (78)

It is her looking and refusing to turn away that links Sula to artistic consciousness. Sula's gaze defines Morrison's anxiety about the role of the artist; like Soaphead Church, Sula responds with a disinterested interest— a paradoxical attitude that leaves the viewer largely disinterested in the pain or suffering witnessed as pain and suffering yet keenly interested in the aesthetic possibilities represented by that pain.[11] Sula's gaze, fundamental to understanding her as the artist manqué, continues throughout her life, even to the liminal moment of her own death at which she still acts as the disinterested spectator. Despite Nel's incomprehension and assertion of moral superiority in their final meeting, Sula's only interest in her own death is as an opportunity for representation—what she might relate to Nel about the experience of death.

This scene seems to register reflexively Morrison's problem with imagining herself as the artist. Eva critiques Sula (and later Nel) for her distanced gaze, and yet it is Morrison herself who is caught in the amorality of disinterested interest as the author of the scene in which Hannah dies.[12] Although focalized by Eva and narrated by a mediating third-person narrator, Morrison is ultimately the author: "The flames from the yard fire were licking the blue cotton dress, making her dance" (75). Morrison's figure of the dance recurs as Eva struggles to save Hannah: "Cut and bleeding she clawed the air trying to aim her body toward the flaming, dancing figure" (76). It is the disinterested interest of the artist that not only can imagine for the reader the blue dress and the tight red tomatoes but also describe Hannah "there on the wooden sidewalk planks, twitching lightly among the smashed tomatoes" (76). One could quote the scene at greater length but the point is that Morrison is inevitably caught in the very debate between ethics and aesthetics that *Sula* stages. While one may argue that Morrison aligns herself with Eva's situational ethics, the author is implicated in Sula's aesthetic gaze, which operates apart from ethics.

Sula, though, is no writer (as Morrison curiously claims not to have been even as she writes *Sula*). Because Sula lacks the outlet of artistic expression, the novel marks her dangerousness as her obsession with discovering "the other half of her equation"—that relationship with another that would complete self—though she has intuited "that no one would ever be that version of herself which she sought to reach out to and touch with an ungloved hand" (121). And yet, despite lacking an art form, Sula still doubles her author in a significant fashion. Strikingly, Morrison's "dirty habit," her pleasure in her text, parallels Sula's pleasure in her sexual habits.[13] Although Sula is far from secret about her sexuality, she certainly is compulsive and uses her sex as Morrison uses writing—as an empowering means to define self; in the act of coitus was the "utmost irony and outrage in lying under someone, in a position of surrender, feeling her own abiding strength and limitless power" (123). Such a focus on Sula's heterosexual activity might for some readers be reason enough not to give much credence to the lesbian reading of the novel. Yet despite her supposed inheritance of the Peace women's "manlove":

> Whenever she introduced her private thoughts into [men's] rubbings or goings, they hooded their eyes. They taught her nothing but love tricks, shared nothing but worry, gave nothing but money. She had been looking all along for a friend, and it took her a while to discover that a lover was not a comrade and could never be—for a woman. (121)

This passage explicitly states Sula's belief that a man, particularly a woman's sexual partner, cannot serve as the other half of the equation, the completion of identity Sula seeks. (Oddly, in the text's symbolic logic, there is a man who might complete Sula, if only the link could be made between the ungloved hand of Sula's private thoughts and the thoughts of Private Shadrack regarding his monstrous hands.) The implications of identity in the above passage collapse the space between homosociality and homosexuality. Comradeship apparently is available between men, yet could the male lover also be a comrade—for another man? Because this quotation implies that a woman's communion with another woman is the only and ideal possibility for comradeship (and something more?), the description of Sula's discovery needs to be read against Morrison's rejection of the lesbian interpretation of a novel. As a step in this direction, one might note that what Sula searches for sexually serves as a figuration for the artist's ongoing construction of self. Men are merely a means to end for Sula, and the act of having sex seems to substitute metaphorically for an author's producing text:

Sexual aesthetics bored her. Although she did not regard sex as ugly (ugliness was boring also), she liked to think of it as wicked. But as her experiences multiplied she realized that not only was it not wicked, it was not necessary for her to conjure up the idea of wickedness in order to participate fully. During the act of lovemaking she found and needed to find the cutting edge. (122)

If one substitutes "texual" and "text" for "sexual" and "sex," in the above passage, one can refigure the final sentence so that it articulates what may be seen as Morrison's reflexively coded comment on her production: during the *writing* of *Sula* she found and needed to find the cutting edge. For Sula, this authentic identity is oddly elusive. Apparently it is found in sexual activity. Yet Sula's experience of discovering authenticity through sex creates simultaneously the desire to try to find that identity again, a dynamic that suggests that her "cutting edge" identity is never fully present and that is only constituted in the act of seeking itself. But men are extremely marginal in this process.

In all the description of Sula's heterosexual activity, what is apparent is that she finds men's sexuality unpleasant and their unwanted presence after the act is something to block out:

When her partner disengaged himself, she looked up at him in wonder trying to recall his name; and he looked down at her, smiling with tender understanding of the state of tearful gratitude to which he believed he had brought her. She waiting impatiently for him to turn away and settle into a wet skim of satisfaction and light disgust, leaving her to the postcoital privateness in which she met herself, welcomed herself, and joined herself in matchless harmony. (123)

The postcoital moment serves as a renunciation of men and affords her a momentary sense of completeness that she had previously experienced only with Nel. What is important to take from this is that, although she performs heterosexual acts, they are not central to, and indeed seem apart from, Sula's experience of personal identity. Sula seeks identity not with men but, as the postcoital moment suggests, in a solitude that is figured as two women together—her self and her other self—which completes the equation.

Morrison herself comments on the way her character enacts a kind of gender shifting in comments she makes about Sula in 1976:

She really behaves like a man. She picks up a man, drops a man, the same way a man picks up a woman, drops a woman. And that's her thing. She's masculine in that sense. She's adventuresome, she trusts herself, she's not

scared, she really ain't scared. And she is curious and will leave and try anything. So that quality of masculinity—and I mean this in the pure sense—
in a woman at that time is outrage, total outrage. (Stepto 27)

But even as she articulates Sula's gender bending, Morrison does so in very
conventional terms, collapsing the space of sex and gender and seeing man
as typically active and woman as usually passive. Still by having her title
character and primary artist manqué function as the stereotyped male,
Morrison, in trying to secure her position as author by writing a second
novel, arguably confronts what there is about authority that might be
troped as masculine.

Given Morrison's characterization of Sula as masculine, the novel presents a rather complex gendered space in the relations between and among
Sula, Jude, and Nel. Jude, for example, explicitly notes that he is not physically attracted to Sula: "A funny woman, he thought, not that bad-looking.
But he could see why she wasn't married; she stirred a man's mind maybe,
but not his body" (104). What prompts this thought is Sula's humorous use
of language in response to his desire for womanly sympathy; instead she
turns the oppression of the African-American male into an ironic account
that makes the black male the thing the world loves the most. What can one
say then about Jude's having sex with a woman whom he identifies as masculine? It would seem that homoerotic affect emerges in such a moment.
But the more important question is "What does Sula think she is doing by
having sex with her best friend's husband?"

From what we have seen about the way Sula uses men, it is clear that
she does not hope that Jude will leave Nel and marry her. Sula's having sex
with Jude, I wish to argue, is not a function of her interest in him per se
or in men and heterosexuality generally but rather in her desire to better
know her female friend's desire. If the sexes of this triangle were reversed
(two men and a woman), a way of reading the scene would be immediately available, especially in light of Sedgwick's work on same-sex or homosocial relationships. In a culture that endorses a variety of same-sex
relations but demonizes homosexuality, if a male has sex, say, with the wife
of a professor he admires (or of a boss he despises) something more may
be happening than sex; it is quite possibly a homoerotically charged symbolic act in which the woman is merely the medium of a communication
that is strictly between men. This symbolic communication effects a displaced consummation of the homosocial relationship. Literature is certainly full of such representations. In William Faulkner's *Absalom, Absalom!*,
for example, when Henry Sutpen takes pleasure that his twin, Judith, is engaged to marry his passionately admired friend from college, the older,
more sophisticated Charles Bon, the sister serves in Henry's unconscious

as the conduit that will allow a displaced fulfillment of his feared and fantasized unspeakable love for Bon. If, as Sedgwick has demonstrated, one of the ways men use women is as a medium to communicate to other men, then "masculine" Sula similarly attempts a displaced communion/communication through Jude with Nel. Only what Nel "hears" at the moment is filtered through a set of values that can only interpret Sula's act as a betrayal. And of course at the level of the social contract, Sula's act is a betrayal, but Morrison's novel seems finally more interested in the representation of the unconscious, both individual and cultural, that motivates Sula and Nel's misunderstanding, a point I will return to later in my discussion of Nel.

The one apparent exception to Sula's superficial attachment to men is her love for Ajax. But her love for this particular man occurs only because his enactment of masculinity challenges that of his more patriarchal contemporaries who think of women as body rather than mind. Ajax and Sula approach each other as equals; Ajax respects Sula's mind as only one other character previously had—Nel. In this relationship, which appears to give her a completed sense of self, she metaphorically discovers the expressive form that she lacks; in bed with Ajax, Sula imagines herself as the sculptor of his identity, a role that suggests a good modernist and psychoanalytic model of surface and depth.[14] In an extended metaphor of discovery, Sula works through the layers of Ajax's body through language that oddly figures a relation between blackness and whiteness. First she imagines rubbing a cloth on this face that removes the blackness to reveal gold leaf. But taking something more abrasive reveals a layer of alabaster under the gold. What might these colored figurations suggest? Is it that Ajax cannot be reduced to the dominant culture's negative characterization of blackness? Or something akin to the Louis Armstrong lyric in "How Did I Get To Be So Black and Blue?" that says "I'm white inside"? But the whiteness itself proves only another pasteboard mask, as the sculpting metaphor becomes explicit: "*Then I can take a chisel and small tap hammer and tap away at the alabaster. It will crack then like ice under the pick, and through the breaks I will see the loam, fertile, free of pebbles and twigs. For it is the loam that is giving you that smell*" (130). Piercing the surface of whiteness, Sula apparently finds a deeper realm of blackness, one representing Ajax's true essence. In doing so, she has figuratively reversed the roles of the heterosexual act. Literally penetrated by Ajax's phallus, she imaginatively assumes the culturally masculine position, penetrating his idealized body with a chisel. From the point Sula believes that she has penetrated to authenticity, the relationship fails because Sula turns conventionally feminine and dreams of possessing him.

After Ajax leaves her, Sula one day makes an interesting discovery that speaks to the issue of identity when she discovers his driver's license: "His name was Albert Jacks? A. Jacks. She had thought it was Ajax" (135). It is hard not to read this as a reflexive moment from the author presumed to be "A" (Anthony) but who in fact is "A" (Ardelia). This discovery leads to Sula's lament:

> I didn't even know his name. And if I didn't know his name, then there is nothing I did know and I have known nothing ever at all since the one thing I wanted was to know his name so how could he help but leave me since he was making love to a woman who didn't even know his name (136).

In this gap opened in the phonetic misapprehension—a space between signifier and signified—Sula's sense of the stability of both Ajax's and her own identity dissolves, a moment that simultaneously calls into doubt Sula's heterosexual relationship with Ajax as the grounding of her authentic self. In part her attraction to Ajax reflects what he allows her to recall from her youth and the time of her and Nel's budding sexuality. In 1922, seventeen years prior to their sexual relation, Ajax's words, "pig meat," addressed to the passing adolescent girls, mark Sula's and Nel's simultaneous awareness of their sexuality, a time when their intimacy marks them as almost identical. So that, although in a less obvious way than Sula's having sex with Jude, her desire for the apparently unconventional Ajax participates in her unconscious attempt to recover a portion of her lost relationship with Nel.

But Sula is not the only "masculine" character in the novel defined by a lack. As in *The Bluest Eye,* there is a metonymic chain of displaced authorial figurations. Oddly mirroring Sula as the artist manqué is Shadrack, another character whose absence of self results from a psychic wounding; in his case the trauma results from witnessing a particularly gruesome death during combat. Morrison herself has commented on the way Shadrack's "madness" dovetails with Sula's strangeness: "They're both eccentrics, outside the law, except Shadrack's madness is very organized" (Stepto 22). In delineating Shadrack, Morrison again recalls her characterization both of her prewriterly self and of Sula, through the young veteran's catalogue of lacks:

> Twenty-two years old, weak, hot, frightened, not daring to acknowledge the fact that he didn't even know who or what he was . . . with no past, no language, no tribe, no source, no address book, no comb, no pencil, no clock, no pocket handkerchief, no rug, no bed, no can opener, no faded postcard, no soap, no key, no tobacco pouch, no soiled underwear and nothing nothing nothing to do . . . he was sure of one thing only: the unchecked monstrosity of his hands. (12)

And yet unlike Sula, who has no medium for her expression, Shadrack creates an expressive form, not through poetic language but rather through communal ritual—his insertion of National Suicide Day into the consciousness of the Bottom. Each January 3, Shadrack invites the people to kill themselves, and over the years, his creation becomes part of the fabric of the community.

It is worth looking closely at the moment that allows Shadrack to move from total lack to the odd place he occupies in the Bottom—a kind of paradoxically empowered marginality. But his achievement of this marginal empowerment comes at considerable cost. Although the narration represents his thoughts in 1919, the Shadrack who is shipped home from the European War is unable to speak or feed himself; in a sense he has returned to infancy in his posttraumatic state. Released from a veteran's hospital and jailed for vagrancy, Shadrack experiences an odd moment of narcissistic recognition by gazing into water. The myth of Narcissus, of course, has profound implications in psychoanalytic thinking. For Freud, the youth who falls in love with his own reflection and drowns in the water of that reflection, suggests both auto- and homoerotic identifications.[15] In Jacques Lacan's refiguration of Freud, narcissism becomes the mirror stage, the child's necessary internalization of the ideological mirage of self, a moment that mediates the prelinguistic stage with the subject's entry into language. Wishing to see his own face but having no mirror in the jail cell, Shadrack solves his problem in the moonlight by seeking his reflection in the toilet bowl:

> There in the toilet water he saw a grave black face. A black so definite, so unequivocal, it astonished him. He had been harboring a skittish apprehension that he was not real—that he didn't exist at all. But when the blackness greeted him with its indisputable presence, he wanted nothing more. (13)

Shadrack's self-recognition, an odd representation of the birth of the "author," may link his madness to that of Pecola Breedlove, which is engendered by a racial self-loathing. Only by putting his face where his bottom should be can he return to the Bottom with a useable identity. His joyful recognition of a narcissistic twin links blackness with the bodily abject, the repository of feces, urine, and menstrual blood, an identification all the more significant inasmuch as water elsewhere is constellated with death and female sexuality.[16] If the "nigger joke" that begins the novel explains how whites treat blacks like shit, the master giving the slave the inferior hilly land instead of the promised bottom land, Shadrack's moment of self-recognition embraces this figuration to reconstruct a small portion of the symbolic order.

At the site of abjection, Shadrack's excremental self is born, which allows him to conceive of National Suicide Day.[17] The idea for such a day is born out of his "struggle to order and focus experience" (14). What this annual ritual gives the outcast Shadrack is something that liquidates his lacks for that one day. If Morrison's pre-artistic self is marked as one with "no power," Shadrack's insanity "did not mean that he didn't have any sense or, even more important, that he had no power"; his empowerment gives him a voice "full of authority" (15). What the otherwise mad Shadrack achieves is a marginal position within the community, one paralleling Soaphead Church's marginality. But more than paralleling each other in the ritualistic role each plays in their community, Shadrack and Soaphead allegorize what Morrison fears about such narcissistic author/ity. They actively embrace their marginality within a racial group already marginalized in America. These characters may play an important (even a constitutive) role within the community, healing in ways they cannot fully comprehend, but they themselves are beyond healing.

Despite this authority Shadrack achieves through his ritual, his one attempt to construct a human bond through his use of language stands as the quintessential modernist moment of the failure of the medium as a form of expression. Concerned that Shadrack witnessed Chicken Little's drowning, Sula enters his well-ordered house. Before she can frame the words to voice her fear, "[h]e nodded his head as though answering a question, and said, in a pleasant conversational tone, a tone of cooled butter, 'Always.'" (62). In his one-word message, we see the gap between a speaker's intention and a listener's reception. Sula can only read this as the ultimate in detached interest since she assumes he watched and will have the child's death simply as pleasurable image and can at any time pleasurably expose her implication. Only near the end of the novel does one learn that Shadrack intends his "always" as solace to ward off the fear of death (clearly a reflection of his own memories of the wartime death he witnessed) and to help her stabilize identity; misreading the question in her eyes "he had said 'always,' so she would not have to be afraid of the change—the falling away of skin, the drip and slide of blood, and the exposure of bone underneath. He had said 'always' to convince her, assure her, of permanency" (157). The moment, however, only helps create in Sula a sense of the contingency of identity. Even though his "always" fails to communicate Shadrack's intent, the word nevertheless fulfills a portion of his desire inasmuch as it does create a psychological link between speaker and listener. And though it makes Sula fearful of Shadrack in life, on her deathbed, she thinks once again of the veteran's "always." Although she cannot remember the speaker, she recalls it as the promise of "a sleep of water" (149); these words, along with her unrealized fear that her dying will be accompanied by "a gasping for breath," return us to Chicken Lit-

tle's drowning and the final moment Sula and Nel experience of themselves as an undifferentiated whole.

If Shadrack's "always" is crucial to Sula's development as an artist manqué,
then so too is what Nel teaches Sula in the aftermath of Chicken Little's
death. Just as it takes Nel and Shadrack to construct Sula's artistic consciousness, so similarly does it take Eva and Shadrack to force Nel to confront her retreat from artistic consciousness. We learn about the specifics of
Nel's response to Chicken Little's death not at the time, a scene focalized
by Sula, but rather near the end of the novel when in 1965 Nel visits Eva
in the nursing home. What this conversation reveals is that Nel is implicated not so much in Chicken's death as in the artist's stance toward such
human drama. Sula is nearly hysterical but Nel is the one who evidences
the disinterested interest of the artistic gaze. The moment quickly turns
uncomfortable for Nel as Eve accuses her of killing Chicken Little. To
Nel's response that Sula was responsible, Eva says, "You. Sula. What's the
difference? You was there. You watched, didn't you? Me, I never would've
watched" (168). In the fiery deaths of Eva's two children she does not
watch but acts. Her attempt to claim the ethical high ground may or may
not make Eva the text's ethical center. Yet ethics is not aesthetics and this
will be one of Morrison's recurring problems in her subsequent fiction—
how to reconcile ethics with an aesthetic consciousness that may be necessarily ethically impaired. Although caught, Nel tries to deny her
implication in the aesthetic gaze of disinterested interest, but Eva insists on
the identity of Sula and Nel: "[n]ever was no difference between you"
(169). Although she quickly leaves the nursing home, Nel cannot escape
the old woman's address, which—given Eva's conflation of Sula and Nel—
speaks as much to Sula's act of watching her mother burn as it does to
Nel's watching Chicken Little drown. Nel confronts the "good feeling she
had had when Chicken's hands slipped": "Now it seemed that what she
had thought was maturity, serenity and compassion was only the tranquil-
lity that follows a joyful stimulation. Just as the water closed peacefully over
the turbulence of Chicken Little's body, so had contentment washed over
her enjoyment" (170).

Nel's memory begins to point us toward the desiring subtext in her relationship with Sula. Water and wetness, as we have seen, are recurring figures in Morrison's descriptions of moments of heterosexual coupling, so
that, in the larger context of the novel, the river setting of the boy's death
suggests both sexuality and narcissism. What Sula's act does at a literal level
is to rid the girls of the unwanted male who intrudes on their play at a
moment in their development when they stand between innocence and

experience; that is, they are aware of their budding sexuality, though they have not yet experienced sex. But their play, though literally innocent, seems figured as sexual experience. Running to the river, they throw themselves to the ground "to taste their lip sweat and contemplate the wildness that had come upon them so suddenly" (57). Beginning with "their foreheads almost touching":

> Nel found a thick twig and, with her thumbnail, pulled away its bark until it was stripped to a smooth, creamy innocence. Sula looked about and found one too. When both twigs were undressed Nel moved easily to the next stage and began tearing up rooted grass to make a bare spot of earth. When a generous clearing was made, Sula traced intricate patterns in it with her twig. At first Nel was content to do the same. But soon she grew impatient and poked her twig rhythmically and intensely into the earth, making a small neat hole that grew deeper and wider with the least manipulation of her twig. (58)

Although not of course literally denoted by the words, the connotative excess of the figurative language suggests that Sula and Nel's innocent play, during which "neither one had spoken a word" (59), enacts a kind of symbolic mutual masturbation.[18] When they are finished playing with their holes, they stand together "gaz[ing] out over the swift dull water as an unspeakable restlessness and agitation held them" (59). Like Shadrack who discovers identity in the water, Sula and Nel in their narcissistic play are on the verge of sexual identity, precisely the moment they are interrupted by Chicken Little.

The boy's death becomes Nel's "joyful stimulation" that follows the unspeakable agitation resulting from her sexually figured grass play with Sula. Similar to the "matchless harmony" (123) that Sula experiences in the aftermath of her man-irrelevant heterosexual acts, Nel experiences a bliss that segues into contentment and tranquility. How does this sexualized water close? Peacefully. Confronting the long-repressed desire in relation to the boy's death leads to another moment of psychic recovery. Unconsciously walking toward the cemetery and Sula's grave, Nel reflects on her past. As she leaves, she passes Shadrack, and though there is no overt recognition, the chance passing seems to serve as a catalyst producing an instance of clarity for Nel:

> Leaves stirred; mud shifted; there was the smell of overripe green things. A soft ball of fur broke and scattered like dandelion spores in the breeze.
>
> "All that time, all that time, I thought I was missing Jude." And the loss pressed down on her chest and came up into her throat. "We was girls

together," she said as though explaining something. "O Lord, Sula," she cried, "girl, girl, girlgirlgirl." (174)

In order to understand better what is at stake in the figuration of the mud shifting, it is useful to place it in relation to the two other moments in which it appears. This means first returning to the scene of estrangement between Sula and Nel. Sula, as I have suggested earlier, assumes that Nel, the teacher of disinterested interest, will understand the communication implied by her having sex with Jude; but while Nel crucially participates in engendering Sula's artistic gaze, Nel herself in the years of her marriage has retreated from the artist's marginality into the conventionality of the community. In effect, the misunderstanding between Sula and Nel mirrors the missed communication between Shadrack and Sula, only now it is Sula's attempt to communicate that fails, so to speak. Sula, in "addressing" Nel by undressing Jude, assumes she hails another who accepts (and indeed the one who helped teach) the radical contingency of identity. But Sula's sexual address only pushes Nel toward a rigid sense of self inasmuch as she fixes her identity as the wronged victim for the next twenty-eight years.

Nel's retreat to the bathroom after the shock of seeing Jude and Sula together introduces mud as a figure. Morrison again is playing in the dark, since Nel enters the well-lighted bathroom "to throw into relief the dark things that cluttered her." As she waits for something to happen, "[t]here was stirring, a movement of mud and dead leaves" (106). She is on her knees next to the toilet, site of Shadrack's epiphany of excremental black identification. But Nel, while waiting for something to happen inside her body, fails to look into the toilet, to face up to the bottom, as it were. Meditating on the private hell of her existence, she realizes that she does so in terms of Sula's language; Nel waits for a cry to express her pain: "The mud shifted, the leaves stirred, the smell of overripe green things enveloped her and announced the beginnings of her very own howl" (108). But it is a howl delayed and deferred that allows the mud to settle into a "gray ball hovering just there" (109). The metaphor residing in mud is obviously underscored by its repetition, and its significance becomes clearer in the context of a third appearance, as Sula thinks about her relation to Ajax.

Earlier I directed attention to the scene in which Sula senses she is sculpting her way to the most authentic layer of Ajax's identity. Her discovery of the blackness under the whiteness under the blackness occurs as she is engaged in coitus, and her thoughts finish as follows:

I will put my hand deep into your soil, lift it, sift it with my fingers, feel its warm surface and dewy chill below. [. . .]

I will water your soil, keep it rich and moist. But how much? How much water
to keep the loam moist? And how much loam will I need to keep my water still? And
when do the two make mud? (131)

Sula's sexual experience allows her gift for metaphor free range. In particular, she reverses the mythic figuration generally associated with earth and
sky.[19] In her rendering, sky is female; earth, male. Moreover, Sula figures
herself the almost godlike creator, the one whose nurture is essential to
Ajax's soil/soul. But most crucial to this instance of the figure is that it clar-
ifies mud as a sexual symbol.

Returning now to mud's initial appearance, we see that it occurs in relation to Nel's conscious sense of heterosexual loss and the promise never
to be able to look at a man again. Yet as "1937" ends, there appears a coun-
tercurrent to her lament over heterosexual suffering: "And what am I supposed to do with these old thighs now, just walk up and down these
rooms? What good are they, Jesus? They will never give me the peace I
need to get from sunup to sundown [. . .]" (111). Here Nel's unconscious
speaks, since the symbolic logic of the narrative reveals that the Peace she
needs is Sula. Reading the pun in the word "peace" here might seem
forced if Nel herself did not play off the doubled signification in the grave-
yard. Looking at the grave markers of the Peace family—each marked only
by dates and the patronymic "Peace"—Nel thinks, "They were not dead
people. They were words. Not even words. Wishes, longings" (171). This
desire for peace cannot be contained by the denotative meaning of "peace"
as harmony or tranquility of mind, since as we have seen from Nel's tranquility in the aftermath of Chicken Little's death, such peace carries an
extra valence. For Nel, her nonverbal longings so often have been for a
sexual pleasure long absent: "the smell of overripe green things," not a desire for Jude Greene but for that smell arising from Sula's and Nel's tear-
ing grass in their "innocent" play by the river—their one presexual sexual
encounter. Read in relation to the final image of shifting mud and the or-
gasmic release of the soft ball of fur, the wishes and longings Nel experiences are for the Peace absent from her thighs. Nel's epiphanic
cry—girlgirlgirl—serves as the climax to narrative desire.[20]

So although there may be no overtly homosexual acts in *Sula,* there is
certainly homoerotic figuration that encrypts same-sex desire. My point in
saying this is not that Barbara Smith was right about *Sula* and that Morrison's understanding of her own text somehow lacks self-knowledge. Indeed the very notion of self-knowledge is limited by the postmodern sense
that the self is always unavoidably elsewhere, only emerging in the act of
inscription. In writing *Sula,* then, Morrison perhaps discovered the kind
of book she could not write, at least not if she wanted to avoid being iden-

tified by certain feminist critics as a lesbian author, an identification that may have seemed in this early stage of her writing career detrimental to her aspiration to speak broadly for African-American experience. Still Morrison was not finished with her need to scrutinize the development of the artistic self, and so one can see her next novel as a daring continuation of *Sula*'s project by constructing a portrait of the African-American woman artist as a young man. If Sula, the artist manqué, gives Morrison one avenue to explore the relation between author-ity/ship and masculinity, her next central character, Milkman Dead, one apparently uninterested in forging the uncreated consciousness of his race, becomes the novelist's strongest and most modernist expression of authentic blackness. In so doing, Morrison turns her intertextual gaze from Woolf to Faulkner.

Chapter 4

Song of Solomon, Narrative Identity, and the Faulknerian Intertext

A
s the title of this chapter suggests, I believe that Morrison's intertextual engagement with canonical white modernist writing tells us something about her ongoing construction of authorial identity in her first four novels. Although I have speculated on Morrison's relation to Virginia Woolf in the previous chapter, I have waited until this moment to consider more fully the implications of what it means to read an African-American writer in the context of white writing. My reason for doing so is largely pragmatic. Since completing her master's thesis in 1955, Morrison has had much more to say about William Faulkner's fiction than about Woolf's; the very quantity of Morrison's commentary on Faulkner, therefore, provides the source material for developing an understanding of her relation to high modernism.

In fact it was at the 1985 Faulkner and Yoknapatawpha Conference in Oxford, Mississippi, that Morrison once again elaborated a self-representation regarding her relation to her published fiction, the story in which she continues to be the writer who was almost a writer. Although in 1983 she claimed she knew she was a writer after completing *Sula*, in 1985 Morrison gives a different account of when her sense of herself as a writer emerged:

> And it was only with my third book, *Song of Solomon,* that I finally said [. . .] "this is what I do." I had written three books. It was only after I finished *Song of Solomon* that I thought, "maybe this is what I do *only.*" Because before that I always said that I was an editor *who* also wrote books or a teacher *who* also wrote. I never said I was a writer. ("Faulkner" 301)

But even without a consideration of the way her third novel gives access to a portion of her aesthetic autobiography, one can still acknowledge that *Song of Solomon* intensely foregrounds the processes of identity formation in the novel's central character, Milkman Dead. It does so, unlike her first two novels, on decidedly male grounds. From the novel's one-word dedication (Daddy), Morrison draws upon a transfigured representation of her own family history, emphasizing male genealogy. The novel's very title derives from what Morrison herself has called the "genuinely autobiographical," as I discussed in chapter 1, since her maternal grandfather was John Solomon Willis.[1] The portrait of "Lincoln's Heaven," the farm that had belonged to Milkman's grandfather in Pennsylvania, is in fact drawn from stories Morrison knew about her own grandfather's farm, eighty-eight acres given to Morrison's great-grandmother during Reconstruction. "The land got legally entangled," Morrison tells Colette Dowling, "because of some debts my grandfather, who inherited it, owed—or, rather, didn't *know* he owed. It was like the old man in *Song of Solomon*. Those people didn't really understand what was happening. All they knew is that at one point they didn't own the land anymore and had to work for the person who did" (54). Like Morrison's family, the Dead family migrates to the Midwest in order to escape racism and violence.

The locale of the novel's opening initially suggests a distance from Morrison's Lorain, Ohio, set as it is in Michigan. For years I have assumed that the setting of part I was Detroit, though that does not seem to square with the geography of the state. On closer examination, it appears that it is a Michigan of the imagination, not one locatable on any map. The novel's first sentence creates a problem when Robert Smith announces his intention to fly "to the other side of Lake Superior" (3). This implies that his point of departure is on the opposite side of the lake, yet the only part of Michigan touching Superior is the Upper Peninsula, a place where very few African Americans live. While it does seem significant that Smith wishes to fly to Canada, that site of freedom for African Americans escaping slavery, it probably is a pointless exercise attempting to name the precise Michigan locale (could it be working-class Marion or Port Huron?). What this ambiguous geographical reference points to is that, fictively speaking, Morrison hasn't left home yet. Morrison seems to confirm the irrelevance of specific locale in a comment she makes to Jane Bakerman at the time of *Song of Solomon*'s publication: "I think I call [the setting] Michigan; they sort of travel around a little bit. But all of mine start here in the Midwest!" (39). Milkman's Michigan, Morrison's comment suggests, is but a minor displacement from the novelist's Ohio and her own working-class, Great Lakes town of Lorain. Yet although Morrison metaphorically stays at home, leaving home is precisely what Milkman Dead thinks he wants.

In this regard, *Song of Solomon* participates in and arguably completes Morrison's fictive meditation on those aspects of authorship that are linked to the cultural masculine. Soaphead Church opens the space of writerly self-examination; Shadrack pushes this reflexive examination into the realm of communal ritual. But Morrison's third novel is a departure from the first two in its focus on a male character, Milkman Dead, a name that had served as the working title for *Song of Solomon*. In bringing African-American male identity to the foreground, Anthony/Toni has performed a daring experiment with gender that her act of self-naming suggests: *Song of Solomon* is a portrait of the African-American woman novelist as a young *man*. Beginning on Morrison's date of birth, the novel takes us through the first thirty-two years of Milkman's life. What is striking is how this time frame corresponds to the fictional Milkman's real-life double, Toni Morrison. Milkman's story stops at the moment of a completed project of self-discovery, authenticity, and connection to his ancestors. Like another novel published in 1977, Leslie Marmon Silko's *Ceremony, Song of Solomon* tells of a movement from alienation to authenticity. In Morrison's life, the time of the novel's ending (1963) corresponds to a time of upheaval—a marriage that had soured, an impending divorce, and an almost therapeutic turn to fiction as she joins a writer's group. In short, Milkman is represented as having achieved an authentic identity at the very moment when Morrison begins her search for identity through her writing, and he undergoes the same self-examination crucial to other Morrison characters, such as Soaphead Church, Sula, Pilate, and subsequently Jadine Childs in *Tar Baby*.

In a novel that focuses on matters of African-American masculine identity, it is worth speculating on such identity as it may relate to Morrison's sense of authorial identity. If Morrison engages Ralph Ellison intertextually in *The Bluest Eye,* a similar project of reclamation occurs in *Song of Solomon*. Only now it is Faulkner, whose major texts examine the forces that shape the identity of Southern white men, who is the focus of Morrison's gaze.

The Faulknerian intertext, however, is not as overtly signaled as the biblical intertext of *Song of Solomon*. Morrison's act of naming her third novel at first suggests the kind of mythic intertext that James Joyce invokes in *Ulysses.* But the biblical intertext of Morrison's title does not supply the kind of narrative context that *The Odyssey* provides Joyce. In this regard, Morrison's act of titling her third novel may be more akin to E. L. Doctorow's titling his fictive reexamination of the Rosenberg executions *The Book of Daniel*—that is, an evocative rendering of the narrator's stance toward the story related. The biblical poem of Solomon does suggest certain ways of thinking about Morrison's novel: both Solomon's song and the song Milkman discovers that sings his family's African genealogy detail sexual suffering. The dialogue between the lovers in the biblical text speaks to Milkman's relationship with Hagar, just as Morrison's meditation on American culture's reification of color makes the woman's assertion, "I am very dark, but comely" (Song Sol. 1.5), resonate in a culturally fresh way. At the same time, the verse also points to the way that skin color can signify in the African-American community. But in *Song of Solomon,* the explicit intertext of Morrison's act of titling deflects attention away from her reading and recasting of Faulkner, a project that continues even into Morrison's later fiction, which is more invested in recovering African-American history. To approach Morrison with Faulkner as one context is to hear a critical dialogue that can be taken as an African-American reclamation of canonical modernism.

In a novel as obsessed with names and naming as *Song of Solomon,* including the potential of names to subvert white authority, one passage particularly suggests one way to begin thinking about Morrison and Faulkner. Macon Dead, who bears his father's name (itself the product of a mistake on a post–Civil War form), walks by his sister's house: "Surely, he thought, he and his sister had some ancestor, some lithe young man with onyx skin and legs as straight as cane stalks, who had a name that was real. A name given to him at birth with love and seriousness" (17).

Macon's desire for an authentic name is shared by a character in Faulkner's *Go Down, Moses:*

> not *Lucius Quintus* @c @c @c, but *Lucas Quintus,* not refusing to be called Lucius, because he simply eliminated that word from the name; not denying, declining the name itself, because he used three quarters of it; but simply taking the name and changing, altering it, making it no longer the white man's but his own, by himself composed, himself selfprogenitive and nominate, by himself ancestored [. . .]. (269)

Faulkner's Lucas Beauchamp, the descendant of a white plantation owner's incestuous miscegenation and perhaps Faulkner's most complex rendering of African-American masculinity, speaks to the possibilities of self-fashioning. Like Morrison, Faulkner changed his name, adding the "u" to his patronymic as a symbolic act of self-fathering. Morrison's reference to John Solomon Willis, her maternal grandfather, is interesting, inasmuch as she appropriates his middle name. It is, as I pointed out previously, the middle name of her maternal grand*mother* Ardelia Willis, that Morrison transforms into the masculine "Anthony" to provide the ostensible genesis for "Toni." This curious need to construct identity through the name links

Billy Falkner/William Faulkner to Chloe/Toni and serves as a metonymy for a larger relationship between the two Nobel prize-winning authors.

Any discussion of Morrison's work in relation to modernism (or postmodernism) in general or to Faulkner in particular is likely to be met with misunderstanding. To speak of a Faulknerian intertext in Morrison's fiction runs the risk not only that some readers will see this as an attempt to question her genius, but also of calling up images of racial and sexual abuse in the American past.[2] Does not the very positing of such a relationship imply that, without a white Southern male's seminal texts, those of an African-American woman would never have come to fruition? But arguing for an intertextual relationship between Morrison and Faulkner does not require granting Faulkner's the status of master text. In fact, my purpose is not a discussion of Faulkner's influence on Morrison but rather to suggest how reading Morrison reshapes the way one reads Faulkner.[3]

The point of examining the relation between Morrison and Faulkner certainly should not be to measure Morrison on the yardstick of a Faulkner but rather to understand how her texts reclaim those of the modernists.[4] The broader notions of intertextuality, emphasizing the infinitely resonating signification of language, mean that one can validly read not only Faulkner's influence on Morrison, but also Morrison's influence on Faulkner—how her fiction and literary criticism may cause one to rethink Faulkner in a fundamental way. This is a point Aldon L. Nielsen has made in his work on race and intertextuality:

> We read Melville within the text of Ralph Ellison's *Invisible Man,* but we must also read Melville differently because of Ellison's text. We must read the transcendence of Ralph Waldo Emerson alongside our reading of the blackness of Huck Finn. We must attempt to understand what the Middle Passage means in black consciousness, and how it means differently in the texts of Harriet Beecher Stowe, and how her texts figure differently when read by black writers. (24)

Nielsen's insistence that the texts of black and white writers must be read against each other develops both from his critique of the way liberal pluralism maintains a sub rosa racial essentialism and from his understanding that race is an unstable social construction:

> The races, and their signifiers, exist only in relation to all other points in our systems of racial signifying. Just as the terms *black* and *white* serve, not, as observation will always confirm, to denote clearly demarcated differences in skin pigmentation, but to organize the meanings of human lives beneath constructed racial rubrics, so do language practices recognized as racially

motivated among native speakers serve to carve up territories of racial con-
notation rather than to reflect preexistent cultural facts. (7)

In this chapter, my intertextual reading hopes to extend Nielsen's project
to the specificity of Toni Morrison and William Faulkner. Both Faulkner's
and Morrison's representations of racial identity emerge in the liminal
space between blackness and whiteness and the communal urge (both
black and white) to deny the brute material fact of the mixture of the
races.

African-American literary theory and criticism, however, frequently
make problematic the issue of race and intertextuality through a politically
understandable urge to focus solely on African-American texts, a part of
the aesthetic past that historically has not received equal status or attention.
Taking their cue from Morrison herself, some argue that the most appropriate frame for assessing her literary work is an African-American folk
and oral tradition.[5] In his work on the theory of African-American literature, Henry Louis Gates, Jr., does acknowledge that African-American
writers revise texts by white writers with "a sense of difference based on
the black vernacular" (*Signifying* xxii). His project, however, is to understand the "web of filiation" created when black writers reinvent the tropes
of other black writers (*Signifying* xxii). This is precisely the work Michael
Awkward takes up in *Inspiriting Influences,* an illuminating study of African-
American women writer's use of the black aesthetic past.

In her book on Morrison, Denise Heinze follows Gates's and Awkward's position on what texts should be read as the intertext of African-
American fiction. Using W. E. B. Du Bois's famous discussion of black
American "identity" in *The Souls of Black Folk* as an always divided "double-consciousness," Heinze notes that double-consciousness may intersect
with Bakhtin's double-voicedness, the Russian theorist's trope for intertextuality. Still, for Heinze, the issue is quite clear: "Morrison's double-
consciousness cannot ultimately be explained in terms of her relationship
to the dominant culture" (10). She turns to Awkward's reading of *The
Bluest Eye* to support this claim; for Awkward, Morrison's novel needs to
be understood in relation to other African-American texts that represent
Du Bois's notion of double-consciousness, particularly Hurston's *Their
Eyes Were Watching God.* Despite Morrison's claim not to have read
Hurston until after the publication of *The Bluest Eye,* Heinze concurs
with Awkward's thesis that Morrison's novels function as refigurations of
the African-American aesthetic past (Heinze 10–11). Awkward's linking
of Morrison and Hurston does not need to depend on Morrison's reading of Hurston, since such a reading strategy is already legitimated by the-

ories of intertextuality, whether Eurocentric (Bakhtin's double-voiced-ness, Kristeva's mosaic of quotations, Barthes' authorless text) or Afrocentric (Gates's Signifyin[g]).

While not wishing to gainsay the value of Heinze's approach, I would nevertheless suggest that the converse of her claim also has a legitimacy: *the double-consciousness of Toni Morrison's work cannot ultimately be understood without some consideration of its relation to the dominant culture.* More overtly than any relation to Hurston's work, Toni Morrison's fiction resonates with that of William Faulkner, a writer whose canonical status clearly marks him as a part of the dominant culture. Before considering some of these fictional resonances, however, I would like to examine a different sort of evidence. Morrison herself in a number of forums has commented upon Faulkner's fiction. Morrison's remarks about the relation of her work to Faulkner's show a decided ambivalence. His influence is at times affirmed, at times denied, at times simultaneously affirmed and denied. That she has read Faulkner closely and carefully is undeniable, so the question of Morrison's relation to Faulkner in some sense turns on what it means that a writer is always inescapably also a reader. In 1955, as a master's student at Cornell, Morrison completed her thesis, "Virginia Woolf's and William Faulkner's Treatment of the Alienated." Her sixteen-page chapter on Faulkner focuses primarily on Thomas Sutpen and Quentin Compson. In *Absalom, Absalom!* and *The Sound and the Fury,* Morrison sees "elements of Greek tragedy," such as "the fall of a once great house" and "old family guilts inherited by an heir"; moreover, "the fact that incest plays such an important part . . . is evidence that Faulkner patterns these histories after the Greeks" ("Virginia" 24). What these comments point to, I believe, is that any piece of writing (even the academic prose of a master's thesis) is always unavoidably a form of intellectual autobiography, no matter how little the autobiographical impulse forms part of the writer's intentions. We might say, for example, that Morrison's previous work on the classics as an undergraduate at Howard University prepared her to make the kinds of claims she does in her master's thesis about Faulkner. So that when one sees incest and family history as elements of Morrison's fictional matter in, say, *The Bluest Eye* or *Song of Solomon,* one need not attribute this presence to Faulkner per se nor even to Greek tragedy. The relation between Morrison's texts and those of the aesthetic past, therefore, is not determined but overdetermined. What this means from a reader's perspective is that numerous cultural texts examine incest and that this whole matrix of prior representations becomes available for a critical examination of what and how incest might mean in Morrison's work.

In the first published interview in which Morrison mentions Faulkner, she bristles at Thomas LeClair's suggestion that some readers—white readers—will not understand a certain scene in *Sula;* says Morrison:

> There is a level of appreciation that might be available only to people who understand the context of the language. The analogy that occurs to me is jazz: it is open on the one hand and both complicated and inaccessible on the other. I never asked Tolstoy to write for me, a little colored girl in Lorain, Ohio. I never asked Joyce not to mention Catholicism or the world of Dublin. Never. And I don't know why I should be asked to explain your life to you. We have splendid writers to do that, but I am not one of them. It is that business of being universal, a word hopelessly stripped of meaning for me. Faulkner wrote what I suppose could be called regional literature and had it published all over the world. It is good—and universal—because it is specifically about a particular world. That's what I wish to do. (LeClair 124)

Her mild approval of Faulkner's fiction—its goodness depends on its representation of particularity—nevertheless signals her desire to put distance between herself and Faulkner, as well as other canonical novelists, and to position herself specifically as an African-American woman author writing the specificity of African-American experience. At the same time, the particular authors Morrison mentions (Tolstoy, Joyce, and Faulkner) reveal the scope of her ambition as a writer.

Morrison reiterates her difference more forcefully in an interview with Nellie McKay in 1983:

> Our—black women's—job is a particularly complex one [. . .]. We have no systematic mode of criticism that has yet evolved from us, but it will. I am not *like* James Joyce; I am not *like* Thomas Hardy; I am not *like* Faulkner. I am not *like* in that sense. I do not have objections to being compared to such extraordinarily gifted and facile writers, but it does leave me sort of hanging there when I know that my effort is to be *like* something that has probably only been fully expressed perhaps in music, or in some other culture-gen that survives almost in isolation because the community manages to hold on to it. (152)

In distinguishing herself from Faulkner, Hardy, and Joyce, Morrison stresses the particularity of African-American experience, from its aurality to its investment in the supernatural (152–53).

Both the LeClair and the McKay interviews, however, serve as a prelude to Morrison's much fuller treatments of the ways Faulkner may have influenced her. Morrison's remarks framing her reading from her then work-in-progress *Beloved* at the 1985 Faulkner and Yoknapatawpha Conference serve as one of the clearest instances of her ambivalence toward Faulkner. Prior to her reading she said, "there was for me not only an academic interest in Faulkner, but in a very, very personal way, in a very personal way as a reader, William Faulkner had an enormous effect on me, an enormous effect" ("Faulkner" 296).[6] But after her reading, in answer to the first question put to her regarding the effect Faulkner had on her literary career, Morrison responds:

> Well, I'm not sure that he had any effect on my work. I am typical, I think, of all writers who are convinced that they are wholly original and that if they recognized an influence they would abandon it as quickly as possible. [. . .] My reasons, I think, for being interested and deeply moved by all his subjects had something to do with my desire to find out something about this country and that artistic articulation of its past that was not available in history, which is what art and fiction can do but sometimes history refuses to do. [. . .] And there was something else about Faulkner which I can only call "gaze." He had a gaze that was different. It appeared, at that time, to be similar to a look, even a sort of staring, a refusal-to-look-away approach in his writing that I found admirable. At that time, in the '50s or the '60s, it never crossed my mind to write books. But then I did it, and I was very surprised myself that I was doing it, and I knew that I was doing it for some reasons that are not writerly ones. I don't really find strong connections between my work and Faulkner's. ("Faulkner" 296–97)

Morrison's attempt here to make Faulkner a "was"—to relegate his influence to her pre-writerly past—seems (especially in light of her subsequent comments about him) as unreliable as Faulkner's frequent claim to those who did not know better that he had never read Joyce, a claim undercut by others who heard Faulkner recite long passages of Joyce's work from memory (Blotner 287).

Still, in *Playing in the Dark,* Morrison's discussion of racial figuration in canonical literature by white authors—Cather, Poe, Twain, and Hemingway—appears to give some credence to her claim that Faulkner has receded from her consciousness. His work is mentioned twice in passing, with only a brief elaboration in the conclusion of her discussion of *The Narrative of Arthur Gordon Pym* and *Huckleberry Finn:*

> We are reminded of other images at the end of literary journeys into the forbidden space of blackness. Does Faulkner's *Absalom, Absalom!,* after its protracted search for the telling African blood, leave us with just such an image of snow and the eradication of race? Not quite. Shreve sees himself as the inheritor of the blood of African kings; the snow apparently is the wasteland of unmeaning, unfathomable whiteness. (58)

This general omission of Faulkner's texts in *Playing in the Dark,* however, does not mean that Faulkner has fallen away from her field of vision; indeed at another level Faulkner reappears in Morrison's critical text through her reading of Faulkner criticism.[7] Her development of "the common linguistic strategies employed in fiction to engage the serious consequences of blacks" draws liberally on James A. Snead's book on Faulkner, *Figures of Division* (*Playing* 66–69).

If Faulkner belongs only to Morrison's past, then what does one make of her comments regarding her experiences teaching *Absalom, Absalom!* from a 1993 interview in *The Paris Review?*

> Faulkner in *Absalom, Absalom!* spends the entire book tracing race, and you can't find it. No one can see it, even the character who *is* black can't see it. I did this lecture for my students that took me forever, which was tracking all the moments of withheld, partial or disinformation, when a racial fact or clue *sort* of comes out but doesn't quite arrive. I just wanted to chart it. I listed its appearance, disguise and disappearance on every page, I mean every phrase! [. . .] Do you know how hard it is to withhold that kind of information but hinting, pointing all of the time? And then to reveal it in order to say that it is *not* the point anyway? It is technically just astonishing. As a reader you have been forced to hunt for a drop of black blood that means everything and nothing. The insanity of racism. So the structure is the argument. [. . .] No one has done anything quite like that ever. So, when I critique, what I am saying is, I don't care if Faulkner was a racist or not; I don't personally care, but I am fascinated by what it means to write like this. (Schappell 101)

Clearly, Morrison still reads Faulkner. And if she still turns to Faulkner's texts, how is she to contain that "very personal" and "enormous effect" ("Faulkner" 296)? Does Faulkner exist for her as a reader, as a teacher, as a critic, but not as writer? This writerly desire to deny influence leads Morrison to a compartmentalizing of self and identity that belies her portrayals of characters who overcome such fragmentation.

Indeed, Morrison's denial of Faulkner's influence on her as a writer contradicts one of the central enabling claims of her critical project in *Playing in the Dark.* She contends that she developed the ability to see moments of racial figuration that literary critics cannot only after she stopped "reading as a reader and began to read as a writer" (*Playing* 15). It is this fundamental difference, she believes, that allows her, as "a writer reading," to understand that "the subject of the dream is the dreamer"; her insistence on a special understanding of "how language arrives" for a writer produces insightful speculations regarding how Cather may have struggled over her representation of Till in *Sapphira and the Slave Girl* or what writerly conflict Hemingway might have experienced by silencing an African-American character in *To Have and Have Not* (*Playing* 17). If one removes the burden of authorial consciousness from these two moments, Morrison's insights still stand, perhaps more clearly, as instances of the way racial ideology functions both in Cather's and Hemingway's texts and more broadly in their particular cultural moment. My point is, simply, that when Morrison claims, as she does in *The Paris Review* interview, that her classroom critique of Faulkner proceeds from being "fascinated by what it means to write like" Faulkner, she is reading the same way she reads Cather and Hemingway—as a writer reading. It may be a useful and enabling fiction for Morrison to see her novels as unmarked by Faulkner. Nevertheless, the rhetorical separation between reader and writer that Morrison wishes to maintain in her critical discourse largely collapses.

As a step toward seeing Morrison as a writer reading Faulkner, I wish to consider her *Song of Solomon* as a rewriting of Faulkner's *Go Down, Moses*. The critical dialogue in which *Song of Solomon* engages *Go Down, Moses* suggests that she reclaims Faulkner in ways that question the male-centered world of the hunt and that refuse the gambit of tragedy.

In her master's thesis, Morrison's characterization of Thomas Sutpen's and Quentin Compson's alienated relation to history also accurately describes Isaac McCaslin's alienation from his past as he comes of age in a defeated South and discovers in the ledgers the horror of his grandfather's incest and miscegenation ("Alienation" 24). Her own character, Milkman Dead, in *Song of Solomon,* similarly comes of age alienated from his family's history, almost as a result, one might say, of patriarchs such as Lucius Quintus Carothers McCaslin, whose forced mixture of the races in Mississippi results in the special status accorded lighter-skinned African Americans in Milkman Dead's Michigan. In other words, Ike's family problem, as he confronts the racism of the white community, is too much history; Milkman's difficulty in seeing the racism within the African-American community (at least in part I) is not enough history. But while *Go Down, Moses* is another tragedy (inasmuch as Roth Edmonds repeats his great-great-great grandfather's incestuous miscegenation, the act that motivated Isaac's repudiation in the first place), *Song of Solomon,* although similarly structured by intergenerational repetitions, finds Milkman ultimately breaking free of certain destructive cycles of the Dead family and Western patriarchal social organization.[8]

A number of other parallels invite a consideration of these two narratives together. In both novels, the male protagonists apparently come to some transcendent moment while hunting, for hunting is something more than the literal stalking of animals; the hunted animals in both are totemic substitutes for characters. Both novels blur boundaries between the natural and supernatural worlds. But perhaps most important, the creation of the adult subjectivity of Isaac McCaslin in *Go Down, Moses* and Milkman Dead in *Song of Solomon* serves as the site of conflict and competition. Certainly those who struggle to create Isaac's and Milkman's subjectivities bear certain parallels. Macon Dead, for example, approximates McCaslin Edmonds, while Guitar and Pilate split the function of Sam Fathers.[9]

In *Go Down, Moses*, McCaslin Edmonds speaks the paternal voice of the Old South, inviting Isaac to take his rightful place in L. Q. C. McCaslin's patriarchal design. Similarly, Macon hopes to create in Milkman a son who will approve of the middle-class values Macon has adopted. Undoubtedly, Macon's perspective on life is best summarized in his words to his twelve-year-old son upon finding that Milkman has disobeyed him by visiting Pilate:

> After school come to my office; work a couple of hours there and learn what's real. Pilate can't teach you a thing you can use in this world. Maybe the next, but not this one. Let me tell you right now the one important thing you'll ever need to know: Own things. And let the things you own own other things. Then you'll own yourself and other people too. (55)

What of course is chilling in Macon's pedagogical moment, teaching his son the path toward self-possession, is that the father, himself the son of a former slave, advocates owning others as a component of self-possession. Macon's teachings are subverted, however, from two directions—by his sister Pilate and by Milkman's friend Guitar—and their presence together seems to constitute a play on Faulkner's Sam Fathers, the former slave who ultimately teaches Ike McCaslin an alternative to owning things. Both Pilate and Guitar act as Milkman's guides to ostensibly different world pictures—Pilate, the part-Native American advocate of the rights of ghosts, and Guitar, the materialist who wishes to awaken Milkman to African Americans' real conditions of existence. Although Macon, the bourgeois fetishizer of material, seems to recognize the threat Pilate poses to his desire to shape his son, the unacknowledged threat that resides in Guitar's friendship with Milkman forms the basis of much of the novel's plot.

Guitar Baines, removed from the well-heeled world of Not Doctor Street, acts as Milkman's guide to the wilderness of Southside, where the African-American underclass lives. The novel's opening underscores the importance Guitar will have as Milkman's guide and mentor. When Milkman's mother, Ruth, goes into labor, Guitar is sent around to the emergency room to fetch help (7). Later, at age seventeen, Guitar befriends the twelve-year-old Milkman and from that moment, Guitar is always there for his young friend. That the older boy befriends a younger one is unusual, but the friendship is odder still when we recall that approximately seven years earlier Macon turned Guitar's family out on the street for not paying their rent.

Why, then, does Guitar want to claim Milkman? As a member of the Seven Days, a secret society that hunts down and kills whites for the murders of African Americans that go unnoticed by white justice, Guitar is forbidden to marry and will never have a son. Milkman represents the possibility of creating an ideological heir, just as Sam Fathers sees Ike as the hope for a spiritual heir. (Sam, the son of a light-skinned slave woman and a Chickasaw chief, has a genealogy similar to what Milkman discovers about racial mixing in the Dead family. Faulkner's novel, however, emphasizes male genealogy, so that despite Sam's racial mix, he clearly identifies himself through his father as "Indian.") The childless and dispossessed Sam Fathers effects a refiliation by subverting the teachings of McCaslin, offering instead both practical and mystical knowledge of the wilderness. In effect, Sam has managed to make an heir of a member of the dominant class that dispossessed the Chickasaws; as a consequence of Ike's appropriating Faulkner's conception of a Native-American world picture, the young man repudiates his white past and patrimony. Guitar's coup would be just as great as Sam's were he to succeed. Milkman's status as a member of the African-American middle class makes him an attractive conquest to Guitar. What finer ideological offspring could Guitar wish for than the son of the man who dispossessed the Banes family? What is at stake, then, in Macon's and Guitar's struggle to claim Milkman is whether Milkman will grow up to be "white" or a "black"; that is, will Milkman accept the values of the African-American middle class, which models itself on white middle-class American culture, or will Milkman cast his lot with the African-American community? Here again, Morrison seems to equate black authenticity with black poverty, for the only African-American communities in the *Song of Solomon* are economically distressed.

One particular moment when Guitar tries to comfort his friend occurs after Milkman strikes Macon for hitting Ruth, Milkman's mother. Guitar's sympathy takes the form of a brief narrative based on his hunting experience:

> Anyway I stayed on the trail until I saw some bushes. The light was good and all of a sudden I saw a rump between the branches. I dropped it with the first shot and finished it with the next. Now, I want to tell you I was feeling good. I saw myself showing my uncles what I'd caught. But when I got up to it—and I was going real slow because I thought I might have to shoot it again—I saw it was a doe.[. . .] I felt . . . bad. You know what I mean? I killed a doe. A doe, man. [. . .]

So I know how you felt when you saw your father hit your mother. It's
like that doe. A man shouldn't do that. You couldn't help what you felt. (85)

Guitar's story would certainly be understood by Ike McCaslin, who knows
that the hunter must not kill does because they, more than bucks, insure
that there will be deer to kill in the future. But in "Delta Autumn," doe
hunting takes on a number of meanings. For one of the men, it is a way to
tease Roth Edmonds about the young African-American woman with
whom Edmonds has had an affair. Does, however, take on a different significance for Ike (who does not yet know of Roth's affair) in the context
of America's imminent involvement in World War II: "It's a good time to
mention does [. . .]. Does and fawns both. The only fighting anywhere
that ever had anything of God's blessing on it has been when men fought
to protect does and fawns" (323). But from the protection of women and
children, the metaphor returns by the story's end to the specificity of the
young African-American woman. After learning that his kinsman Roth
Edmonds has repeated the very act—incestuous miscegenation—that
caused him, Ike, to repudiate his patrimony, he intuits that the deer Roth
has killed is a doe.

In both *Go Down, Moses* and *Song of Solomon,* then, killing a doe
metaphorically suggests hurting an African-American woman. Yet in Guitar's realization that Milkman doesn't grasp the metaphor ("Chances were
Milkman didn't even know what a doe was" [86]), there seems a kind of
wry intertextual gloss that calls into question the efficacy of the metaphor,
a metaphor that suggests that the female's safety depends upon the honor
of good male hunters. In particular, Guitar's metaphor sheds a different
light on his membership in the Seven Days and his work of hunting and
killing white people.

I wish to approach an understanding of Guitar's involvement in the
Seven Days somewhat obliquely, holding in suspension the doe hunting
metaphor and drawing temporarily on a different metaphor—that of urinating. On one of the Dead family's weekly Sunday drives when Milkman
is a little boy, he asks his father to stop so that he can relieve himself. Milkman's sister Lena accompanies the boy. She returns in tears because Milkman has peed on her (34–35). By itself the moment is not significant. But
at the end of part I, Lena, more than twenty-five years later, recalls the moment for Milkman and turns it into a metaphor for the thoughtless way he
has treated the women of the family, since "there are all kinds of ways to
pee on people" (214):

You've been laughing at us all your life. Corinthians. Mama. Me. Using us,
ordering us, and judging us. . . . You don't know a single thing about either

one of us—we made roses; that's all you knew—but now you know what's best for the very woman who wiped the dribble from your chin because you were too young to know how to spit. Our girlhood was spent like a found nickel on you. When you slept, we were quiet; when you were hungry, we cooked; when you wanted to play, we entertained you; and when you got grown enough to know the difference between a woman and a two-toned Ford, everything in this house stopped for you. You have yet to wash your own underwear, spread a bed, wipe the ring from your tub, or move a fleck of your dirt from one place to another. And to this day, you have never asked one of us if we were tired, or sad, or wanted a cup of coffee. You've never picked up anything heavier than your own feet, or solved a problem harder than fourth-grade arithmetic. Where do you get the *right* to decide our lives? (215)

When Milkman fails to answer the question, Lena continues: "I'll tell you where. From that hog's gut that hangs down between your legs" (215). Something more than Milkman's literal phallus, however, grants him authority within the family, and Lena recognizes this too. Again we are pointed back to the moment Milkman strikes his father. Lena concludes: "You are exactly like him. [. . .] You think because you hit him once that we all believe you were protecting [our mother]. Taking her side. It's a lie. You were taking over, letting us know you had the right to tell her and all of us what to do" (215–16). The reproduction of the father-function and the preservation of patriarchal privilege reside in Milkman's striking Macon. Milkman claims his privilege as an adult male to control and select the sexuality of "his" women.[10] Lena's anger boils over in this moment, after all, because Milkman has determined that it is inappropriate for his sister Corinthians to see Porter. Although Milkman might have a legitimate reason for his objection to Porter (namely, his involvement with the Seven Days), Milkman goes about breaking off his sister's relationship in a heavy-handed way, telling Macon, and thus, once again, aligning himself with the authority of the father.

Milkman is not the only male who pees on women. In fact the three men—Milkman, Macon, and Porter—in conflict over Corinthians are joined by moments of urination. When Macon discovers the gold of the old white man he presumably has killed in the cave, he "like a burglar out on his first job, stood up to pee" (170). Here too Macon is linked to the peacock ("luxury fanned out before him like the tail-spread of a peacock" [170]), a recurring figure that in this context suggests a pun lurking in the bird's name.[11] Macon's urinating signals the shift about to take place in his relationship with his sister Pilate. His insistence that the gold will allow them to recoup the loss of their farm in the aftermath of their father's murder meets her equally strong belief that it would be wrong to take the gold of the man Macon has just killed. This moment, in which brother and sister come to blows, creates a permanent break between the two.

Porter's act of urinating is by far the most spectacular of the three. Standing in the window of his attic apartment (an apartment Macon owns), the drunken Porter threatens suicide. His drunken shouts turn from a demand that the crowd of women "Send me up somebody to fuck!" (25) to his assertion that "I love ya! I love ya all" (26). Between the former and the latter, Porter "leaned his shotgun on the window sill, pulled out his penis and in a high arc, peed over the heads of the women, making them scream and run in a panic that the shotgun had not been able to create" (25). Porter's mixed messages—one of self-interest, the other suggesting altruism—take on special significance when we recall that his attempted suicide results from his work as a member of the Seven Days. His ambivalent utterances, spoken in drunkenness, reveal the ideological fraternity of Porter, Macon, Milkman, and Guitar; despite differences of class and political perspective, each acts on the assumption of male privilege that is grounded in the possession of women. Moreover, Porter's assertion to the women below that "I love ya" casts an odd light on Guitar's insistence that his killing of whites is motivated purely by love of African-American people. To link Milkman and Guitar in ideological brotherhood might seem particularly objectionable given Milkman's lack of social or race consciousness and Guitar's deep awareness of the injustices suffered by the African-American underclass. Nevertheless, the way these males position themselves in relation to the female points to a profoundly similar world picture.

In order to elucidate my meaning, we need to ask, "What precisely is the Seven Days, and does the group's stated mission correspond to its praxis?" As Guitar explains to Milkman, the Seven Days enacts an Old Testament, eye-for-an-eye form of justice:

> when a Negro child, Negro woman, or Negro man is killed by whites and nothing is done about it by *their* law and *their* courts, this society selects a similar victim at random, and they execute him or her in a similar manner if they can. If the Negro was hanged, they hang; if a Negro was burnt, they burn; raped and murdered, they rape and murder. (154–55)

Although Guitar stresses the indifference of the members of the group, it is clear that the Seven Days began as a particular response to a particularly personal kind of sexual violence against African-American men: "It got started in 1920, when that private from Georgia was killed after his balls were cut off and after that veteran was blinded when he came home from France in World War I" (155). What Guitar leaves unsaid is crucial. The one man was castrated and the other blinded because white American males perceived a threat to their possession of white women. The returning veterans had experienced a radically less segregated world in France, a world in which white women would have been available to them sexually. (One of the members of the Seven Days, Empire State, in fact married a white woman in France and becomes mute when he discovers her in bed with another black man.) The white males responsible for the violence against African-American men were sending a particular message—one form of miscegenation, African-American men and white women, would not be tolerated.

Tellingly, the kinds of crimes the Days avenge include a number that involve sexual possession, such as the rape of an African-American woman by a white man or the lynching of an African-American man for his interest in a white woman. One day at Tommy's barbershop, the men of the Days passionately discuss the news regarding the murder of the Emmett Till, a black teenager from Chicago who was murdered in Mississippi by three white men for whistling at a white woman; the three men were acquitted by an all-white jury.[12] Morrison's inclusion of the historical figure Till gives weight to the discussion the members of the Seven Days have regarding the plight of African-American men; the history of violence against black men is no fiction. Guitar notes, "Ain't no law for no colored man except the one sends him to the chair" (82).

In the Seven Days' focus on African-American men, African-American women (and hence African-American people as a whole) tend to get lost. One of the more extended passages in which we hear the teachings of Guitar Baines occurs in chapter 10. Milkman complains that everyone in his family wants something from him, to which Guitar responds:

> Look. It's the condition our condition is in. Everybody wants the life of a black man. Everybody. White men want us dead or quiet—which is the same thing as dead. White women, same thing. They want us, you know, "universal," human, no "race consciousness." Tame, except in bed.[. . .] But outside the bed they want us to be individuals. You tell them, "But they lynched my papa," and they say, "Yeah, but you're better than the lynchers are, so forget it." And black women, they want your whole self. Love they call it, and understanding. "Why don't you *understand* me?" What they mean is, Don't love anything on earth except me. (222)

In Guitar's view, the African-American man is the supreme marginal figure, silenced not only by whites, but undermined and unmanned even by African-American women. Milkman here objects to Guitar's major premise—that his killing is motivated by the love of African-American people—pointing out that "except for skin color, I can't tell the difference between what the white women want from us and what the colored women want. You say they all want our life, our living life. So if a colored woman is raped and killed, why do the Days rape and kill a white woman? Why worry about the colored woman at all?" (223).

Guitar's angry response to this question cuts to the heart of the matter in much the same way as Porter's drunken shouts do, revealing a level of meaning unavailable to the speaker: Guitar's "nostrils flared a little: 'Because she's *mine*'" (223). As the chief spokesman for the Seven Days, Guitar here makes it abundantly clear that all the Days, not just Porter, pee on women, particularly African-American women. In his response we see the issue of race bracketed momentarily and instead discover what is really at issue—male possession of women. Thus the Seven Days' "heroic" stance on saving the African-American race parallels Milkman's "defense" of his mother. Both are about males staking claim to woman-as-property, so that we might say that the rule of Milkman in the family or of the Days in society is one and the same—perpetuation of patriarchal authority, pea/e-cock power.

The Seven Days epitomizes patriarchal organization. The group is all male and does not permit its members to marry or to form permanent attachments with women. The very name suggests the originating authority of the monotheistic God the Father of the West who created the heavens and earth in six days and rested on the seventh.[13] But there is no rest for the Seven Days (Guitar's day is the Christian Sabbath) in its unarticulated effort to establish masculinity as violent mastery and manhood as the right to say what one's women do. African-American male violence does not simply imitate white male violence, the former *self-consciously* imitates the latter. Thus, the unrecognized mission of the Seven Days seems to be the following: if white male violence works to keep African-American men from white women, then African-American men need to organize to insure continued property rights in African-American women.

Guitar's emphatic reason for "protecting" African-American women ("Because she's *mine*") resonates with another moment in *Go Down, Moses.* In part 5 of "The Bear," a year and a half after the death of Sam Fathers, Lion, and Ben, Ike goes one last time to the hunting camp before the timber company to which Major DeSpain has sold the timber rights begins to denude the area. On his way to meet Boon under a sweet gum tree in a clearing, Ike encounters a huge rattlesnake, over six feet long, that he addresses as Sam in "The Old People" had addressed the spirit of the big buck six years earlier: "'Chief,' he said: 'Grandfather'" (314). This address prepares us for what we suppose will be another transcendent moment where Ike communes with his ideological parent, Sam Fathers. However,

the part-Chickasaw he next sees is the inept hunter Boon, sitting under
the gum tree with his disassembled rifle, while in the tree forty or fifty
squirrels are trapped with no chance of escape. Boon shouts at the ap-
proaching figure that he does not recognize as Ike: "Get out of here! Dont
touch them! Dont touch a one of them! They're mine!" (315). Boon,
speaking a message antithetical to the wisdom of Sam Fathers, has been co-
opted by the values of the timber company to which he owes his job as
town marshal and can see in the absurd plenty in the gum tree only something to be hoarded.

In turn, then, the sweet gum tree under which Boon sits in *Go Down,
Moses* takes us to the sweet gum in chapter 11 of *Song of Solomon* where
Milkman sits, exhausted from hunting with the men of Shalimar, Virginia.
As Milkman rests, he begins to question the self-centered attitude he carries with him. In this moment, Milkman very nearly becomes the ideological heir to Guitar in much the same way that Ike becomes the spiritual
heir to Sam Fathers—via the male communion of the hunt. Listening to
the hunters signal their dogs, Milkman feels that he understands hunting
and, by knowing what hunting is, that he understands Guitar:

> Down either side of his thighs he felt the sweet gum's surface roots cradling
> him like the rough but maternal hands of a grandfather. Feeling both tense
> and relaxed, he sank his fingers into the grass. He tried to listen with his fin-
> gertips, to hear what, if anything, the earth had to say, and it told him quickly
> that someone was standing behind him and he had just enough time to raise
> one hand to his neck and catch the wire that fastened around his throat. (279)

This epiphany shatters with Guitar's attempt on Milkman's life. But something larger ruptures in this moment and its aftermath. On the verge of accepting Guitar's worldview in which "does" need the protection of good
male hunters, Milkman is nearly killed by his mentor. Milkman escapes to
find that the hunters have treed a bobcat with its "glistening night eyes"
(280). From the outset, Guitar is described as "a cat-eyed boy" (7), so that
the bobcat's death and subsequent butchering at King Walker's gas station
take on a special significance.

As the hunters butcher the bobcat, the scene alternates between the
graphic details of the way the cat is dismembered and Milkman's memories, which are italicized, of pieces of the teachings of Guitar Baines.[14] Each
cut rends another hole in the fabric of Guitar's patriarchal world picture:

> Luther reached into the paunch and lifted the entrails. He dug under the rib
> cage to the diaphragm and carefully cut around it until it was free.
> *"It is about love. What else but love? Can't I love what I criticize?"*

Then he grabbed the windpipe and the gullet, eased them back, and sev-
ered them with one stroke of his little knife.
"*It is about love. What else?*"
They turned to Milkman. "You want the heart?" they asked him.
Quickly, before any thought could paralyze him, Milkman plunged both
hands into the rib cage. "Don't get the lungs, now. Get the heart."
"*What else?*"
He found it and pulled. The heart fell away from the chest as easily as
yolk slips out of its shell.
"*What else? What else? What else?*" (282)

As the hunters finish their work, Milkman asks them what they plan to do
with the bobcat. The hunters' two-word response ("Eat him") returns us
to an earlier key moment in Milkman and Guitar's friendship, when they
prepare to steal Pilate's "gold," the bag that actually contains the remains of
Jake, Milkman's paternal grandfather. Milkman and Guitar, passing a Buick
dealership, see a white peacock, which Milkman notes for its strutting and
inept flying. Guitar suggests catching it and to his friend's puzzled question
("What we gonna do if we catch him?"), he replies: "Eat him!" (179). Here
Milkman asks Guitar why the peacock "can't fly no better than a chicken"
and Guitar responds:

"Too much tail. All that jewelry weighs it down. Like vanity. Can't nobody
fly with all that shit. Wanna fly, you got to give up the shit that weighs you
down."
    The peacock jumped onto the hood of the Buick and once more spread
its tail, sending the flashy Buick into oblivion. (179)

Macon, as I noted earlier is linked to the peacock, but in this passage we
begin to see Milkman as the peacock, for Milkman from the time he is
fourteen also struts (62). That the bird stands on the Buick seems suggestive, since Macon purchases a new Buick every two years; thus, the peacock
on the car indicates the way Macon's wealth props up Milkman. Guitar's
description of the peacock's failure to fly well certainly is apropos of the
Milkman who flies off to Danville, Pennsylvania, to find the gold, since
Milkman carries with him all the markers of comfortable middle-class life,
notably, his Cutty Sark, a gold Longines watch, and his Florsheim shoes.
And, after offending the men at Solomon's store in Shalimar by his showy
display of wealth and inquiries about their women, Milkman is linked both
metonymically and metaphorically to another cock, "a black rooster [that]
strutted by, its blood-red comb draped forward like a wicked brow" (265).
    Song of Solomon's drama of the peacock and the bobcat raises questions
about the nature of the male world of the hunt—a world *Go Down, Moses*

celebrates—through a complex series of self-reflexive turns: while hunting for gold, which only slowly reveals itself as a hunt for his heritage, Milkman goes on a coon hunt during which he becomes the "coon" who is hunted. Milkman's hunt is play and sport. He doesn't really need the gold. But Guitar and the men of Shalimar play for keeps; their hunting is deadly serious: the poor men of Shalimar need the meat they kill and Guitar's killing is, he believes, for a higher cause. In King Walker's gas station, Milkman finally sees through the falseness of Guitar's teachings, a new state objectified by the final image of the dead bobcat's head: "The tongue lay in its mouth as harmless as a sandwich" (283). No more will Guitar's words and language on race influence Milkman's thinking. Guitar's claim to kill for love ("It is about love. What else?") stands exposed; it's not about love but something else indeed—male power and possession. Milkman does not jettison entirely his relationship with Guitar, for he takes up the hunters' offer to get the heart—that which was nurturing and sustaining in his friendship with Guitar. The entrails of that cat Guitar, both his racism and nostalgia about hunting, are part of the shit that has weighed Milkman down and will not let him fly. But after the attack of his cat-eyed friend and the subsequent death and dismemberment of the bobcat, Milkman loses the limp that looks like a strut and ceases to be both the vain peacock and the cock who pees on women.

Milkman's encounter with the prostitute Sweet neatly objectifies his transformation, since her occupation would normally position her as a commodity, her sexuality bought, not shared; she is the kind of woman men routinely treat with no consideration. And yet Milkman interacts with her in a way that directly addresses the catalogue of shortcomings Lena had pointed out to him at the end of part I and serves almost as reparation for the thoughtless way he had used his cousin Hagar:

> He soaped and rubbed her until her skin squeaked and glistened like onyx. She put salve on his face. He washed her hair. She sprinkled talcum on his feet. He straddled her behind and massaged her back. She put witch hazel on his swollen neck. He made up the bed. She gave him gumbo to eat. He washed the dishes. She washed his clothes and hung them out to dry. He scoured her tub. She ironed his shirt and pants. He gave her fifty dollars. She kissed his mouth. He touched her face. She said please come back. He said I'll see you tonight. (285)

But what exactly allows Milkman now to engage in reciprocal relations with women, and if he can achieve some distance on the male hunt metaphor, why can't Ike? Neither his mother nor his wife provide Ike an alternative to the metaphor of the hunt. Yet almost simultaneous with

Milkman's rejecting the excesses of Guitar's thinking, we see Milkman's unconscious movement toward the other mentor of his youth, Pilate, inasmuch as he imagines the bobcat's heart pulling out of its chest cavity "as easily as yolk slips out of its shell" (283). This image takes us back to the first meeting between Milkman and Pilate during which she makes for him the perfect soft-boiled egg. And so over his breakfast eggs the next morning he specifically asks his new friends in Shalimar if they have ever heard of Pilate Dead.

In moving toward the perspective of Pilate, Milkman aligns himself with the one character in the novel who has achieved a special purchase on patriarchal forms of social organization. Because she has no navel, she is prevented from joining a community in the prescribed fashion, as a woman claimed in marriage by a man; to have sex with a man is to reveal she has no navel and thus to be shunned for her difference. After her split with Macon, she is taken in by a preacher's family and begins her new life as a female Huck Finn. (The preacher's house, she tells Ruth, was "a nice place except they made me wear shoes" [141].) She quickly discovers the problems associated with her sexuality. Pilate becomes the object of the preacher's advances, which causes the preacher's wife to send her packing. Twice cast out from groups of migrant farm workers, Pilate finds things no better in towns: "All her encounters with Negroes who had established themselves in businesses or trades in those small Midwestern towns had been unpleasant. Their wives did not like the trembling unhampered breasts under her dress, and told her so" (144). And in such towns Pilate finds that the only economic opportunity available to an unmarried African-American women is working either as a laundress or as a prostitute.

Continually rejected, Pilate reevaluates life in a way that places her in the tradition of Emersonian self-reliance, making her a kind of cross between Henry David Thoreau and Hester Prynne. Performing Thoreau's call to reassessment, Pilate "threw away every assumption she had learned and began at zero" (149) in order to ask herself fundamental questions about how to live in the world. And like Hester, who places her hair under her cap, Pilate cuts her hair signaling a repression of her sexuality, since that is what has caused her the most trouble. Again like Hester, Pilate sets up housekeeping on the margins of the community. While Hester only dreams of a time when women's and men's roles will be reformulated, Pilate establishes a woman-centered alternative community that consistently operates without regard for middle-class conventions or the expectations of men.[15] Her house, as critics have noted, is the site of funkiness where people can eat, act, and be authentically, and contrasts with the middle-class repressions of the Dead household. But although Pilate represents an alternative to the ideology of masculine possession, her alternative family's repudiation of middle-class conventions (which constantly serves as a reminder that Macon Dead's values are inauthentic) links her representation of authentic blackness to black poverty every bit as much as Guitar Banes's politics that locate authenticity in the impoverished community of South Side.

Still, just as Faulkner attempts to represent an alternative to white masculinity in Native American spirituality through Sam Fathers, who communes with his spirit ancestors, Morrison uses Pilate to underscore the possibilities of non-Western spirituality. In doing so, the novelist begins to link the aesthetic to the ethical. As I noted in the previous chapter, there is a significant parallel in Sula's and Pilate's moments of self-reflection on the nature of their lives, yet Pilate creates a more useable identity out of that moment of philosophical reduction. Like Sula, Pilate figures a part of the artist's relation to the community. Both are eccentric and, though nominally a part of their communities, are also apart from them. Although one of the characters best loved by readers of Morrison's fiction, Pilate herself, while respected and sometimes feared, is not beloved by the community. When Hagar comes in late to get her hair done, neither beautician wants to do her hair, but as Marcelline rationalizes, it's best not to turn Hagar down because Pilate "wouldn't like it" (312). If people turn to Pilate, it is because she has conjure powers and potions, can defeat apparently physically stronger men, and can also make fools of the police.

In addition to her spiritual powers, she also has an expressive form—the song she sings at Milkman's birth that is the secret genealogy of the Solomon family. But although figuring elements of artistic identity, she is not the artist whole and complete; she may be the keeper of the oral text and its medium, but she does not know its meaning. Nevertheless, by expressing both the spiritual and the aesthetic, Pilate makes a turn that Sula cannot. Sula's limitation is that her artistic gaze cannot encompass the moral and the ethical; her sexuality is her only textuality. But Pilate insists on the realm of morality, perhaps best indicated by the bag of bones she keeps with her to remind herself of her implication in what she believes to be the death of the white man whom Macon struck in the cave. The bones, of course, turn out to be actually those of her father, but that does nothing to diminish the genuineness of her belief that one must claim responsibility for one's acts.

If his ancestors are important to Faulkner's Sam Fathers, who addresses their spirits in the form of the animals of the forest, the departed dead are equally important to Pilate. In fact, there is a ghostly visitor to Pilate's wine house, that—had they known of it—would have been taken by the people of South Side as a far surer sign of Pilate's unnaturalness than that stigmatized by the missing navel. For Pilate speaks with her dead father,

Jake/Macon, who comes to her wearing "a white shirt, a blue collar, and a brown peaked cap" (150). Pilate's relation with the spirit world is an index of the alternative spirituality she represents, and—along with her matrilineal household—creates a link between American and West African culture, a link that Morrison develops more fully in *Beloved* through Baby Suggs's religion of the maternal body. Throughout part I and a significant portion of part II of *Song of Solomon,* Milkman consistently fails to recognize the possibility of ghosts. Freddie's claim that his mother died of ghosts only elicits Milkman's laughter. Later he will not credit his own senses when the ghost of his paternal grandfather witnesses Milkman's and Guitar's attempt to steal Pilate's "gold"—actually the bones of the grandfather. Indeed, even when face to face with a possible ghost, Milkman does not believe. Having arrived in Danville, Pennsylvania, and trying to discover where Circe lives, Milkman asks direction of a man whose description matches Jake's above: "One of them was a Negro. A tall man, elderly, with a brown peaked cap and an old-fashioned collar" (227)—Oleh, Chief, Grandfather indeed![16]

Milkman's encounter with Circe is even more decidedly ghostly, marked by a particular recurring smell that announces the onset of possible supernatural moments in *Song of Solomon:* "a sweet spicy perfume. Like ginger root—pleasant, clean, seductive" (239).[17] The odor of ginger masks what had seconds earlier been an overwhelming stench of decay. From this dreamlike encounter with a woman who, as Milkman notes, "*had* to be dead" (241), he gets decisive clues both to the reality of ghosts and to uncovering his family's history—the names of his paternal grandfather and grandmother, Jake and Sing. (Milkman knows that Pilate claims her father appears to her speaking a single word—sing—which she takes as a command to sing.)

Like Ike McCaslin, who as a youth is granted his desired glimpse of Old Ben, the mythic bear, only after relinquishing his watch and compass, Milkman solves the riddle of his family's past in the song the children of Shalimar sing only after losing his watch, the final marker of his allegiance to his father's middle-class world. The parallel between Isaac and Milkman points to Milkman's developing artistic consciousness. The dense and difficult part 4 of "The Bear" reveals that Ike's quest is not simply for knowledge of the woods. Sitting in the commissary of his father's farm, he examines the ledgers of the old plantation and learns to read between the lines of the cryptic dialogue between father and uncle; connecting the fragments, he interprets the hidden secret of McCaslin genealogy—old McCaslin's incestuous rape of his black daughter. Clearly a defining moment for Isaac, he repudiates a particular enactment of Southern white identity as inauthentic and embraces instead that of his Native-American/African-American mentor, Sam Fathers. Just as Faulkner uses his character Ike, the one who produces an active interpretation of a coded text, to allegorize the eccentricity of artistic consciousness, Morrison also uses Milkman's act of interpretation to suggest his path toward artistic production. In terms of artistic identity, by reading correctly the meaning of the children's song of Solomon, Milkman becomes the other half of the equation, completing Pilate's reproduction of the text by supplying its latent meaning. In the novel's allegorizing of authorship, it seems that one does not get to be Pilate unless one has also been Milkman. In 1963 Morrison, like her fictive double Milkman, is poised to make a turn toward family history and genealogy in her personal quest to begin writing herself through *The Bluest Eye.* As we have seen in Morrison's texts from her first novel through *Playing in the Dark,* the space between thoughtful interpretive reading and writing is never very great, whether we think of that dream interpreter turned writer, Soaphead Church, or Toni Morrison herself who reads as a writer.

The Milkman, then, who returns to Michigan is a changed man. Spiritually renewed, he believes in ghosts.[18] More importantly, he acknowledges his implication in Hagar's death.[19] Like Pilate, who keeps the sack of bones because she maintains that one is responsible for one's dead, Milkman will now possess a box of Hagar's hair, a sign that in addition to being the heir to Pilate's relation to the aesthetic, he will also continue to link ethics to a developing artistic consciousness.

In almost a mirror reflection to the way Milkman becomes the spiritual heir to Pilate, Pilate's granddaughter Hagar is seduced by the worldview of Macon Dead. Chapter 13, which interrupts and delays Milkman's triumphant return, chronicles what happens to Hagar after Milkman leaves her still standing in Guitar's apartment after her failure to kill Milkman. And while Milkman moves slowly away from his father's and Guitar's teachings, Hagar loses her hold on the alternative formation represented by Pilate's house. Indirectly, one might argue, Hagar's death may be traced to Macon Dead inasmuch as she becomes crazy as a result of loving Macon's son, who is raised to reproduce Macon's middle-class values. (Milkman in name is, of course, quite literally another Macon Dead.) Milkman's rejection of Hagar precisely because she does not fit his middle-class design causes her to desire to be like the women Milkman desires—light-complexioned and possessing all the totemic markers of middle-class feminine beauty. So at the very time that Milkman on his journey through Pennsylvania and Virginia progressively loses all the signs of middle-class gentility (his Cutty Sark, Florsheim shoes, and Longines watch), Hagar gathers to herself its feminine counterparts (an Evan-Picone skirt, Con Brios, and Van Raalte gloves). It would, however, be inappropriate to label Macon as the sole or final author of Hagar's desire, for he merely embodies the larger metaphysical system that informs men that they have priority over women and that tells African Americans that white is good and black is bad.

If all he learned was that his great-grandfather reputedly could fly, then Milkman's joy at the novel's ending would be trivial. *Song of Solomon*, Morrison's first novel to foreground the activity of men, however, raises a tough question—one that cannot be answered fully by one novel: is it possible for African-American men to reconceive their masculinity in a nonpatriarchal fashion, that is, in a way that does not reduce African-American women to objects of possession? The example of Milkman Dead suggests that the possibility is open for such a reconception. Ike McCaslin fails to provide the key to a nonpatriarchal society because his renunciation—his refusal to profit from a system of male power that perpetuates racial injustice—is just that, simple negation and refusal, a withdrawal from life. He generates no alternative vision of how to live in the world, and the transmission of patriarchal authority is in no way disrupted by Ike's refusal to be its embodiment; his passivity leads to Roth Edmonds's tragic reenactment of the incestuous miscegenation that so horrified Ike when he read the McCaslin ledgers.

But Milkman has his Pilate/pilot, a woman who opens paths more sustaining than Sam Fathers's hunting trails, even though those trails lead him once again to African-American poverty as the only site of authentic black identity. Nevertheless, she teaches him how to treat women as fully human and that flying is a state of being rather than a physical act: "Now he knew why he loved her so. Without ever leaving the ground, she could fly" (336). As she lies dying in Milkman's arms, she tells him: "I wish I'd a knowed more people. I would of loved 'em all. If I'd a knowed more, I would a loved more" (336). The kind of flying Milkman ultimately understands and values is Pilate's flying, the ability to transcend self and self-love. And surely Pilate's claim serves as an intratextual critique pointing out the inauthenticity of Guitar's claim (one echoed by Porter and Robert Smith) that the Seven Days' killing is done for love. What weighed Milkman down for so much of *Song of Solomon* is male ego (much as Hagar is destroyed by her desire to be the desire of male ego), forged in the structures of a patriarchal society.

The novel's conclusion is noteworthy for its ambiguity that has occasioned a variety of critical response.[20] Does Milkman actually fly? Does he live or die following his struggle with Guitar? Finally, I believe, it does not matter whether Milkman survives. He has achieved the very connection to an African-American community that Guitar all along has criticized his friend for lacking. Guitar may believe himself to be the one acting from higher principles, yet Milkman, who even in this moment sees Guitar as his brother, now achieves the transcendence he wrongly felt he had won under the sweet gum tree. Guitar's adherence to the vision of masculinity as violent mastery may win the day, but Milkman's transformation suggests that masculinity can be conceived in tropes other than those of deadly possession.

But perhaps another reason why the novel's denouement is so ambiguous is that Morrison could not easily imagine Milkman after the moment of his sense of authentic identity as completed project. Could Milkman find permanent happiness in Shalimar? Should he take the spirit of Shalimar back to Michigan? Would he repudiate the economic advantage represented by his father's property? Clearly the funk has erupted in Milkman but the question remains: Can the funk rise economically? Despite his sense of triumph at having found the site of authenticity in rural black poverty, it is hardly a triumph in which Morrison could fully participate or with which she could identify, especially in the aftermath of publishing her best-selling third novel. And that is because Morrison herself does not choose black poverty as the location of her cultural identity. Put another way, in a heated exchange between Milkman and Guitar, Guitar attacks his younger friend for hanging out with the black middle class. Milkman responds, unconsciously echoing his father, "What's wrong with Negroes owning beach houses?" (103). In 1977 and in terms of the logic of *Song of Solomon*, Morrison's answer is fairly straightforward: quite a bit is wrong with such ownership because it inhibits the possibility of authenticity. Yet in a 1998 profile of the author, Morrison's attitude toward possession seems markedly different:

> Even without the upcoming tour [to promote *Paradise*], Morrison's life seems hectic. She rents an apartment near Princeton University in New Jersey [. . .]; another apartment in lower Manhattan; and a stone house in Rockland County, N.Y. Plus, she is having rebuilt the house she owned on the Hudson River just north of New York City, which burned to the ground on Christmas Day 1993. Three residences? Or four, counting the house in progress? "I was a child of the Depression," she shrugs and laughs. "I have bad dreams about eviction." (Gray 68)

How might one account for this changed attitude from the time Morrison was composing *Song of Solomon* in the mid-1970s to this more recent and relaxed position?

Her third novel was the main selection of The Book of the Month Club, the first African-American novel so designated since Richard Wright's *Native Son*. Additionally, *Song of Solomon* won awards from both the National Critic's Circle and the American Academy and Institute of Arts and Letters. Morrison's success as an author, over and above her work as an editor (a position she left following the publication of her third novel), meant that she finally was earning an income that placed her very comfortably in the middle class by any purely economic measure. Perhaps, then, the lived contradiction between her fictive resolutions—which had consistently made black poverty the only place in which an African American could hope to attain an authentic identity—and her certain recognition of her own sharply rising income led her to rethink her early fiction's identifications. Clearly she must have realized that having money does not necessarily mean that an African American is "white" or a sellout. What she would need was a way to reimagine blackness that allowed for the individual to develop economically as well as spiritually.

The chapter that follows explores *Tar Baby*, the novel that Morrison wrote after *Song of Solomon* and that begins the author's attempt to rethink blackness and its relation to class. Like her previous novel's title, *Tar Baby* overtly signals one of her intertexts, this time the African-American folk tale. And just as in *Song of Solomon*, Morrison rewrites a modernist, but now it is neither Ellison, nor Woolf, nor Faulkner. In *Tar Baby*, Morrison rewrites Morrison. This rewriting critically engages—in ways as striking as her use of *Invisible Man* and *Go Down, Moses*—the triumphant achievement of completed authenticity (Milkman) and the valorization of the black agrarian community (Shalimar). In rewriting her modernist novel, as well as her fictively imagined self, Morrison points the way to an understanding of her later novels as the product of postmodern blackness. Morrison's exploration of African-American identity through a transfigured meditation on her male genealogy in *Song of Solomon* becomes in *Tar Baby* a coded meditation on descent through the female side of her family. Morrison's intensely reflexive fourth novel crucially participates in her fictive project of reclaiming both modernist technique and personal identity. Near the end of *Song of Solomon*, Milkman's voice echoes across the valley as he calls to Guitar, a moment suggesting the hinge that joins the doubled worlds of these two novels: *tar, tar, tar*—*Tar Baby*.

Chapter 5

Descent in the "House of Chloe": Race, Rape, and Identity in *Tar Baby*

T*ar Baby* seems for a number of readers an aberration in Morrison's development as a writer, and yet its importance in her canon can be underscored by a peculiar logic that makes this novel the first one published by Toni Morrison the Writer. As I have pointed out in the previous chapters, Morrison in various interviews maintains that she did not fully identify herself as a writer—or see that writing was her life's work—until she had completed her first three novels. Despite her newly found comfort with identifying herself as a writer, her fourth novel, concerned for the first time with representing rounded white characters, paradoxically remains somewhat marginal; it is less frequently taught and receives relatively less critical attention than her other novels. Nevertheless, the kind of aesthetically layered text Morrison creates in *Tar Baby* reveals a particular link to *Song of Solomon* and its engagement with canonical modernist narrative technique. Like her previous novel, *Tar Baby* overtly signals an explicit intertext, the African-American folk tale of the tar baby, a white farmer's trap to catch that trickster, Br'er Rabbit.[1] This story is in fact recounted at a key plot moment. But there is in the novel an equally explicit intertext, the account of the fall in Genesis.[2] Set initially on the private island of retired Philadelphia candy maker Valerian Street, the novel examines the unlikely relationship between Son, a dark-skinned intruder, and the light-skinned Jadine, a young woman whom the wealthy man has patronized and the niece of Valerian's two most intimate servants, Sydney and Ondine. Son and Jadine must flee this Caribbean paradise when they bite into the apple of knowledge. Only now the apple is baked into a pie for Christmas dinner. Valerian reveals at this dinner that he fired three part-time island servants for stealing a few of his apples that he had imported especially for the holiday. Son, incensed by Valerian's insensitivity to class difference, excoriates his host. This moment releases years of underlying tensions between master and servants, as well as husband and wife, revealing the following suppressed knowledge—Valerian's wife, Margaret, abused their son when he was a child. Morrison's ironic inversion of Genesis, then, is that the tree of knowledge proves to be the undoing primarily of the island's self-appointed "god," because Valerian is forced to recognize his implication in the abuse of his son. Jadine and Son's breakup depends at least as much on the narrative logic of the tar baby story, but in a way that leaves one wondering: who is the tar baby, who is the rabbit, and might there be a rise after the fall?[3] Morrison herself has directly given a doubled meaning to the designation "Tar Baby." On the one hand, she uses the negative meaning in relation to Jadine, who as the white man's creation functions to entrap Son, the African-American man. On the other hand, a different kind of tar baby is positively marked. Morrison also speaks of Jadine as having "lost the tar quality" that the women whom Son identifies as the church pie ladies have. In this second meaning, Morrison casts "tar" as these women's ability "to hold something together" and to "nurture" (Wilson 131). Jadine's problem, then, in this doubled significance of the word is simultaneously being the tar and lacking the tar. One way to cast Son's dilemma is that he is in different ways stuck on both kinds of tar babies—erotically attached to Jadine and emotionally bonded too tightly to his memories of nurturing rural earth mothers.

These doubled intertexts of *Tar Baby*—both the folk tale and the biblical story—might serve as a metonymy for the novel's representation of the doubleness of African-American racial identity. Notably there is the issue of how the media constructs Western beauty as a universal standard. In this regard, Pecola Breedlove in Morrison's first novel, *The Bluest Eye,* points the way to Jadine Childs in *Tar Baby.* Both accept a Western valuation of beauty, although for opposite reasons: Pecola, a dark-skinned black girl, because she cannot approach the cultural imperative and Jadine, a light-skinned black, because she can embody its image on Parisian fashion runways. But in addition to the folk tale and Genesis, *Tar Baby* has a more complex, less overt intertext; the novel is closely related to the project in *Song of Solomon.* In fact, if Morrison challenges Ellison's modernism in *The Bluest Eye,* recasts Woolf's representation of same-sex desire, and reclaims Faulkner's narratives of race in *Song of Solomon,* then she may be recasting her modernist song of authentic black identity in *Tar Baby.* Both novels focus on young African Americans—Milkman Dead and Jadine Childs— whose identities are fragmented. The two characters occupy a debilitating psychic space between the desire to assimilate to the values of the white middle class and the voices that urge them to acknowledge a black racial identity, voices that seem almost to equate authentic blackness with black poverty. In both novels, Morrison seems engaged in a form of self-fashioning, using these two characters, albeit in different ways, to figure her own struggle to construct an identity as an African-American woman. Growing up in the working-class town of Lorain, Ohio, Morrison's youth and adolescence were largely free of race consciousness. Her accounts of her relation to *The Bluest Eye,* as I pointed out in chapter 2, invite speculation on how that first novel begins a project of racial self-discovery. If *Sula* and *Song of Solomon* continue the fashioning of self, then *Tar Baby,* in its coded scripting of self, completes that project by overtly giving up the project of ever achieving a completed self.

In *Song of Solomon,* as we saw previously, the autobiographical gesture is overt. The novel opens on (and Milkman is born the day after) Morrison's birthday, February 18, 1931.[4] The action of the novel covers thirty-two years, ending in 1963 when Milkman finally achieves a racialized identity, a time that corresponds in Morrison's life to a marriage that was soon to end and the beginning of her career as a writer. *Tar Baby,* I will argue, for all its distance and displacements from Morrison's maturation in Lorain, Ohio, is as deeply personal as *Song of Solomon,* which more directly draws on her family history.[5] To say that these novels register the personal is not to deny the ways in which they comment on larger social and political issues; nevertheless, Morrison's fourth novel allows her to examine fictively her success as a novelist in a white dominated publishing and literary establishment, especially as that success impinges on her identity as an African-American woman.[6] If there is a novel of Morrison's that fully registers W. E. B. Du Bois's sense of the double-consciousness of African-Americans, it is *Tar Baby.*[7] Even more than *Song of Solomon, Tar Baby* represents Morrison's struggle to fashion a useable identity. Figuring her self as male in *Song of Solomon,* Morrison's Milkman can embrace a sense of Africanized identity in the all-black agrarian community of Shalimar, Virginia, but his acceptance into this community is hardly gender neutral; the men signal their approval of Milkman by their willingness to share their prostitute, Sweet. In *Tar Baby,* however, figuring the self as female, Morrison creates a more ambivalent and troubled relation to that novel's black agrarian community, Eloe, Florida; the African-American woman, the text suggests, may not be able to identify with agrarian community in the same way that the African-American man does.

Jadine Childs, with her Sorbonne education and her modeling career, is overtly marked as a woman whose identity is in crisis; she becomes aware of that crisis in a Parisian supermarket when a black woman wearing a yellow dress (who exemplifies a mesmerizing non-Western beauty) looks at Jadine and spits. Jadine's retreat to her benefactor's island signals her attempt to step back and assess the competing demands of the white world and of racial identity. Morrison, herself a relatively light-complexioned black, who in 1981 was coming fully into her own as a major figure in American literature, seems to have created the honey-colored Jadine, whether consciously or not, as a figuration of her own subject position: not a Sorbonne degree, but an M.A. from Cornell; not a black model, but a model of black success—as editor at Random House, as winner of numerous literary prizes, and as a figure much sought after by the popular print media for interviews and photos.[8] Jadine may be a cover girl for *Elle,* but Toni Morrison appears on the cover of *Newsweek* when *Tar Baby* is published. But perhaps the most significant evidence for pursuing the homologies between author and character occur on the novel's penultimate page; an "authentic" black, Thérèse, an island woman whose "magic breasts" symbolize her nurturing and maternal role, identifies Jadine as a woman who has "forgotten her ancient properties" (305). This phrase—"ancient properties"—first appears prior to the novel's first page. Morrison dedicates her novel to

> Mrs. Caroline Smith
> Mrs. Millie MacTeer
> Mrs. Ardelia Willis
> Mrs. Ramah Wofford
> Mrs. Lois Brooks
> —and each of their sisters,
> all of whom knew
> their true and ancient
> properties

Morrison's rewriting of *Song of Solomon* arguably begins at this point, given the earlier novel's focus on masculine genealogy and its dedication to "Daddy." By naming the women in her family—her mother, sister, aunts, and grandmother, Morrison indirectly includes herself as one of those sisters who has remained true to her identity as an African-American woman. Yet the very need to declare her authenticity suggests that she also has questioned herself regarding the validity of this claim, especially given the name changes that transform Chloe Wofford into Toni Morrison.[9] The productive tensions that leads to this dedication may be charted by juxtaposing two statements Morrison has made regarding the relation between the contemporary and the traditional African-American woman. In the first, she speaks about Jadine's problems with older African-American women:

> She feels left out from that environment. She is not afraid of the male world, but she is afraid of the female world. It's interesting to see such women who

have gone away put into that situation. I have seen them extremely uncomfortable in the company of church ladies, absolutely out of their element. They are beautiful and they are competent, but when they get with women whose values are different and who judge competence in different areas, they are extremely threatened. (Ruas 106)

Although beginning specifically with Jadine, Morrison then extrapolates a type of woman from her personal experience. And this experience may be quite personal indeed. In a conversation with Colette Dowling in 1979, Morrison comments on why she did not return home to Lorain, Ohio, after the publication of *Song of Solomon:* "I didn't want those people to look at me funny. I didn't want to experience myself as separate from them. I couldn't bear the fact that old ladies who used to tell me, 'Chloe, cross your legs' would look at me any other way than that they had the right to tell me that still" (59). Morrison, like the type she delineates, has "gone away" and now senses a distance from the church ladies of Lorain. Once again we see Morrison's difficulty with her identity as "Chloe," only the above instance is much more concrete than my speculations in chapter 2 on how she may have experienced her birth name in light of stereotyped portrayals in earlier American literature, such as Aunt Chloe in *Uncle Tom's Cabin.* Morrison's sense of a barrier—the result of her newfound fame—that has arisen between herself and the authoritative older women from her Lorain past seems to find its fictive expression in Jadine's anxiety over black female identity when she accompanies Son on his return home to Eloe. It is hard not to think reflexively about an intellectual such as Morrison who has had such a successful career as a writer and editor when she says of Jadine, "she cannot nurture and be a career woman. You can't get rid of the pie lady and the churches unless you have something to replace them with" (Ruas 105). Since Morrison herself experiences a distance from the pie ladies of her past, *Tar Baby* may be in part about what she has replaced these women with.

Here we might again recall Morrison's claim to have changed her name in college "[b]ecause the people at Howard seemed to have difficulty pronouncing" Chloe (Dowling 50).[10] A curiously covert commentary on this substitution appears to take place in the intertextual dialogue between the dedication to the women in her family, quoted above, and the epigraph Morrison chooses to preface *Tar Baby,* the first novel to appear after her claim regarding her name: "For it hath been declared unto me of you, my brethren, by them which are of the house of Chloe, that there are contentions among you." This quotation from the King James Bible (1 Cor. 1:11) resonates in ways over and above the private meaning Morrison encodes regarding her name change from Chloe to Toni.[11] The "contentions among you," for example, registers Morrison's attempt to address African Americans and their divisions, especially between women and men.[12] But the epigraph refuses to point forward into the fictional world exclusively, since Morrison, in fact, just has named a group of women who, in Morrison's childhood, would have been literally in the "house of Chloe" Wofford.

Although *Tar Baby* is much more about female descent than male genealogy and does not thematize naming to the extent that *Song of Solomon* does, the depiction of Son's relation to his name suggests that all of Morrison's meditations on self are not limited to Jadine. After captured in Valerian's house, Son identifies himself as William Green. But prior to his discovery, he ruminates about his name:

> In eight years he'd had seven documented identities and before that a few undocumented ones, so he barely remembered his real original name himself. Actually the name most truly his wasn't on any of the Social Security cards, union dues cards, discharge papers, and everybody who knew it or remembered it in connection with him could very well be dead. Son. It was the name that called forth the true him. The him that he never lied to, the one he tucked in at night and the one he did not want to die. The other selves were like the words he spoke—fabrications of the moment, misinformation required to protect Son from harm and to secure that one reality at least. (139)

Like her character, William Green, Toni Morrison has a name that serves the "Son" function. Here it seems worth recalling Morrison's comment from 1992 about her true identity: "I am really Chloe Anthony Wofford. That's who I am. I have been writing under this other person's name. I write some things now as Chloe Wofford, private things" (Bigsby 28). Morrison's oblique references to her own name change in *Tar Baby* resonate strongly with the way her early fiction repeatedly examines the possibility for African Americans to forge an authentic identity for themselves. For a novelist who has hidden her name, Morrison seems at some level to almost want the reader to catch the concealment through fairly overt acts of self-referentiality. For example, in chapter 4 Margaret remarks to Jadine, "Look. Chloé has four new parfumes. Four" (84). Chloé, of course, is a well-known brand of perfume, but since *Tar Baby* is Morrison's fourth novel, this otherwise disposable comment takes on much greater significance. What a certain symbolic logic—introduced at the outset through the intertextual play between the novel's epigraph and dedication—reveals, then, is the way Morrison uses this fiction to respond to doubts, whether her own or those of others, about her authenticity, even as she questions the existential implications of authenticity.

The overtly personal dedication and the coded reference to personal identity in the biblical epigraph prefacing *Tar Baby,* therefore, imply that the personal does not drop out when one turns the page and enters Morrison's novel proper. Taken together, dedication and epigraph create a curious parallel between Morrison's relation to her women relatives (as well as to the older African-American women of Lorain, Ohio) and Jadine's struggle with the "night women" in *Tar Baby* who haunt her dreams and demand her acceptance of a particular enactment of black female identity. To the extent that this parallel is valid, the plot implies that Jadine, as an African-American woman, has not yet achieved a racialized adult identity but that an important precondition for a more fluid enactment of identity has been reached; namely, she recognizes that black female identity need not accept its construction by black men, particularly when that construction is complicitous with the assumptions of white patriarchy.

In *Tar Baby,* whatever racialized identity Jadine may be able to conceive is marked in its inception by rape. But this rape seems almost to resist the resisting reader; that is, it is a rape that is rhetorically constructed to deny the reader's awareness of the violence.[13] In this regard, the rape in *Tar Baby* produces an oddly homologous relation to Toni Morrison's act of self-naming that intentionally obscures the origins of her name. Yet Morrison provides clues in her novel about both the hidden rape and her hidden name. Taken together, these two gestures of concealment speak to the profoundly difficult negotiation of black female identity Morrison performs. As a successful black woman whose work is validated by white corporate and academic culture, she does not wish to dismiss the constructions of identity and community made by black men, who are largely excluded from those same structures that confirm her success, but at the same time she wishes to maintain that the black woman cannot be forced to return, either sexually or psychologically, to the agrarian past.

Like Jadine, who is physically violated, Morrison in a sense has been violated metaphorically by the white corporate/publishing world that forced her to put Chloe undercover. But there may also be elements in black male culture that participate in that violation. Morrison provides a fictive account of tensions between African-American women and men. These tensions are the focus of Michele Wallace's study of black machismo, published in 1979, a year that places it directly between Morrison's own meditations on African-American masculinity in *Song of Solomon* and *Tar Baby.* Wallace acknowledges the real and horrific oppression of African-American men during slavery but argues that this has lead to a contemporary construction of black masculinity that sees its manhood as dependent on the subservience of the African-American woman; from a black male perspective, black women's subservience is in part penance for their complicity with white men during slavery (Wallace 13–16). So it seems there would be equally good reasons for Morrison to wish to abandon the agrarian implications of Chloe for either white men's or black men's mythologizing of black women. What plays the role of the violating male in Morrison's life may not be a particular individual (as it is for Jadine) but rather a kind of cultural destinator—the intersection of racial and sexual ideology that makes the rape of a black woman by a black man practically unimaginable: "To black people, rape means the lynching of a black man. Obsession with the lynching of the black man seems to leave no room in the black male consciousness for any awareness of the oppression of black women" (Wallace 120).

Morrison learned a number of techniques from the modernists, and her fiction contains numerous scenes in which the main thing that is not represented is the main thing. Thus it is with the crucial violation that occasions the demise of Son and Jadine's relationship. Many critics note the impasse that Son and Jadine come to when the narrator says: "Each knew the world as it was meant or ought to be. One had a past, the other a future and each one bore the culture to save the race in his hands. Mama-spoiled black man, will you mature with me? Culture-bearing black woman, whose culture are you bearing?" (269).[14] In the heated argument that ensues, lines are crossed not merely rhetorically but also physically. The first telling detail comes immediately prior to Son's telling Jadine the story of the tar baby when he "tore open his shirt" (270). This gesture is the prelude to a rape. As he tells her the story of tar baby that identifies her as the creation of a white man, Jadine speaks the following lines; for emphasis, I will cite only Jadine's half of the dialogue:

"Don't touch me. Don't you touch me."
"Quit! leave me *alone!*"
"You better kill me. Because if you don't, when you're through, I'm going to kill you."
"I am going to kill you. *Kill* you."
"As sure I live," she said. "I'm going to kill you." (270–271)

After Son leaves, Jadine "lay in wrinkled sheets, slippery, gutted" (271) and is unable to use her hands to remove a piece of hair from her mouth. More telling is Son's response when he returns four hours later; he is "repentant, terrified that he had gone too far" (271). During their final conversation, Jadine is wearing only a T-shirt, which leads to this description of her from Son's point of view: "The Cheech and Chong T-shirt was up around her waist and her nakedness below embarrassed him now. He had produced that nakedness and having soiled it, it shamed him" (272). Son's sexual violation of Jadine is startling in two ways: first, for the way that critics have commented upon this key scene without noticing the sexual violation; and second, for the way that Morrison's own less-than-candid remarks on her novel have helped to conceal the rape.[15]

Speaking of Son and Jadine in an interview, Morrison cryptically notes: "I may have some attitude about which one is more right than the other, but in a funny sense that book was very unsettling to me because everybody was sort of wrong. (Laughter) Some more wrong than others" (Jones and Vinson 178). What the rape suggests is that the one who is "more right" counterintuitively may be Jadine, even though she still has much to learn. At the very least, the scene should make problematic those discussions that identify Son as the source of value in the novel.[16] Morrison's ambivalent discussion that refuses to name the rape points to a similar deflection of attention away from the act in *Tar Baby*.

There are good reasons for readers to miss Son's rape of Jadine because the text is at pains to construct Son as nonrapist by questioning stereotypes about black male sexuality. When Son is first "introduced" to Valerian's household, it is with a gun at his back and with a general presumption that he was planning to rape Margaret, Valerian's wife, since he had been hiding in her closet. Having jumped ship and lived on next to nothing on the island for several days, he is unkempt, dirty, and (from a white perspective) the very image of criminality—"a black man with dreadlock hair" (80).

The next day, Sydney Shield, Jadine's uncle, who is the Streets' very proper butler, is outraged that Valerian has extended his hospitality to the stranger. Ondine, Sydney's wife, tries to calm him and their conversation helps undermine the possibility that Son can ever be named as a rapist.[17] Ondine notes that Valerian had been drinking, but Sydney replies:

"Ain't that much whiskey in the world make a man sleep with a wife-raper down the hall."

"He didn't rape anybody. Didn't even try."

"Oh? You know what's on his mind, do you?"

"I know he's been here long enough and quiet enough to rape, kill, steal—do whatever he wanted and all he did was eat." (99)

Sydney is not satisfied because Son has been given the guest room next to his niece and he fears for Jadine's safety. His fears, apparently, are not unfounded, for the next day Son appears in Jadine's room and grabs her from behind and buries his face in her hair. The ensuing dialogue, precisely because of the parallels to the scene in which Son does rape Jadine, serves to disguise rather than highlight the later scene:

"You rape me and they'll feed you to the alligators. Count on it, nigger. You good as dead right now."

"Rape? Why you little white girls always think somebody's trying to rape you?"

"White?" She was startled out of fury. "I'm not . . . you know I'm not white!"

"No? Then why don't you settle down and stop acting like it."

"Oh, God," she moaned. "Oh, good God, I think you better throw me out of the window because as soon as you let me loose *I am going to kill you*. For that alone. Just for that. For pulling that black-woman-white-woman shit on me. Never mind the rest. What you said before, that was nasty and mean, but if you think you can get away with telling me what a black woman is or ought to be . . ." (121, emphasis added)

Important here is that Jadine looks for safety in "they"—the men (Sydney, Valerian) who will protect her from rape. The sexual insult culminates when Son tells Jadine that he smells her, suggesting that over and above the smell of his unwashed body he can smell her response to him as a woman. However much she wishes to deny it, this moment implicates Jadine and makes her unable to tell Valerian of Son's insult.

But even Son's overt sexual aggression is diffused beforehand by the way that Son, in the days before his discovery, has been entering Jadine's room at night to gaze on her sleeping features. Surely here is his opportunity to rape her, and yet he restrains himself physically, content with an apparently innocuous goal:

he had thought hard during those times in order to manipulate her dreams, to insert his own dreams into her so she would not wake or stir or turn over on her stomach but would lie still and dream steadily the dreams he wanted her to have about yellow houses with white doors which women opened and shouted Come on in, you honey you! and the fat black ladies in white dresses minding the pie table in the basement of the church and white wet sheets flapping on the line [. . .] (119)[18]

Again the text insists on Son as nonrapist, and yet clearly his goal is penetration/insertion, the penetration of Jadine's unconscious, in order to get this "yellow" to think the world in terms of the black woman in the yellow dress whose insult sends Jadine scurrying back to Valerian's island in the beginning. The question is whether Son's penetration will be forced or consensual. Son's vision of a black pastoral has its origins in his memories of his agrarian home, Eloe, Florida.

One effect of Son's sexual advance is a moment of self-reflexivity in which Jadine is aware of her double-consciousness. Intending to tell Valerian of Son's insult, her thoughts lead her to how she enacts a subject position for whites: "She needed only to be stunning, and to convince them she was not as smart as they were. Say the obvious, ask stupid questions, laugh with abandon, look interested, and light up at any display of their humanity if they showed it" (126–27). This moment of reflection helps define Son's function as a mentor figure to Jadine, just as Guitar's insistence on racialized identity forces Milkman to question his urge to assimilate to middle-class culture in *Song of Solomon*.

The protracted courtship that precedes Son and Jadine's consummation of their desire again seems to show how restrained Son can be. Jadine certainly is more attracted to Son after he has bathed, shaved, cut his hair, and donned some of Valerian's old clothes. She agrees to go down to the beach with him for lunch. In the ensuing conversation he is able to persuade Jadine to allow him to touch the arch of her foot, a curious moment of sexual simulacrum; she asks him to stop, "but his forefinger stayed where his finger had been in the valley of her naked foot. Even after she laced up the canvas shoe" (179–80). This moment of sexual foreplay marks Son's initial success in his desire to restructure Jadine's unconscious; when the jeep runs out of gas and Son leaves Jadine to get fuel, she encounters for the first time an eerie presence that in this scene is only subliminal but which will later become the nightmare vision that attends her relationship with Son. Walking along a part of the island known as Sein de Veilles, or Witch's Tit, Jadine falls into a black tarlike jelly that threatens to engulf her. Although Son is literally absent, he remains present in the sketch Jadine has made of him. From the trees, spirit women look down at Jadine's struggle:

> They were delighted when first they saw her, thinking a runaway child had been restored to them. But upon looking closer they saw differently. This girl was fighting to get away from them. The women hanging from the trees were quiet now, but arrogant—mindful as they were of their value, their exceptional femaleness; knowing as they did that the first world of the world had been built with their sacred properties [. . .]. (183)

Although Jadine is unaware of these women, whose sacred properties are most centrally the ability to bring forth new life, their presence marks the extent to which Son's agenda with Jadine seems to be advancing. These women are the mythologized version of Son's pie ladies, nurturing mothers all. What Jadine's encounter with the women in the tree suggests is that Son's mentoring, while it has something important to teach her, is also fraught with danger.

But what is dangerous about Son is hidden by the way he seems the antithesis of everything Valerian represents. Son crushes his host's racist/classist assumptions at the Christmas dinner on the island and thus destroys Valerian's illusion of mastery. Shortly after this abortive dinner, Jadine and Son consummate their relationship in a scene that shows Son's tender, careful treatment of Jadine. The new couple then fly to New York, where Son's desire to remake Jadine is countered by her equally strong urge to reshape him. In an effort to complete his restructuring of her unconscious, Son insists on their going to the origin of his image of black agrarian bliss, Eloe, Florida.

By taking Jadine to Eloe, Son hopes to reveal to her an authentic African-American community, one that will cause her to abandon her investment in white culture. In this regard, Son again plays the same role for Jadine that Guitar plays for Milkman. But as I have argued in the previous chapter, Guitar can only lead Milkman so far, and ultimately Milkman must reject Guitar's notion that killing white people is about "loving" black people because the Seven Days, against their stated intentions, turns out to be about black men protecting their property interests in black women. In this regard, Guitar, who initially seemed to present an alternative to the paternalism of Macon Dead, Milkman's father, stands revealed as another embodiment of the patriarchal impulse.

Eloe also reveals itself to be a far more appealing place for men than for women, in that everyone seems to accept that what men do is more important. Jadine is estranged from this close-knit community that seems to foster segregation of a different type—not race-based, but sex-based. The men of Eloe immediately absorb Son into themselves, leaving Jadine in the company of rural women; these same men regard the light-skinned Jadine as Son's trophy. It is in Eloe that Son's goal, a fundamental reshaping of the way Jadine imagines the world, seems to be nearly complete; Jadine, however, does not experience her new dreamscape as soothing but rather as a nightmare populated by the night women. Earlier, trapped in the tar pit on Valerian's island, Jadine could not see the women of Witch's Tit watching her; now in Eloe, making love to Son, she alone can see a fantastic group of women, including Son's former lover Cheyenne, Thérèse, his Aunt Rosa, Jadine's dead mother, Ondine, and the woman in the yellow dress, crowd into the room: "they each pulled out a breast and showed it to her. Jadine started to tremble. They stood around in the room, jostling each other gently, gently—there wasn't much room—revealing one breast and then two and Jadine was shocked" (258). But Jadine's biggest fright comes when the woman in the yellow dress "stretched out a long arm and showed Jadine her three big eggs," the clearest sign of the nurturing and fertility of these women (258–59). To commit to the community of Eloe and the enactment of female identity represented by the night women and the pie ladies comes at too high a price for a woman such as Jadine, for it is to acquiesce to a form of patriarchal agrarianism that strictly limits woman's role to the natural creation of motherhood. Son's father decrees that Jadine may not sleep with Son because they are not married, and though this may seem an innocuous representation of the moral values of a more traditional community, the father's decision points to a more sinister set of assumptions behind such tradition regarding the need for male control of female sexuality. Cheyenne's presence in this group of night women particularly underscores the patriarchal nature of this community and serves as the metaphorical hypertext link, as it were, to *Song of Solomon,* an intertextual gloss on Milkman's encounter with Sweet, the woman whom the men of Shalimar all know. Milkman's ritual of filliation is completed in the spectacular bodily pleasure he takes with Sweet; the bath and massage she gives him lead him to think:

> If this bath and this woman [. . .] are all that come out of this trip, I will rest easy and do my duty to God, country, and the Brotherhood of Elks for the rest of my life. I will walk hot coals with a quart of kerosene in my hand for this. I will walk every railroad tie from here to Cheyenne and back for this. But when the lovemaking came, he decided he would crawl. (285)

The signifier "Cheyenne" takes us from here (Milkman and the spectacular sex Sweet offers) to *Tar Baby* and Son's attempt to gain sole ownership of a woman whose sexuality, like Sweet's, is the common experience of Eloe's men. Son "accidentally" kills Cheyenne in a moment of male rage: he drives a car through their house because of her infidelity. This act exists in a logical continuum with the general patriarchal assumptions of Eloe, where a man is expected to limit the autonomy of "his" woman. But the very attempt to take exclusive possession of Cheyenne was Son's mistake, according to what Soldier, Son's friend, tells Jadine. Cheyenne, with "the best pussy in Florida" (254), cannot, after her communal circulation, be owned privately. A number of readers, though, are willing to forgive Son his killing Cheyenne—a violence that might otherwise anticipate his rape of Jadine—as an understandable male response.

What Son wants to do to the fashion model Jadine is what Valerian already has done to Margaret, the former Maine beauty queen; namely, construct a female subjectivity that effaces itself the better to serve male identity.[19] If Valerian has made Jadine a tar baby in one sense (a black woman more cathected to white culture than black), Son surely wishes to make her a tar baby in another (a nurturing black mama who will never ask to share a male authority or autonomy). On this particular point, what's so African about Son or Eloe for that matter? Just as Morrison refashions Chloe, with its connotations of stereotyped black agrarian identity, into

Toni, so must Jadine distance herself from Eloe and its patriarchal agrarianism. Given Morrison's other clues regarding her name, Eloe seems almost a pun (visual at least) on Chloe; this link is symbolically suggestive, for just as Jadine rejects agrarian Eloe, Morrison denies the agrarian implications of Chloe by taking Toni as her public name.

Before Son returns to New York, Jadine's dreams are so completely consumed by the night women that Jadine feels "the helpless victim of a dream that chose" her (262). When Son does return to New York, their relationship quickly deteriorates, so much so that during an argument Son picks up Jadine and dangles her out the window of their apartment while he tells her she must cease her classist assumptions and be kinder to her aunt and uncle. His violent "pedagogy" anticipates his attempt a few pages later to rape her into a "correct" subject position.

As she lies in bed in the immediate aftermath of Son's rape, her thoughts turn not to her sexual violation but rather to the sense of lack that coalesces around a particular image—a beech tree on her undergraduate campus and an annual mother-daughter day each April in which girls in pastel skirts sway arm in arm with their mothers: "Pale sulfur light sprinkled so softly with lilac it made her want to cry. [. . . B]ut her tears were not because there was no one to sing with under the biggest beech in the state, but because of the light, pale sulfur sprinkled with lilac" (271). Jadine's tears are not an orphan's cry for the mother's body but rather an acknowledgment that she has been unable to participate in a ceremony that, whatever elements of "bourgeoisie sentiment and alumni hustling" (271) it may include, still signifies the ancient properties, the intergenerational linkage of women nurturing women. It is precisely this recognition of her lack that suggests it may be possible for Jadine to forge a new identity as she returns to Paris.

Crucially, Jadine exits the novel on a plane, a gesture that recalls Milkman's plane flight that begins part II of *Song of Solomon*. Milkman's flight initially represents an entirely selfish desire for Pilate's gold but becomes transformed during the course of his journey into a quest for familial and racial identity.[20] Classist to the end, Jadine in the airport rest room still addresses Alma Estée as Mary, the generic name given all women servants at Valerian's house. The Jadine who leaves for Paris is certainly monstrous, but it is the monstrousness of a narcissism perhaps necessary to become an artist. Morrison's comments on Jadine in published interviews are contradictory, though she is careful to distance herself from her character's shortcomings. For example, unlike Jadine, who in the aftermath of Son's rape feels unable to provide emotional support for the aunt who raised her, Morrison makes clear her difference: "My mother took care of me when I could not go to the bathroom or feed myself.

When she gets in that position, I have to do that for her" (Wilson 131). Perhaps the need to distance herself from Jadine arises because there is so much of Morrison in her character. Both are educated in a Eurocentric tradition; Morrison's response to the question, "At what time in your life did you form specific judgments about the value of being Black?" creates a curiously homologous relation between author and character:

> I came to that as a clear statement very late in life, I think, because I left home, say at 17 and went to school, and the things I studied were Western and, you know, I was terrifically fascinated with all of that, and at that time any information that came to me from my own people seemed to me to be backwoodsy and uninformed. You know, they hadn't read all these wonderful books. You know how college students are. And, I think, I didn't regard it as valuable as being Black. [. . .] But the consciousness of being Black I think happened when I left Cornell and went to teach at Texas Southern University. [. . .] So I think it was as a novice teacher, and that was in 1957 or 1958, that I began to think about Black culture [. . .]. (Jones and Vinson 173–74)

Morrison here has identified herself as a young woman who only comes to a racialized consciousness at an age very close to the twenty-five-year-old Jadine.

What remains unclear in both *Tar Baby* and Morrison's subsequent commentary is whether an African-American woman's right relation to the "ancient properties" is innate or learned. In two separate interviews conducted in 1981, Morrison seems to agree with Thérèse's evaluation of Jadine, which asserts that this young woman has lost her ancient properties.[21] Yet what Ondine despairs of in her final conversation with Jadine is that she has failed to *teach* her niece those nurturing properties: "Jadine, a girl has got to be a daughter first. She have to learn that. And if she never learns how to be a daughter, she can't never learn how to be a woman" (281). In a 1983 interview, Morrison maintains her character *has* learned something when Nellie McKay asks, "Is Jadine ever going to know who she is?" Morrison responds: "I hope so. She has a good shot at it[,] a good chance. Now she knows something she did not know before. She may know why she was running away. And maybe, the biggest thing that she can learn, even if she never gets back to Son, is that dreams of safety are childish" (150). Again Morrison's comments deflect attention away from Son's violence. Her characterization of Jadine also contradicts Thérèse's (as well as Morrison's earlier assessment of Jadine) as a woman who has *forgotten* her ancient properties; in this version, whatever properties constitute identity are not innate but rather are *learned*. And if they are not innate, can we speak of Jadine losing what she never had or forgetting what she never knew?

On the plane to Paris, Jadine thinks about the aftermath of Son's rape. Her thoughts reveal her as pregnant with the possibilities of a new identity that can sort through the competing claims of African-Americaness and womanhood. Unable to determine which of the possibilities might account for the failure of her relationship with Son, Jadine muses:

> Having sixteen answers meant having none. So none it was. Zero. She would go back to Paris and begin at Go. Let loose the dogs, tangle with the woman in yellow—with her and with all the night women who had *looked* at her. No more shoulders and limitless chests. No more dreams of safety. No more. Perhaps that was the thing—the thing Ondine was saying. A grown woman did not need safety or its dreams. She *was* the safety she longed for. (290)

Strikingly, the word "rape" is again absent, since that would seem to provide a single immediate answer to the question of what went wrong. But this does not mean that Jadine does not take the rape seriously; rather, she is thinking about the reasons that lead to the violation. She can and must leave Son, but she still loves Son. Throughout her meditation on the plane, the rape is, as in its initial representation, a trace—more absent than present. Although she does not wish to become a woman like Ondine, her aunt's words still lead her to a realization. Jadine's dissipated dream of safety was her belief that good men would protect her from bad men; earlier she believed that Valerian and Sydney could protect her from Son's potential rape. In Son the categories good man/bad man have collapsed so thoroughly that the distinction becomes meaningless. Jadine's reflections echo the language of the decision Pilate comes to when she has been shunned because she lacks a navel (a discovery that only happens when she has sex with men):

> Although she was hampered by huge ignorances, but not in any way unintelligent, when she realized what her situation in the world was and would probably always be she threw away every assumption she had learned and began at zero. First off, she cut her hair. That was one thing she didn't want to have to think about anymore. Then she tackled the problem of trying to decide how she wanted to live and what was valuable to her. When am I happy and when am I sad and what is the difference? What do I need to know to stay alive? What is true in the world? [. . .] Throughout this fresh, if common, pursuit of knowledge, one conviction crowned her efforts: since death held no terrors for her [. . .], she knew there was nothing to fear. (*Song* 149)

It initially may seem odd to compare the self-centered Jadine to Pilate, who perhaps more than any character in Morrison's fiction represents the ability to transcend self-love; nevertheless, Jadine seems poised at the same moment of Thoreauvian self-scrutiny that Pilate experienced. It is important to remember that Pilate only becomes Pilate *after* this fundamental reassessment. For both Pilate and Jadine, their recognition is that they cannot look toward men for their safety or authentic identity. Tellingly for Jadine, she takes the words of her surrogate mother, Ondine, as a way to begin her rethinking. *Song of Solomon,* then, may provide one way to read Jadine's exit from the novel. Milkman learned about African-American male identity from Guitar to a certain point, beyond which he had to reject Guitar and turn to Pilate for guidance. So too Jadine has had Son to take her part of the way toward a racialized identity but she, like Milkman, must reject her initial mentor when that mentor's version of African-American identity specifically denies equality to black women. The Jadine who flies to Paris appears to have the potential to become self-piloted/Pilated.

Ironically, the very reason that Jadine must leave Son—his sexual violation of her—produces her resolution to confront the night women who suggest she has failed to achieve an appropriately nurturing gendered identity. In this regard, Son perhaps has performed his rescue of Jadine, but not in the way that he had hoped to with her focusing that nurturance on him. Immediately following Jadine's realization that her dream of safety is over, there is a conceit that initially appears to be directly introduced by the narrator; however, the extended metaphor follows Jadine's thoughts as they shift (through a good modernist representation of the workings of the unconscious) from the words of Ondine, her aunt, to the life cycle of soldier ants. The soldier ants point as much to Son as to her aunt, for it was Son's chocolate eating that drew the soldier ants to Valerian's green house. But Jadine's vision is of a society that is almost exclusively female, since the male ant's only role is to impregnate the queen, after which the male dies. Jadine's conception of this female society is harsh, but needs to be read with an awareness of her as a rape victim:

> She seals herself off from all society and eats her own wing muscles until she bears her eggs. When the first larvae appear, there is nothing to feed them so she gives them their unhatched sisters until they are old enough and strong enough to hunt and bring their prey back to the kingdom. That is all. Bearing, hunting, eating, fighting, burying. No time for dreaming [. . .]. (291)

Previously terrified of the woman in the yellow dress who held up the chicken eggs, Jadine now appropriates eggs for herself.[22] Her vision of a matriarchy governed by a self-isolated queen, however, is far from a utopia. It is a world of clear purpose but no play. Yet for all its grimness, this conceit, which anthropomorphizes the insect world, reiterates the notion of self-reliance while insisting upon female fecundity; Jadine here confronts the ancient property of female nurturance in its starkest, most primal form. This figuration of the mother in a sense anticipates Sethe's thick love in *Beloved* that kills one daughter only then to suckle another with a combination of mother's milk and sister's blood. The return at the end of the chapter from the insect to the human world shows how traumatic it has been for Jadine to have been sexually violated by the man she loved. At the same time, her memory of Son as "the man who fucked like a star" points back to the consensual moment on Valerian's island when they initially consummated their love. In that first sexual union, Son tells Jadine to imagine herself as a star feels itself: "Star throbs. Over and over and over. Like this. Stars just throb and throb and throb and sometimes, when they can't throb anymore, when they can't hold it anymore, they fall out of the sky" (214). By explicitly ending the chapter with Jadine's recollection of Son's gentleness, the novel implies that, despite her pain, Jadine will be able to retain that which has been nurturing in her relationship with Son. Rejecting Son (and by extension his patriarchal vision of women) will be painful because it means a repudiation of certain forms of romance, girlishness, and desire. Yet Jadine is ready to move toward a woman-centered community because she realizes that the physical and psychological abuse is too high a price to pay to be granted authenticity within Son's patriarchy. Because Jadine is able to imagine herself in such an extended metaphor, one that posits female solitude as a necessary condition for productivity, it is possible to see her as arriving by the novel's end at the nascent moment of artistic consciousness.

Consistent with Morrison's drawing upon the life cycle of the male soldier ant, which dies once it has mated, Son metaphorically dies after raping Jadine. His one role—to initiate her struggle to attain a more self-conscious racialized and gendered identity—is over. Although he attempts to pursue Jadine back to Valerian's island, Thérèse rows him to the back side of the island where Son essentially ceases to be representational, becoming instead a kind of cartoon rabbit and escaping back into his same-as-it-never-was briar patch. Son is relegated to the trash heap, not of history but of mythology. Morrison, speaking of Son's end, claims that he "may identify totally and exclusively with the past, which is a kind of death, because it means you have no future, but a suspended place" (Ruas 112).

My reading both of Morrison's self-fashioning through her name change and of the origin of Jadine's adult subjectivity in a moment of sexual violation necessarily is speculative; nevertheless, the evidence that joins these two realms of fiction suggests that Morrison, while writing her fourth novel, was wrestling with her own "night women," those internalized voices that might question her for layering nontraditional roles onto her maternal one. In 1981, when *Tar Baby* appeared, Morrison had left behind Lorain, Ohio, along with her birth name; she was raising two sons by herself, while giving a high priority to a career that made her as much the cultural as the natural creator. The identity Morrison was fashioning for herself obviously exceeded the boundaries of Son's version of black female subjectivity. Despite the reluctance of the novel (and subsequently the author) to name the violation, Morrison's representation of his rape of Jadine illustrates that any reading that unreflexively yearns for Son's nostalgic vision is inadequate. Reading this fiction as a form of authorial self-fashioning allows one to see that *Tar Baby*, like *Song of Solomon*, confirms Morrison's refusal to endorse an African-American identity that would allow black men—in unacknowledged complicity with white patriarchy—to assume property rights in black women. Black women, the text also suggests, need not be tied to agrarian community in order to partake in the ancient properties but, like Jadine (or indeed like Morrison herself), may migrate freely, with or without men, to the city and beyond.

If the intertextual dialogue between *Song of Solomon* and *Tar Baby* (in which self is figured first as male and then as female) allows Morrison to fashion a useable racial identity by narrating the difficulties of coming to such an identity, she then takes that newly purchased authorial identity to her next novel, *Beloved*. The critique of African-American masculinity and femininity in the earlier novels now moves toward a rapprochement between African-American women and men. Morrison portrays the Sweet Home men allowing the new slave, Sethe, time to choose which of them she will have as a husband; white men are the rapists in this novel of both black women and black men. Morrison's narrative sets out to recover cultural memory regarding an American holocaust about which there has been much forgetfulness. In *Song of Solomon* and *Tar Baby,* Morrison's coded references to her own family history suggest the movement her subsequent fiction would make toward engaging the intertext of African-American history. In *Beloved, Jazz,* and *Paradise,* that history becomes explicit, even as she continues to engage the aesthetic past and, at times, to write reflexively of self.

Chapter 6

The Authorized Morrison:
Reflexivity and the Historiographic

With *Tar Baby,* Morrison lays to rest much of her anxiety about her identity as an African-American woman novelist. This is what I mean by "the authorized Morrison." She has in the course of her preceding fictions largely authorized herself, constructing a powerful position from which to write and speak. If this study contributes anything to an understanding of Morrison, it is the way her identifying fictions—her first four novels—do not simply thematize identity formation, they perform it. As I have argued, it is a highly self-reflexive process: as Morrison writes, she enacts the identity she was not certain she had, thereby constituting that very identity. The Morrison who writes *Beloved, Jazz,* and *Paradise* is more confident that the funk can rise economically; in other words, she feels less inclined to celebrate a black identity exclusively linked to poverty.

No longer needing to allegorize her struggle to become an authentic African-American woman, Morrison nevertheless, at various moments in her later historiographic trilogy, continues to meditate on authorship and the social role the artist may play in relation to the community. I do not intend my discussion of Morrison's latest three novels to be full and complete readings; rather, I want to place these fictions in the context that this study has emphasized—the autobiographical impulses that animate various moments within the writing. Although no longer as prominent a feature as it was in her earlier novels, the reflexive contemplation Morrison begins on authorship with Soaphead Church in *The Bluest Eye* continues through such characters in her historiographic trilogy as Baby Suggs, Sethe's mother-in-law in *Beloved;* the unnamed, disembodied narrator of *Jazz,* who is strong enough to question her own productive powers; and a final marginal figure from *Paradise,* Patricia Best, the light-complexioned black woman whose historical writing interprets the hidden meaning of genealogy in the all-black town of Ruby, Oklahoma.

No Uncle Tom:
Baby Suggs, Artist of the Bodily Spirit

> Certainly no American text of the sort I am discussing was ever written for black people—no more than *Uncle Tom's Cabin* was written for Uncle Tom to read or be persuaded by.
>
> —Toni Morrison, *Playing in the Dark*

Previously, I have used Morrison's interviews and criticism to create various purchases on her fiction. I would like, however, to move in a different direction here to suggest that *Beloved* may provide clues about Morrison's developing critical sensibility, a sensibility that would manifest itself a year after the publication of her fifth novel in her lecture, "Unspeakable Things Unspoken: The Afro-American Presence in American Literature." In other words, how does Morrison's fifth novel look if one reads it for her development of a critique of Enlightenment impulses in nineteenth-century American literature? For Morrison, Stowe's failure to acknowledge the black reader means that *Uncle Tom's Cabin* exemplifies the larger failure of the American novel to recognize its implication in the construction of racism (*Playing* 16–17). Certainly in Morrison's fictional rendering of slavery, the African-American reader is always addressed. But Morrison's relation to Stowe, I wish to argue, goes beyond a passing comment to the intertextual fabric of *Beloved.*

In *Beloved,* Morrison begins to make a clearer turn to a fiction that is historiographic in the sense Linda Hutcheon has identified as postmodern. For Hutcheon, novels such as *Beloved* "juxtapose what we think we know of the past (from official archival sources and personal memory)" with alternative representations that emphasize "the postmodern epistemological questioning of the nature of historical knowledge"; such an emphasis allows the reader to ask, "Which 'facts' make it into history? And *whose* facts?" (*Politics* 71). Morrison's turn toward alternative history is signaled by *Beloved*'s most immediate intertext, the archive of slave narratives in general and more particularly the story of Margaret Garner.[1] While working at Random House, Morrison served as the unacknowledged editor for an alternative history of everyday African Americans, *The Black Book* (1974), a portion of which included excerpts from slave narratives. Later Morrison came across Garner's story. While working on *Beloved* in

1985, Morrison claims to have known about Garner only through a "newspaper clipping"; however, as the novelist continues discussing Garner's escape from Kentucky, Morrison reveals a familiarity that seems to exceed a single newspaper clipping:

> [Garner] lived in a little neighborhood just outside of Cincinnati and she had killed her children. She succeeded in killing one; she tried to kill two others. She hit them in the head with a shovel and they were wounded but they didn't die. And there was a smaller one that she had at her breast. The interesting thing, in addition to that, was the interviews that she gave. She was a young woman. In the inked pictures of her she seemed a very quiet, very serene-looking woman and everyone who interviewed her remarked about her serenity and tranquility. She said, "I will not let those children live how I have lived." (Naylor 206–207)

Morrison goes on to tell about Garner's mother-in-law's reaction to the killing. More recently Morrison responded to a question regarding her reading of slave narratives and their relation to *Beloved:*

> I wouldn't read them for information because I knew that they had to be authenticated by white patrons, that they couldn't say everything they wanted to say because they couldn't alienate their audience [. . .]. Their narratives had to be very understated. So while I looked at the documents and felt *familiar* with slavery and overwhelmed by it, I wanted it to be truly *felt*. I wanted to translate the historical into the personal. (Schappell 103)

Claiming little specific knowledge (nor wanting more regarding Garner), Morrison can presumably merge fiction and history in a fashion that will personalize and politicize the past. The earlier quotation, however, suggests that Morrison is more aware of the historical record concerning Garner than she admits, and the reason may have something to do with a desire to conceal another intertext, Harriet Beecher Stowe's *Uncle Tom's Cabin.*[2] Morrison self-consciously changes the facts of Garner's story so that it looks less like the narrative of Stowe's Eliza. Margaret Garner, like Eliza, escapes across the partially frozen Ohio River; Morrison, however, changes this detail in Sethe's crossing of the Ohio.[3] This is an interesting twist on an author-directed form of intertextuality. Her earlier titles *Song of Solomon* and *Tar Baby* explicitly invite the reader to think about the biblical chapter and the folk tale; now, however, Morrison's novel directs the reader's attention to *Uncle Tom's Cabin* because of the fictive moves that create difference and seem almost to say, "Don't think of Stowe's novel." Yet Stowe's narrative insists on manifesting itself.[4] But what specifically identifies this nineteenth-century novel as an intertext of *Beloved?*

In chapter 39 of *Uncle Tom's Cabin,* Simon Legree's abused mistress, Cassy, develops the plan whereby she and Emmeline (whom Legree plans to succeed Cassy) will escape by hiding in the attic of the cruel master's house. Her stratagem is based on "the memory of an old ghost legend" (396), which in turn is rooted in the death of a woman slave whom Legree apparently tortured and killed in that garret. By clever contrivances, Cassy convinces Legree that the attic is indeed haunted, so that when she and Emmeline appear to escape into the swamp, they may safely return to hide in the garret until Legree exhausts himself searching the swamp.

While actually carrying out the first part of this plan (the apparent escape into the swamp) with Legree in hot pursuit, Emmeline falters: "O Cassy, I'm going to faint!" Cassy responds, pulling a stiletto and says: "If you do, I'll kill you!" (401). This moment, in which a woman who has lost her daughter threatens the young woman who is that lost daughter's metaphorical substitute, resonates particularly with a central moment in Toni Morrison's *Beloved*—Sethe's successful killing of her baby daughter, Beloved, when the mother realizes she and her children will be taken back into slavery. Cassy's relation to Sethe becomes even clearer in the life history that Cassy narrates to Tom. She tells him how she killed a son out of love. Cassy's first son, fathered by the master whom she loved, had been taken from her after the master sold her; she reasons, therefore, that her second son's life—given the violent disruptions of the black family under slavery—would not be worth living and so gives the baby laudanum (364). Taken together, Sethe's and Cassy's infanticides suggest the way *Beloved* rewrites *Uncle Tom's Cabin,* a rewriting that refuses the vision of Stowe's Christian world and simultaneously posits an Africanist realm of spirituality. Unlike spirituality in Stowe's novel, in which the tortured black body of Uncle Tom can be released only by death into eternal salvation, whatever paradise can be achieved in Morrison's novel must happen in relation to the body.

Several other overt parallels between *Beloved* and *Uncle Tom's Cabin* remain despite Morrison's apparent attempt to deflect the reader's attention from the connection.[5] Like Eliza, who lives in comfort and apparent security from the market economy of slavery at the Harris farm in Kentucky, Sethe also lives on a Kentucky farm where the human dignity of the slaves appears secure. In both novels, this tranquil state terminates suddenly: in *Uncle Tom's Cabin,* Mr. Shelby must sell two of his slaves or risk losing his farm; in *Beloved,* the death of the good master allows the sadistic schoolteacher to take over. In response, both Eliza with her child and Sethe, pregnant with Denver, escape to Ohio. But here the parallels begin to break down. Eliza's story quickly moves toward comedy. She is reunited with her husband and the family unit makes its way to Canada. In fact, except for the Christian martyr Tom, all of Stowe's major characters find integration into a larger community. Eliza is reunited with her mother, just as Cassy is reunited with her daughter. Even the sting of Uncle Tom's death is mitigated by the narrator's certain knowledge that Tom goes to meet his Maker. In a novel that purports to reveal the horrors of slavery, it oddly becomes a sort of fairy tale, a wish fulfillment nominated as "truth stranger than fiction. How can it be otherwise, when a system prevails which whirls families and scatters their members, as the wind whirls and scatters the leaves of autumn? These shores of refuge, like the eternal shore, often unite again, in glad communion, hearts that for long years have mourned each other as lost" (424). *Beloved*'s reunions, on the other hand, are far from easy or fortunate. Paul D finds Sethe only accidentally and after years of wandering. And he is not her husband. Moreover, Morrison's novel addresses ambiguously the mother–daughter reunion. Not all haunted houses lead to happy homes.

Chapter 42 of *Uncle Tom's Cabin* claims, with Stowe's Fieldingesque irony, to be "An Authentic Ghost Story." Cassy, who, unlike Sethe, is not haunted by the killing of her child, decides to "haunt" Legree as part of her plan to escape with Emmeline. She begins leaving the garret at night dressed in a sheet and appears to Legree one night thus attired. In doing so she brings to bear an understanding of Legree's fear of the slave he killed in the attic and of his recurring dread of the rough way he treated his dying mother. Cassy's action drives Legree into insanity that hastens his death. So in one sense, the figure of the ghost in Legree's plantation house is the simplest of the three. Cassy, as the reader is well aware, is the "ghost," a ploy she uses to defeat an evil man.

In another sense, though, the ghost in Legree's house is complicated by Stowe's Christian world picture.[6] Speaking of Legree, who returns from a night of drinking, the narrator tells us: "let a man take what pains he may to hush it down, a human soul is an awful, ghostly, unquiet possession for a bad man to have" (417). To figure the soul as a ghost, however, pulls against the narrator's assertion that Legree's superstitious nature is a trait "common to coarse and uninstructed minds" (367–68), for what is Legree's superstition but an intimation of his ghostly soul? That is to say, it is precisely Legree's superstition that is closest to his spirituality and the possibility of his redemption. In Legree's house, then, ghosts are simultaneously affirmed and denied: the narrator's overt rhetoric makes the idea of ghosts laughable, while Stowe's Christian vision assures us of a different supernatural, the realm of heaven and angels.

Stowe's Christian supernatural emerges in the contrasting yet parallel death scenes of two of Tom's masters—the good New Orleans master, St. Clare, and the vicious planter, Legree. On St. Clare's deathbed in Stowe's aptly titled chapter "Reunion," the good man has a vision of his mother: "Just before the spirit parted, he opened his eyes, with a sudden light, as of joy and recognition, and said, '*Mother!*' and then he was gone!" (318). Not only does St. Clare encounter his mother's ghost in the moment of his dying, he himself is denominated as one—"spirit." Just as Tom's good master is ushered into eternity by his mother, so too is Legree met by his mother who will lead him to eternal damnation. Although initially it was Cassy's acting that drove Legree to distraction, it is Legree's mother who comes to his deathbed, "a stern, white, inexorable figure, saying, 'Come! come! come!'" (418).

The distinction, we might say, is between ghosts and holy ghosts or angels, which—as appearance of these two mothers at the deaths of their sons would suggest—aligns these maternal ghosts with a feminine principle in Stowe's discourse. This feminine principle has everything to do with an opposition between reason and feeling.[7]

And those with the most natural relation to feeling in Stowe's world are women, children, and African Americans. The dying Eva's relation to her father, St. Clare, and Tom's relation to his various masters underscore Stowe's world picture. Eva, for example, leads her father to Christ, but only by the assertion of her belief, a belief that cannot be grounded on reason. Tom's relation to St. Clare duplicates Eva's, since Tom vows never to leave until "Mas'r St. Clare's a Christian" (306). Tom, like Eva, bases his appeal not on reason but on faith. From the outset we are told that Tom is simple. His stature as Christian tragic hero resides in his spiritual greatness, his ability to feel the logos, not to reason with it:

> Uncle Tom was a sort of patriarch in religious matters in the neighborhood. [. . . H]e was looked up to with great respect, as a sort of minister among them; and the simple, hearty, sincere style of his exhortations, might have edified even better educated persons. But it was in prayer that he especially excelled. Nothing could exceed the touching simplicity, the childlike earnestness of his prayer, enriched with the language of Scripture, which seemed so entirely to have wrought itself into his being as to have become a part of himself, and to drop from his lips unconsciously. [. . .] And so much did his prayer always work on the devotional feeling of his audiences, that there seemed often a danger that it would be lost altogether in the abundance of the responses which broke out everywhere around him. (37)

Tom's religion, like Romantic poetry, is the spontaneous overflow of powerful emotions. Tom, however, readily grants St. Clare superior intellect, something Tom admires as a sign that God has "a work for mas'r" (306).

Tom's ministrations to his masters never deviates, no matter what kind of man his master is. Tom is as good and faithful a servant to Legree as he was to Mr. Shelby or to St. Clare. Refusing only to harm other slaves, Tom is a model of subservience on the Legree plantation. Stowe's Christian world picture, for all its assertion of the moral superiority of true Christian women, slaves, and children, ultimately reinscribes what Jacques Lacan has termed the Name-of-the-Father, paternal authority that functions as linguistic construct (Lacan 199). The faithful wife, the humble slave, or the dutiful child may remind the husband, the master, or the father of the good and the true, but authority always resides with the male. And it is the duty of the wife, the slave, and the child to submit to male authority, even when it is questionable, and to leave punishment of the bad man (that is, the failed embodiment of the father function) to that ultimate symbolic Father, God. Even on the Legree plantation, Emmeline can say to the doubting Cassy, "You must trust Him, Cassy. [. . .] He is our Father!" (406). The most persistent contradiction in Stowe's novel, then, is that while it scrutinizes earthly manifestations of patriarchy, in the final instance it resoundingly affirms patriarchy as transcendent design, thus remaining well within the logocentrism of God the Father.

As *Uncle Tom's Cabin* and *Beloved* meditate on community, they begin to chart a parent's possible motivation for sacrificing a child. If *Uncle Tom's Cabin* argues for the efficacy of women in a spiritual patriarchy, *Beloved* functions in part to recover a realm of spirit that is outside and prior to transcendence conceived of in masculine tropes.[8] A key difference is marked by the nature of ghosts in Morrison's novel. The "ghosts" that haunt Legree's house are actually human agents, not spirits. In *Beloved,* 124 Bluestone Road is indeed visited by an authentic ghost.[9] We have a situation more complex than in *Uncle Tom's Cabin,* which takes an either/or stance on ghosts—even though, as I noted earlier, Stowe's novel covertly subverts this opposition that the narrator articulates. *Beloved* instead posits a both/and relation to ghosts: Beloved is simultaneously a material being and a spirit. But whose spirit? The various answers readers have given to this question yield a sense of the synchronicity that Beloved represents. She is Sethe's dead child come home, she is Seth's hanged mother reincarnated, she is spirit of the Middle Passage; Beloved is, in short, a metonymy for the "Sixty Million and more" of the book's dedication, a number representing those killed, raped, or otherwise physically and psychologically damaged in the history of the American slave trade. As such, Beloved is not the Word but rather the "rememory" made flesh. Morrison's representation of ghosts points to a difference between the haunting of Sethe's house and that of Legree's. This difference turns on the way spirituality is articulated through religious language, particularly in *Uncle Tom's Cabin* and *Beloved.* As the intersection of the material body and the spirit, the impregnated Beloved serves as a figure for the religious thinking of Baby Suggs. Her spirituality resonates with the Dogon creation myth that mourns the lost possibilities of androgyny and the female in the fallen world.

In Morrison's rewriting of *Uncle Tom's Cabin,* she apparently omits "the hero of our story" (Stowe 28), Uncle Tom. Tom, the religious patriarch of the Shelby farm, however, is recast in the maternal figure of Baby Suggs. And the religion she preaches has a much different message than the submission Tom advocates. Thinking about the atrocities committed by white people in the aftermath of the Civil War, Stamp Paid asks himself, "What *are* these people? You tell me, Jesus. What *are* they?" (180). But in *Beloved,* Tom's Jesus can neither succor nor explain. Although Tom dies in certainty of meeting his Heavenly Father, Baby Suggs dies in doubt; nevertheless, *Beloved* in its fictive resolution triumphantly affirms her religion of the maternal body. In the clearing where she held her ceremonies, Baby Suggs, shunning the patriarchal Word, "did not tell them they were the blessed of the earth, its inheriting meek or its glorybound pure"; instead, "she told them that the only grace they could have was the grace they could imagine":

> "Here," she said, "in this here place, we flesh; flesh that weeps, laughs; flesh that dances on bare feet in grass. Love it. Love it hard. Yonder they do not love your flesh. They despise it. [. . .] Love your hands! Love them. Raise them up and kiss them. Touch others with them, pat them together [. . .]. This is flesh I'm talking about here. Flesh that needs to be loved. [. . .] And all your inside parts that they'd just as soon slop for hogs, you got to love them. The dark, dark liver—love it, love it, and the beat and beating heart, love that too. More than eyes or feet. More than lungs that have yet to draw free air. More than your life-holding womb and your life-giving private parts, hear me now, love your heart. For this is the prize. (88–89)

If Tom's Christianity is the religion that legitimizes a masculine libidinal economy that privileges the transmission of the patriarchal Word in the father-son relationship (with woman as the ghostly go-between), then Baby Suggs's religion of the body envisions a fleshy and fluid spirit suggestive of the maternal body. In the opening sentence of her sermon, an interesting expression leads in two directions simultaneously—"we flesh." The strangeness of the words points to an irreducible tension. Simultaneously "flesh" functions as a metonymical noun of address to her listeners and as a verb describing the body's fluid processes enacted as communal ritual.

But her role as preacher of the flesh also reveals Baby Suggs as the synthesis of Morrison's previous representations of the artist figure, particularly as this character develops aspects of Pilate Dead. Clearly, Baby Suggs is the master of an expressive form, unlike the many maimed or near artists of Morrison's previous fiction. Having healed herself through the writing of her first four novels, Morrison now figures an artist who can truly heal the community in ways that a Soaphead Church or a Sula cannot. In the female preacher of *Beloved,* one might say, Morrison reveals her aspirations for her art and communal role. Rather than art imitating life, life follows art, for Baby Suggs seems to model the role of public intellectual that Morrison has come to play since the late 1980s. Neither an Uncle Tom nor an artist manqué, Baby Suggs weds the aesthetic to both the spiritual and the ethical, suggesting the enlarged public role Morrison would carve out for herself in order to comment more broadly on racism in America.

But even as Morrison imagines the larger potential for expression, the specter of marginality arises once again, for Baby Suggs, like all of Morrison's artist figures, risks becoming isolated from the community. This of course is precisely what happens when she gives too much of herself in the aftermath of the feast she prepares for her daughter-in-law, recently escaped from slavery. Reproducing the miracle of Tom's Jesus (the feeding of the multitude), Baby Suggs only earns the community's resentment by her fantastic excess. It is in fact this prosperity that marks Baby Suggs's difference from so many of Morrison's earlier characters whose authenticity seems to depend on a life that is economically pinched. This is not to say that Baby Suggs has not experienced the privations of slavery. She may have gained her daughter-in-law but her son is denied her. Moreover, Baby Suggs's prosperity is relative; she is hardly wealthy, but in this all-black, post–Civil War community, she has more than she needs and more than others. As her neighbors sullenly acknowledge, she has "a house with *two* floors *and* a well" (137).

Acknowledging that "she had overstepped" (138) by giving too much of her gifts (thus flaunting her blessings), Baby Suggs senses the ill will of the black community just prior to the arrival of schoolteacher and ensuing tragedy. As she hoes her garden, she recalls her seven children taken from her, naming four of them, and tries to imagine them grown. The last of the four names points to the reflexivity and unfinished business of self-fashioning latent in the moment. She asks herself, "Does Ardelia still love the burned bottom of bread?" (139). By having the novel's central figuration of the artist invoke the first name of Morrison's maternal grandmother, the secret Ardelia of Chloe Wofford, the author seems to come to terms with whatever might be threatening in that name. In a sense Morrison becomes the grandmother's mother and thus claims herself as her own ancestor.

Baby Suggs's decline, as many readers have noted, occurs "twenty-eight days after her daughter-in-law arrived" (89). This time period, the menstrual cycle, anticipates a different flowing of female blood, Sethe's slitting her daughter's throat. The flowing of blood also is linked to another flowing of bodily fluids, Sethe's milk, milk intended for the child whose blood she spills. Here both Luce Irigaray's feminist theory and Baby Suggs's sermon speak together to comment on the crime schoolteacher's nephews perpetrate on Sethe's maternal body. In Halle's telling, schoolteacher and his nephews are good Christians (37), yet the nephews' act of stealing Sethe's milk is a figure of the division of body and spirit, a moment erecting boundaries between self and other. The stealing of Sethe's milk is *Beloved*'s primal scene—that which must be simultaneously repressed and repeated. In fact the novel literally repeats the violation as a moment of Enlightenment discourse: schoolteacher records with the ink Sethe has made for his "scientific" investigation into race his nephews' rape of her; for schoolteacher, Sethe's pain is invisible and serves only as another moment for him to attempt to know her essential racial identity.

Sethe's killing her daughter creates a symbolic economy based on the maternal body in which her act reverses and repays schoolteacher's kinsmen: child's blood replaces mother's milk. The sight of Sethe's holding her slaughtered child renders schoolteacher's nephew unable to explain, paralyzed by "the flow of some shameful liquid" (Irigaray 237). The amazed white male audience of Sethe's act observe from the position of male subjectivity "that finds everything flowing abhorrent": "Horrible to see: bloody. *Fluid* has to remain that secret *remainder,* of the one. Blood, but also milk, sperm, lymph, saliva, spit, tears, humors, gas, waves, airs, fire . . . light. All threaten to deform, propagate, evaporate, consume him, to flow out of him and into another who cannot be easily held on to" (Irigary 237). Sethe's repayment in this fluid economy reverses by asserting that the boundaries of self exceed the individual body, a position figured strikingly by her nursing the infant Denver shortly thereafter so that the baby ingests simultaneously mother's milk and sister's blood.

Beloved's climactic moment—the hot summer day when the community of women comes to purge 124—is the clearest moment of the primal scene's repetition and serves as an ontological unhinging as it blurs the boundary between past and present. The day becomes a chance for Sethe to choose differently than she did eighteen years earlier. In this repetition, a minor character helps us again see the difference between Uncle Tom's God the Father and Baby Suggs's religion of the body. As Edward Bodwin returns to his Sweet Home, the house of his childhood that he and his sister rented to Baby Suggs, he is, for all appearances, a benevolent patriarch and member of "the Society," a local group originally founded to oppose slavery. Yet in his private thoughts he is the excluded son, whose return to 124 is crowded with memories of the tin soldiers he hid from "his father, probably, a deeply religious man who knew what God knew and told everybody what it was" (260). The Society, we learn, had used

Sethe's killing her child as political capital to advance the abolitionist cause. But despite Bodwin's ostensibly progressive politics, his personal vanity regarding his dark mustache and white hair leads to an interesting moment of reflection:

> Twenty years ago when the Society was at its height in opposing slavery, it was as though his coloring was itself the heart of the matter. The "bleached nigger" was what his enemies called him, and on a trip to Arkansas, some Mississippi rivermen, enraged by the Negro boatmen they competed with, had caught him and shoe-blackened his face and his hair. Those heady days were gone now; what remained was the sludge of ill will; dashed hopes and difficulties beyond repair. (260)

The appellation "bleached nigger" points to the way that Bodwin, in Morrison's critical terms, is playing in the dark. The regret in his meditation seems at odds with the fact that the Society's chief objective has been achieved: the slaves are free. Essentially Bodwin longs for the good old days of slavery so that he might again be an abolitionist freedom fighter and media star. In his self-willed incomprehension of what is implied by his desires, Bodwin stands convicted, along with *Tar Baby*'s Valerian Street, of "the crime of innocence" (*Tar Baby* 242). In his desire to return to the pre–Civil War condition of slavery, Bodwin's complicity with schoolteacher is underscored, for both schoolteacher's punishment and Bodwin's (preferably infinitely deferred) liberation of African-American bodies depends on a white male authority.[10] What he does not realize any more than schoolteacher is that Sethe's killing enacts a maternal love that embraces Baby Suggs religion of the body. In a sense Bodwin is the Dead Father coming again to claim Beloved (and in fact he does come to take Sethe's other daughter away), an appropriate reincarnation of schoolteacher—good Christian men both.

Sethe's decision to attack schoolteacher/Bodwin rather than kill Beloved ("spirit" woman)/Beloved (child) serves as a therapeutic reenactment that purges Sethe's haunted memory and signals Beloved's departure. But the moment also allows the community to atone for its guilt at having resented Baby Suggs's good fortune and generosity. In coming forward as a group, the thirty women suggest a different kind of religious thinking, one that affirms Baby Suggs's religion of the body. Even as they are deciding what course of action to take, the language of the women echoes Baby Suggs's message; speaking of Beloved, Ella says:

> "It's sitting there. Sleeps, eats and raises hell. Whipping Sethe every day."
> "I'll be. A baby?"
> "No. Grown. The age it would have been had it lived."

"You talking about flesh?"
"I'm talking about flesh." (255)

The last two lines, suggesting the call-response form of an African-American church service, particularly echo one of Baby Suggs's lines from the Clearing—"This is flesh I'm talking about here" (88). It is particularly significant that Ella speaks at this moment. Although biographical information about Morrison consistently identifies her mother as Ramah Wofford, something curious appears on Morrison's birth certificate. In the space provided for the mother's name, "Ramah Willis" appears but carroted above and before "Ramah" and in the same hand is "Ella." (See Morrison's birth certificate, reproduced in chapter 2.) The legal status of "Ella" is not clear. Is it a nickname by which Ramah Wofford was known? Whatever this name's status, it appears clear that Morrison's mother insisted on its addition to the legal document that is her daughter's birth certificate. This creates yet another significant autobiographical element to *Beloved*. Baby Suggs, mother to Ardelia, is also the spiritual ancestor to Ella, so that Morrison's depiction of the artistic impulse through Baby Suggs becomes even more highly freighted; there is an implied line of metaphorical descent from Baby Suggs through Ardelia and Ella to Chloe. In the symbolic logic of the novel, then, although Baby Suggs is gone, her religion of the maternal body animates the community's movement toward redemption. The afterlife that Baby Suggs's words achieve is what Morrison surely desires for her own words—that they be remembered. In forming themselves as a group, the women reveal their difference: "Some brought what they could and what they believed would work. Stuffed in apron pockets, strung around their necks, lying in the space between their breasts. Others brought Christian faith—as shield and sword. Most brought a little of both" (257). This passage indicates the continuity of older African belief systems in America, even when those beliefs had to survive by going underground and merging with the forms of the master's religion. But the clearest affirmation of Baby Suggs's spirituality is that the group of thirty women goes behind the patriarchal Word of Christianity for origin: "They stopped praying and took a step back to the beginning. In the beginning there were no words. In the beginning was the sound, and they all knew what that sound sounded like" (259). It is precisely this presymbolic sound that gives Sethe the courage to rewrite the ending to schoolteacher's first visit.[11]

Baby Suggs's religion of the maternal body, affirmed by the cry of the community of women, serves as a different point of entry for rethinking the categories of patriarchy than Stowe's affirmation of God the Father. Moreover, *Beloved*'s community of women creates a nuanced sense of gender as it relates to the possibility of religious transcendence, one that will find its fullest expression in *Paradise*. Morrison's engagement of *Uncle Tom's Cabin*, by creating an intertextual space that maps what Morrison finds intolerable about Stowe's representation of race and gender, points to the criticism she would soon write in "Unspeakable Things Unspoken" and *Playing in the Dark*.

The Aut(h)o(r)-Erotics of Narration: Playing with Textual Pleasure

"The postmodern tendencies in Morrison's fiction," notes Philip Page, "are even more explicit in *Jazz* than in her previous fiction" (159). Although Page writes this before the publication of *Paradise*, his assertion about the postmodern quality of Morrison's sixth novel is appropriate. *Jazz* indeed seems to play with and directly thematize "such Derridean concepts as the *différance*, the trace, and the breach" (Page 159). Perhaps the most obvious instance of this is the self-named character, Joe Trace, who derives his name himself from the only secure knowledge he has about his mother, Wild— that she disappeared without a trace. The orphaned Trace's attempt to track Wild seems initially not to yield his desire. Searching for any minimal sign of her acknowledgment, he finds nothing. Nothing, that is, until Felice communicates to him the dying words of the girl, Dorcas, who Joe shot. Dorcas's words make present a verbal trace substituting for the absent maternal body and serve as the long deferred moment of acknowledgment. Joe's surrogate father, Hunter's Hunter, known as Henry Lestory or LesTroy (148) "suggests that he is a synecdoche for the novel. Henry *is* the story in the sense that he has perfected the story's principal metaphor, tracking [. . .]" (Page 164).[12] Between the trace and the story lies the metafictionality of *Jazz*, a story full of improbable reconciliations: between husband and wronged wife, between the wife who mutilated her husband's lover's corpse and that girl's aunt, between the middle-aged lover and the girl he kills, between a son and a father whom the son initially hoped to kill.

One thing to note about the story of *Jazz*, particularly the one in the novel's present (1926), is that the possibilities of black identity are played out in a different economic environment than Morrison uses in her earlier fiction. Harlem in the 1920s with its black-owned businesses represents a prosperous African-American community. Whether she intends it or not, Morrison's sixth novel seems to comment on her first. Like Cholly and Pauline Breedlove, Joe and Violet Trace leave the racism of the rural South for the economic promise of the North. From the time they arrive in New York City in 1906 through the 1920s, the Traces (unlike the Breedloves) are upwardly mobile. Joe finds progressively better paying jobs that afford the Traces a number of life's small comforts. And though both the Breedloves and the Traces experience tragedy in their new homes, the Traces transcend the tragic denouement that the plot wishes to impose. In *The Bluest Eye,* the Breedloves' move to Lorain, Ohio, encodes the loss of one form of authenticity—that of the rural black community. But for the Traces, whatever African-American identity they forge by the end of *Jazz* does not depend exclusively on their embracing rural black poverty.

Despite the undeniable importance of Joe and Violet's reconciliation, the larger reconciliation of this novel happens not at the level of the story but of the discourse—the narration itself and the narrator, Morrison's figuration once again of the artist. Morrison's representation of authorship participates in the profoundly metafictional orientation of *Jazz.* Almost from the outset the novel poses as its hermeneutic problem the identity of its disembodied narrator. When the narrator announces "I haven't got any muscles, so I can't really be expected to defend myself" (8), the reader's hunt for an elusive identity begins. Although there is no definitive evidence that the narrator is either black or female, Eusebio Rodrigues thoughtfully explores the issue of who speaks by looking closely at the novel's epigraph from the gnostic text *The Nag Hammadi.* Since this first-person voice in the epigraph is the goddess Thunder, the first-person narrator's reference to her narration as "my storm" (219) suggests for Rodrigues that the narrator is a "female immanence of the divine" (261). For Vincent O'Keefe, the epigraph "represents not only a form of heresy against or revision of Christianity [. . .] but also a feminist resistance to the masculine domination of Christian spirituality" (334). If one accepts Rodrigues's and O'Keefe's arguments, then there seems to be a clear link from the representation of an alternative spirituality in *Beloved* to the narrative consciousness of *Jazz.* Baby Suggs's project, in effect, is continued by the narrator of *Jazz,* yet the later artist figure has a much more dialogical conception of her authority, one that allows her to transcend the isolation of artistic production. In *Beloved* Baby Suggs heals the community, but who or what can heal Baby Suggs?

The consensus view sees the narrator of *Jazz* as female, and I certainly follow that convention, but I want to retain another sense of the narrator's sexual identity. For Henry Lewis Gates, Jr., the narrator's indeterminacy extends to the matter of a determinate sex: "it is neither male nor female [. . .]. It is *both* and *neither*" ("Jazz" 54). Gates is right to emphasize indeterminacy, and given the novel's conclusion, I wish to stress his claim that the narrator is both male and female, if not always simultaneously so, then alternately.[13] As the narrator's pleasure is delineated, it seems as though this speaker represents the emotional bisexuality of artistic production. Whatever the exact identity of the narrator, as the teller of the story, she certainly figures the author function. Early in her representation of herself she says, "I lived a long time, maybe too much, in my own mind. People say I should come out more. Mix. I agree that I close off in places, but if you have been left standing, as I have, while your partner overstays at another appointment, or promises to give you exclusive attention after supper, but is falling asleep just as you have begun to speak—well, it can make you inhospitable if you aren't careful, the last thing I want to be" (9). Doreatha Drummond Mbalia in fact directly equates the narrator with Morrison on the grounds that, like the narrator who speaks of problems with "a partner," Morrison "experienced problems with her mate"; moreover like the narrator, "the novelist [. . .] may live too much in the mind. It is this similarity that makes narrator and author a part of the narrative structure" (636). Whether one wishes to read this moment quite so autobiographically, Mbalia's reading certainly underscores the way the narrator figures authorship and its discontents.

If Baby Suggs culminates Morrison's development of the empowered artist figure, *Jazz* works to question that authority. This questioning occurs in the narration and the progressive loss of authority experienced by the first-person narrator who is not a character in the story she tells of both parental and sexual love lost and found. The narrator's confident predictions at the beginning (which outline the story and intimate a denouement of violent repetition when Felice again triangulates the relationship between Joe and Violet Trace) turn to uncertain speculation about Golden Gray and finally to a frank admission of error and limitation. But for all the acknowledgment of fallibility, the narrator remains remarkably free from anxiety, a sign of Morrison's fuller comfort with her authorial role. From this new position of comfort, *Jazz* returns us to the collapsed space of sexual and textual pleasure, but now not as that which must be repressed as it was in *Sula*. Instead, *Jazz's* more playful narration suggests that the healing that Baby Suggs imagines in her spiritual art may also flow back to the artist through the person of the reader.

I want to turn, then, to the conclusion of Morrison's sixth novel because it is there that the narrator begins to dismantle her authority. Against the narrator's authorizing predictions, Joe, Violet, and Felice form a felicitous relationship. It is not necessary, of course, to believe that Morrison is fooled in the same way as her narrator is by the unpredictability of these characters; nevertheless, the narrator of *Jazz* encodes the multiple paradoxes of Morrison's own relation to authority. In short, the author seems to use her narrator to comment on the psychic determinism of her early fiction in which the individual often is doomed to repeat later in life the prior insult and injury that defines his or her adult subjectivity. Cholly Breedlove serves as the paradigmatic example of the early type of character in Morrison's fiction for whom "the past was an abused record with no choice but to repeat itself" (*Jazz* 220). Psychologically raped by the white men who interrupt his first attempt at coitus, abandoned by his mother, rejected by his father, Cholly cannot but repeat the insult in his relation with Mrs. Breedlove. Even more devastatingly, he literalizes his psychological rape by raping his daughter, an act that marks the full extent of his limited ability to love. Sula's subjectivity, though aesthetically refined, is marked by her overhearing her mother's claim to love but not like her; as a result, Sula is doomed to repeat the loss of intimacy in her relationship with both Nel and Ajax. Though he discovers authenticity in his journey when he accepts Pilate's values, Milkman's life up to that point has been shaped by his oedipal struggle with the father.

Even beyond the content of her earlier fictions of identity formation, Morrison seems in *Jazz* to comment on her earlier modernist narration in *The Bluest Eye*. That first novel begins with two prefaces, both of which suggest psychic determinism. The repetition of the text of a standard elementary school primer, in which each iteration removes more markers of capitalization and punctuation, suggests the way the racialism of the primer's representation of a white world moves from consciousness to the unconscious. Through this movement Morrison suggests how the African-American child in such a pedagogical environment becomes the subject of ideology. The second preface to *The Bluest Eye* tells the story in miniature, as many modernist texts do, so that the reader must attend not to the pleasure of discovery but to an analysis of the logic of tragedy predicated on psychological repetitions. The first four pages of *Jazz,* of course, by giving a version of the complete story, seem to do what the second prefacing gesture of *The Bluest Eye* accomplishes. But in the later novel this modernist technique is undone.

Only in *Beloved* does Morrison fully imagine a way that the past could be rewritten. Sethe has a chance to choose again and, given her second chance, affirms the maternal religion of Baby Suggs. But if *Beloved* emphasizes the maternal body, *Jazz* points the reader to the erotic female body. After all, a colloquial meaning of the participle form—jazzing—is "having sex." In this regard, what the narrator identifies as her erroneous pride in believing her narration is infallible is linked to an autoerotic sexuality. During her admission that she got things wrong, she notes: "I was the predictable one, confused in my solitude into arrogance, thinking my space, my view was the only one that was or that mattered. I got so aroused while meddling, while finger-shaping, I overreached and missed the obvious" (220). Solitude, as we have seen in so many of Morrison's previous figurations of the artistic subject position—from Soaphead Church to Baby Suggs—is risky, leading to Church's aberrant sexual desires and to Baby Suggs's overreaching. But by the end of *Jazz,* the narrator's sexual object

choice shifts away from the self (as suggested by the controlling and perhaps masturbatory pleasures of finger-shaping) and toward another, a move
in which the narrator announces her previously unspoken desires.

One of the ways this movement manifests itself is Morrison's turn to a
more postmodern poetics that blurs the boundaries between the mimetic—
the world the novel represents—and the diegetic—the telling of the story.
The clearest instance of this blurring occurs near the end when the narrator's meditation turns to the voiceless woman known as Wild, a disturbing
figure to the men of the novel because her presence is known only by her
absence, but whose absence is experienced as an eerie presence:

> I'd love to close myself in the peace left by the woman who lived there and
> scared everybody. Unseen because she knows better than to be seen. After
> all, who would see her, a playful woman who lived in a rock? Who could,
> without fright? Of her looking eyes looking back? I wouldn't mind. Why
> should I? She has seen me and is not afraid of me. She hugs me. Understands
> me. Has given me her hand. I am touched by her. Released in secret. (221)

Here the narrator receives in a clear and unambiguous fashion what Joe
Trace has longed for all his life—Wild's direct and unmediated acknowledgment. But what might this acknowledgment mean? The touch the narrator receives from Wild of course makes no sense in terms of realistic
representation. Wild would be long dead and yet the supernatural possibility that allows Joe's mother to manifest herself through the youthful Dorcas permits one to imagine a Wild who could still be part of the present
time of narration. On the one hand, Wild's touch, read in the context of
Joe's search for his absent mother, seems to make her the timeless goddess
figure's mother—Wild as the ancestor of Thunder. On the other hand, a
different context is established by the novel's concluding paragraphs, one
in which the narrator's being touched and hugged by Wild figures a movement away from a controlling self-arousal toward another sense of erotic
possibility. In this regard, Wild's embrace echoes Sula's desire for the intimate female companion who can complete her; thus one might articulate
a logic of *Jazz:* the character in the story who is body but not voice (Wild)
completes the chief character of the discourse (the narrator) who is voice
without body.

Not only is a boundary crossed when a character within the story embraces the teller of the tale who is outside the story. A further limit is
imaginatively transgressed in the final two paragraphs of the novel. Now
the embrace occurs between the narrator, the character that figures the
author function, and the reader.[14] And although the real reader seems to
be encompassed by the fiction, that reader, I will argue, is positioned in a

particular fashion. One arrives at this sexualized moment from an odd and paradoxical admission on the narrator's part. Commenting on the reconciled love of Joe and Violet, the narrator laments:

> I envy them their public love. I myself have only known it in secret, shared it in secret and longed, aw longed to show it—to be able to say out loud what they have no need to say at all: *That I have loved only you, surrendered my whole self reckless to you and nobody else. That I want you to love me back and show it to me. That I love the way you hold me, how close you let me be to you. I like your fingers on and on, lifting, turning. I have watched your face for a long time, now, and missed your eyes when you went away from me. Talking to you and hearing you answer—that's the kick.* (229)

What is striking in this description is the narrator's assertion of a difference between her passion, which has always remained secret, and Joe and Violet's open heterosexuality. The narrator's closeted passion has remained unnamed, yet paradoxically, in the moment of enunciation, it becomes the unspeakable thing spoken.

But then the final paragraph seems to dissolve the issue of sexuality by turning the matter into a riddle:

> But I can't say that aloud; I can't tell anyone that I have been waiting for this all my life and that being chosen to wait is the reason I can. If I were able I'd say it. Say make me, remake me. You are free to do it and I am free to let you because look, look. Look where your hands are. Now. (229)

Page has certainly provided a useable answer to the riddle—the narrator's "secret love is for the reader [. . .]. She imagines that she is the book and therefore that the reader holds her [. . .]" (173–74). Such a solution does open the novel up in interesting ways. Fully confident regarding her authority (in ways that Morrison was not in her first four novels), the narrator can now risk giving that identity away in the apparent sexual gift that the narrator makes of herself at novel's end. In authorizing the reader to complete the meaning of her text, Morrison reverses Roland Barthes's poetics of pleasure from *The Pleasure of the Text*. Instead of the reader's bliss that results from one's turning one's text of pleasure into writerly activity, Morrison articulates the storyteller's bliss at being remade.

Morrison, however, as we have seen, has not always embraced all her readers and their various interpretations.[15] Here I want to introduce the possibility (only finally to reject it) that *Jazz* may be working to position its ideal reader as female. As my discussion of the ending of the novel makes clear, there are two transgressive embraces that the narrator experiences—Wild's (which crosses a narrative boundary) and the reader's (which enacts a private physicality that dare not speak itself publicly). If one reads the two moments relationally, so that the former (a woman-woman embrace) is the context for understanding the later, then it would be possible to argue that this novel specifically positions its reader as female. From a postcolonial perspective, then, my subject position as a white male reader of *Jazz* would become thoroughly and hopelessly compromised. As Franz Fanon argues in chapter 2 of *Black Skin, White Masks* ("The Woman of Color and the White Man"), the possibility of "authentic love" between such a pair will remain "unattainable" so long as racialized thinking exists. If the novel constructs the ideal reader as female, I should not even be reading Morrison—let alone writing about her—for to do so would position me as the always already colonizing white male who subjugates the sexualized body of the black woman.

It is here, however, that I wish to return to Gates's sense of the indeterminacy of the narrator's sexual identity. If we read the narrator as both female and male, then the embrace between narrator and reader is large indeed, for it recognizes a wide variety of sexual-textual pleasures. The narrator's Whitmanesque acknowledgment of the reader's touch admits that there are a multitude of religions of the body, so that the touch represented in the final sentence may be imagined as occurring between man and woman, man and man, or woman and woman; the embrace, in fact, may even be intergenerational or interracial. The overcontrolling narrator of *Jazz* who learns to accept limitations on "her" authority seems to encode Morrison's recognition that she no longer needs to attempt to control the meaning of her published novels by telling critics what kind of reading is appropriate. The pleasure of the text, both that of the writer and the reader, allows for a polymorphously perverse (con)textuality.

With this sense of the resonance of the novel's conclusion, I want to return briefly to Morrison's relation to William Faulkner, which was the focus of chapter 4 of this study. His novel *Absalom, Absalom!,* one of Morrison's recurring texts of pleasure, seems to have moved her from readerly pleasure to writerly bliss. I began my discussion of *Jazz* by listing the novel's improbable reconciliations. One addition to my earlier list might be Morrison's relation to Faulkner. Her comments published in 1993 in which she speaks of her "fascination" with Faulkner as she details a line-by-line reading she performed of *Absalom* for her students at Princeton provide a specific context for thinking about Faulkner's novel in relation to *Jazz*.[16] Given the time frame of these remarks, Morrison's careful reading of *Absalom, Absalom!,* which led to her classroom lecture, appears to have occurred during the time she was writing *Jazz*.

Morrison's unpublished lecture, then, becomes a crucial intertext to *Jazz,* pointing to her engagement with Faulkner on race and the possibilities of acknowledgement. But if Morrison uses Faulkner's *Go Down,*

Moses as a kind of scaffolding for *Song of Solomon,* her reading of Faulkner manifests itself more playfully in her later novel. This is not to say that her purpose is not serious. Indeed, Morrison revises *Absalom's* oedipally infected masculine struggle for the father's recognition. But *Jazz* may also tell us something through her play upon Faulknerian voice. Particularly in the unnumbered sections six and seven of *Jazz,* Morrison produces a pastiche of Faulknerian style, subject matter, and plot through her narrator's at times uncertain history of the racially mixed Golden Gray. In *Absalom,* lines of family relations are obscured by Thomas Sutpen's refusal to acknowledge the children he fathers by black women. Miscegenation in Faulkner's novel happens exclusively when African-American women have children by white fathers. Within that frame, however, Faulkner teases at the supreme horror of his Southern white community: what if a black man slept with a white woman? This question is central to Quentin and Shreve's construction of Henry Sutpen's motive for murdering Charles Bon. The seductive, charming Charles Bon serves as the white Southern community's repressed ideological horror: if white men can father black men who appear white, then these same "white" black men can beget black children on white women. These are the issues and questions Morrison directly addresses in her critical mapping of the ideological boundaries of Faulkner's already searching examination of "the insanity of racism."

Morrison's Golden Gray starts out by reproducing the desire of Charles Bon but ends perhaps by revising the choice of Etienne Bon. Like Charles Bon, Golden Gray is the product of miscegenation, yet Morrison reverses Faulknerian genealogy: Golden is the son of a privileged white woman, Vera Louise Gray, and a dark-skinned slave, Henry LesTroy (or Lestory). Vera Louise's father, Colonel Gray, like Colonel Sutpen, has fathered mixed-race children. His discovery of his daughter's sexual behavior leaves him devastated, and in an act that recalls Sutpen's repudiation of his Haitian wife, Colonel Gray disavows his relationship with his daughter, giving her a large sum of money to go away.

It is here that one key element of Morrison's rewriting of *Absalom* stands out. Thomas Sutpen, the patriarch who wishes to design a lasting empire, becomes the obsession of all of those—the sons, the daughters, and wife—he denies; however, unlike Faulkner's Southern colonel, Morrison's is peripheral. Sutpen's first wife may live only for revenge, but Colonel Gray's daughter goes off to Baltimore with her servant, True Belle, to raise her son, and never gives her father another thought. Old Gray's money, however, allows Vera Louise to raise Golden Gray as a gentleman, much as Sutpen's money allows his first wife to raise their light-complexioned, mixed-race son, Charles Bon, in luxury.

Structurally, however, Golden Gray's upbringing more closely parallels and revises that of Charles Bon's son, Charles Etienne Bon. Both Gray and Etienne are raised by a white woman and a black woman. Both have their sense of their white identity disrupted by unexpected knowledge of their mixed racial background. Still, in Gray's desire to discover the absent father, he recalls Charles Bon's obsession, though with a difference: Bon seeks Sutpen, the white father, for recognition; Gray initially seeks LesTroy to kill him. Raised culturally white in the code of noblesse oblige, Gray is confronted with Henry Sutpen's dilemma. LesTroy, after all, is the black man who slept with his white mother, and his white identity tells him he should kill the scoundrel. Yet when he enters LesTroy's cabin and sits on his father's bed, Golden Gray is faced with Charles Bon's sense of loss. What Bon desires from his father, is "the living touch of that flesh warmed before he was born by the same blood which it had bequeathed him to warm his own flesh with, to be bequeathed by him in turn to run hot and loud in veins and limbs after that first flesh and then his own were dead" (255). Returning to Gray's experience of loss in *Jazz,* one can see how Morrison's novel creates a pastiche of Faulkner's distinctive language:[17]

> Only now, he thought, now that I know I have a father, do I feel his absence: the place where he should have been and was not. Before, I thought everybody was one-armed, like me. Now I feel the surgery. The crunch of bone when it is sundered, the sliced flesh and the tubes of blood cut through, shocking the bloodrun and disturbing the nerves. They dangle and writhe. Singing pain. Waking me with the sound of itself, thrumming when I sleep so deeply it strangles my dreams away. There is nothing for it but to go away from where he is not to where he used to be and might be still. Let the dangle and the writhe see what it is missing; let the pain sing to the dirt where he stepped in the place where he used to be and might be still. I am not going to be healed, or to find the arm that was removed from me. I am going to freshen the pain, point it, so we both know what it is for. (158)

Does Morrison's pastiche of Faulkner mean that Morrison gains no critical distance on his text?[18] No, but that distance arises not intertextually but intratextually. Having reproduced one version of Faulknerian masculinity, potentially tragic in its sense of fatality and intention, Morrison fashions a way to avoid that tragedy. Gray's rhetorical flight, the double of Charles Bon's, is grounded when LesTroy returns home. He tells Gray that he will accept the young man as a son if he can act like a son but warns, "don't bring me no whiteboy sass" (173), an expression that works to deflate Gray's "Faulknerian" tragic rhetoric.

Morrison, however, in activating the Faulknerian intertext, invites the reader to participate in a reexamination of his work. The only clear intersection between *Absalom, Absalom!* and *Jazz* may be the way Golden Gray's pain parallels Charles Bon's. But having made this move, Morrison authorizes the reader to think in the space between the two novels. If I am less certain of other moments where Morrison gestures to Faulkner, my movement from father (Charles) to son (Etienne), although less sure, remains in the spirit of Morrison's novelistic "reading" of Faulkner.

If one accepts the Faulknerian resonance in Morrison's narrator, then there is a striking passage, one underscoring the metafictional nature of her narration, when the narrator stops to comment on her construction of the story. She claims to have gotten the portrayal of Golden Gray wrong in a way that eerily recalls Morrison's discussion of Faulkner's delayed and disguised portrayal of race in *Absalom,* a portrayal that she characterized in *The Paris Review* interview, quoted earlier, as "*not* the point anyway":

> What was I thinking of? How could I have imagined him so poorly? Not noticed the hurt that was not linked to the color of his skin, or the blood that beat beneath it. But to some other thing that longed for authenticity, for a right to be in this place, effortlessly without needing to acquire a false face [. . .].
>
> Now I have to think this through, carefully, even though I may be doomed to another misunderstanding. I have to do it and not break down. Not hating him is not enough; liking, loving him is not useful. I have to alter things. I have to be a shadow who wishes him well, like the smiles of the dead left over from their lives. (160–61)

The repeated pronouns in this passage—"he" and "him"—seem not simply to describe the relation between narrator and character but perhaps also to point to a commentary from one author to another. In this moment, Morrison appears almost to speak in coded form of her revision of and relation to Faulkner. Whether Morrison here stands to Faulkner as the narrator does to Golden Gray, it is in Morrison's second, revised portrayal of Golden Gray that the figure who seems to be altered is Charles Bon's son, Etienne.

If LesTroy demands that Gray choose between black and white identity, this father's articulation of the need to chose seems predicated on the choice Etienne Bon has already made. Like Golden Gray, Etienne is presented with a clear choice between black and white, but how he chooses sets him apart in Faulkner's depiction of racially mixed characters. Faulkner's most fully developed black male characters of mixed race choose whiteness as the core of their identity. (When they do choose blackness, as Etienne Bon does, it is portrayed as a terrible mistake.) Lucas Beauchamp in *Go Down, Moses,* for example, fixes his genealogical pride in his descent from Carothers McCaslin, the man who has raped Lucas's grandmother and great-grandmother.[19] Etienne chooses blackness through an identification with his mother, but only to emphasize his cultural wounding; Gray also finally chooses blackness, ostensibly through an identification with a black father, though in fact it is as much his union with the voiceless African-American woman, Wild, that creates identity.

Morrison initially leaves Gray's decision much less clear than Etienne's, but through Joe Trace's quest for acknowledgement from Wild, Joe's absent mother, the reader discovers the material trace that reveals Gray's choice. (Joe Trace, one of the central figures of the novel's plot of the present, must be read through his relation to his lost mother, so that his desire for acknowledgement from his mother also comments on and revises Charles Bon's desire for acknowledgement from his father.) The personal items and male clothing belonging to Golden Gray that Joe discovers in Wild's cave reveal that Golden has chosen blackness through cohabitation with Wild.

In this regard, Wild works to reclaim the figure of the nameless black woman whom Etienne Bon marries. Clearly one of Faulkner's most embarrassing representations of race (even acknowledging its source as Mr. Compson), this woman, who never is given a voice, is described as "coal black and ape-like" (166). Etienne's choice of blackness, an act that seems to defy black masculine identity even while proclaiming such identity, suggests a racial self-loathing; his marriage to the African-American woman, as Mr. Compson imagines, is done to injure Judith, the white woman who urges him to pass for white. Etienne's defiance of the white woman who helped raise him serves as an ongoing act of vengeance against white culture. Golden Gray, however, learns to love the black woman whom he initially found disgusting. Once again, "Faulknerian pastiche" seems to be an appropriate way to name Morrison's use of language when she records Gray's immediate nausea at the sight of the obviously pregnant "berry-black woman"; his revulsion at the "black, liquid female" (Faulkner, *Light* 144–45) almost exactly duplicates Joe Christmas's fear and loathing of women. Gray, however, is able to put aside his youthful sense of injury and move past his fear of the feminine. As a result his choice of blackness becomes an act of love, one in which he accepts a new identity and creates his earthly paradise with Wild.

The Anxiety of Writing Your Best: Paradisiacal De-Scription

As I argue previously in this study, *Tar Baby* begins Morrison's critique of the all-black agrarian community as the site of African-American authenticity. Milkman Dead's paradise—Shalimar, Virginia—sours in Jadine

Child's experience of Eloe, Florida. *Paradise* expands this critique by thoroughly exploding Milkman's sense of both completed authenticity and the essential goodness of a racially pure black community. Ruby, Oklahoma, stands as Morrison's most economically prosperous all-black community, one desperately in need of spiritual renewal; that spiritual renewal, however, does not (as her earlier fiction so often did) demand the return to poverty as the ground of identity. Despite this novel's expansion of the critique of *Song of Solomon*'s stand on authenticity, *Paradise* in a number of ways represents Morrison's return to the thematics and tropes of her third novel particularly and of her early fiction more generally. In her early fiction, female subjectivity almost always grows out of violation—child abuse, spousal abuse, molestation, or rape. In particular, *Paradise* returns us to the troubled relation between men and women, particularly when African-American men's sense of identity parallels that of the patriarchal structures of middle-class white culture. *Song of Solomon* criticizes a masculine identity that sees women as property; Milkman may have worked through this problem, but it is an identity that makes Jadine reject even Son and his agrarian community.

Gender politics, however, moves to the background in both *Beloved* and *Jazz*, concerned as they are with building bridges between African-American women and men. In *Beloved*, white men are the rapists of both African-American women and men, and in *Jazz* even the middle-aged man who murders his teenage lover becomes a sympathetic figure.[20] But in the tensions between the patriarchal town of Ruby and the women-centered space of the Convent, Morrison comes back to gender and the issue of who has the right to define and name. "What is ours?" and "what must we protect and defend?" are the questions the men in *Paradise* constantly ask themselves. What the men do, they do "for Ruby" (18). The name itself is a metonymy inasmuch as how the men perceive and protect their town—named for one of their women—is reflected in how they treat each individual wife and daughter.

I argued earlier that *Song of Solomon* uses the figure of doe hunting to define and critique a particular form of patriarchal masculine identity. This figure returns in the opening chapter of *Paradise* in which a group of men from Ruby, good hunters whose ostensible goal is to protect their cult of true black womanhood, makes the seventeen-mile trek to the Convent to slaughter the women who have created a home there. The men who enter the Convent discover what they want to see—"the devil's bedroom, bathroom, and his nasty playpen" (17)—gathering the rumors of the past twenty years into a narrative that make these women the dangerous Other; unlike their decorous women, the Convent women in these men's eyes are child murderers, lesbians, temptresses, and witches who have turned the former Convent in to a coven. What is actually more threatening is that these women have claimed, out of their abuse, the power to name and identify themselves. This is the unspoken reason for the raid on the Convent. The Convent women's proximity to Ruby means that Ruby's women have an alternative model for conceiving of themselves.

In resorting to murder, these men simply take the logic of *Song of Solomon's* Seven Days a step further. Despite claiming to kill white people out of a love for black people, the Seven Days, as I pointed out in chapter 4, actually functions to protect African-American men's property interests in black women. The men of Ruby construct a narrative in which their protection of their black women authorizes their killing of one white girl and four "[b]odacious black Eves unredeemed by Mary" who in the moment of the killing run "like panicked does" (18).[21] The collective male perspective on their task is articulated in the thoughts of one of the men who has invaded the Convent:

> Certainly there wasn't a slack or sloven woman anywhere in town and the reasons, he thought, were clear. From the beginning its people were free and protected. A sleepless woman could always rise from her bed, wrap a shawl around her shoulders and sit on the steps in the moonlight. And if she felt like it she could walk out the yard and on down the road. No lamp and no fear. A hiss-crackle from the side of the road would never scare her because whatever it was that made the sound, it wasn't something creeping up on her. Nothing for ninety miles around thought she was prey. She could stroll as slowly as she liked, think of food preparations, war, of family things, or lift her eyes to stars and think of nothing at all. Lampless and without fear she could make her way. And if a light shone from a house up a ways and the cry of a colicky baby caught her attention, she might step over to the house and call out softly to the woman inside trying to soothe the baby. The two of them might take turns massaging the infant stomach, rocking, or trying to get a little soda water down. When the baby quieted they could sit together for a spell, gossiping, chuckling low so as not to wake anybody else. (8–9)

In his mind, Ruby represents the best of all possible worlds for women, but clearly Morrison exposes through this character's thoughts the central unacknowledged contradiction of the male communal narrative that authorizes the hunting of women in the name of protecting womanhood. The women of Ruby may walk without fear but they also do so without a lamp, and they are, by and large, unenlightened about anything but their domesticity. They walk but do not drive and there is really nowhere to go since the nearest town is ninety miles away. It is a safety based on isolation that approximates the carceral. The safety of the women of Ruby, moreover, depends on the good will of Ruby's men. Any reader familiar with Morrison's fiction knows that women who place their dreams of safety in men are compromised, for this fiction repeatedly illustrates that only when women give up such dreams can they begin to form their own identities. The women who subscribe to the town's patriarchal ideology do so at the cost of limiting their possible identities to that of the tender of a man's home and the nurturer of a man's children. But even this cost may be insufficient to purchase safety, since any woman who ever threatens the male order of things immediately moves from the set of "not prey" to that of "prey."

The attack on the women, set as it is in July 1976, the month of America's Bicentennial, surely serves to remind the reader that the land of the free historically depended on those who were not. Although the historical contraction of American freedom lies in slavery, race is not central to the novel. Race matters, but in an upside down, through-the-looking-glass kind of way. The racially pure black community of Ruby emerges out of the doubled insult of class and colorism. Having migrated from the South to Oklahoma and been denied entry into a community of prosperous, lighter-complexioned African Americans, those who push on to found the town of Haven construct themselves as God's chosen people. After World War II, Haven falls on hard times economically. The sons of Haven's founders move west to form a new town, Ruby, dedicated to the preservation of the same sense of exceptionalism born when their fathers were rejected by the lighter-skinned blacks. Haven and Ruby stand as displaced representations of early American exceptionalism; if the white American male's freedom was enhanced by the presence of the enslaved racial other, as Morrison argues in *Playing in the Dark* (42–44), something strangely similar occurs in *Paradise.* For Ruby's men, their exceptionalism and sense of freedom lies in their genetically pure African heritage, unsullied by any drop of white blood. This need for racial purity, of course, explains why the men pay such careful attention to the morality of their women and why a man must own his woman's sexuality.

Although it is not the dominant matter of *Paradise,* Morrison once again considers the role of artistic production as if to ask what role remains for the artist or writer living in a world with such violent gender and racial politics. Artistic identity—certainly central to Morrison's personal identity—is radically divided in *Paradise,* figured principally in two very different characters—the orphaned Connie of the Convent and the marginalized Patricia Best of Ruby, two women who specifically attempt to appropriate the power to name and narrate, though in very different ways. Patricia analyzes and critiques; Connie becomes a visionary.

Connie once again reminds the reader of the significance of names. Known through most of the novel as Connie, she becomes spiritually re-

born after her encounter with a divine presence, a moment that enables
her to reclaim her birth name, Consolata Sosa. With this renewed identity,
she becomes the spiritual leader of this community of wounded and
abused women. Consolata's spirituality represents a kind of syncretic belief. This belief encompasses, on the one hand, her love for the Reverend
Mother (and by extension for the tropes and rituals of the Catholic
Church) who saved her from poverty and prostitution in her third-world
home. On the other hand, Consolata's faith finds expression in her mirac-
ulous powers to heal the body, a power that precedes the logic of the
Christian Word. In this latter regard, Consolata is the latest in a line of fictional descent that may be traced back through such earlier characters as
Pilate Dead and Baby Suggs. But Consolata takes their spiritualized healing art to another level.

Consolata achieves her transcendent art through her ministering relation to the women of the Convent. In order to initiate the communal
healing and to ritualize her invitation to follow her, Consolata prepares a
feast for the women and tells them that she will attempt to lead them to
the encounter with the divine that she experiences. Outlining the
women's naked bodies in the position they select, Consolata address the
prone women:

> My child body, hurt and soil, leaps into the arms of a woman who teach me
> my body is nothing my spirit everything. I agreed her until I met another.
> My flesh is so hungry for itself it ate him. When he fell away the woman
> rescue me from my body again. Twice she saves it. When her body sickens I
> care for it in every way flesh works. I hold it in my arms and between my
> legs. Clean it, rock it, enter it to keep it breath. After she is dead I can not
> get past that. My bones on hers the only good thing. Not spirit. Bones. No
> different from the man. My bones on his the only true thing. So I wonder-
> ing where is the spirit lost in this? It is true, like bones. It is good, like bones.
> One sweet, one bitter. Where is it lost? Here me, listen. Never break them
> in two. Never put one over the other. Eve is Mary's mother. Mary is the
> daughter of Eve. (263)

Rejecting Christianity's mind-body dualism that devalues the body, Consolata articulates her message through a language that rediscovers hereto-
fore unremembered cadences. (Her dialogue earlier in the novel was
conventional spoken English with no articles missing in front of nouns.)
Consolata's speech to the women is a newer version of Baby Suggs's religion of the maternal body. Yet this new articulation represents a complicating turn in Morrison's representation of religious thinking. This
complication grows out of the fact that one of the ways the flesh works is
sexual. In her address, Consolata conflates the daughterly love she feels for

Mary Magna, the Mother Superior of the former convent, and the sexual love she had with a married man from Ruby, Deacon Morgan. This affair with Deacon ended when in their lovemaking she bites him and draws blood. But in the logic of Consolata's representation, this bodily hunger is simultaneously a spiritual hunger, so that the sexual passion figures the Passion of Christ and the Eucharist—"Take, eat, this is my body"—another instance of the syncretic faith Consolata imagines. Her healing relation to Mary Magna also blurs the sacred and the secular. The biblical references to Eve and Mary are clear, but Consolata is also the fallen Eve who gives life to (indeed almost seems to give birth to Mary Magna) by holding the older woman between her legs.

From this moment, the women of the Convent leave traditionally spoken words behind for a new communion of the body. Morrison describes this practice as their "loud dreaming" (264), a designation that almost seems to describe the "language" used by Sethe, Denver, and Beloved to express their desires when they close themselves off within 124 Bluestone Road. But what is represented in *Beloved* is only described in *Paradise:* "In loud dreaming, monologue is no different from a shriek; accusations directed to the dead and long gone are undone by murmurs of love" (264). From this language/not language, the women move to a different medium, painting, in order to fill in the empty spaces of their bodily outlines that Consolata had traced. Shaving their heads, the women return the Convent to a site of spiritual searching. In the climactic expression of their multimedia spirituality, Consolata leads the women into a perfumed summer rain for a cleansing dance on the eve of the men's attack on the Convent:

> Consolata started it; the rest were quick to join her. There are great rivers in the world and on their banks and the edges of oceans children thrill to water. In places where rain is light the thrill is almost erotic. But those sensations bow to the rapture of holy women dancing in hot sweet rain. They would have laughed, had enchantment not been so deep. (283)

In her combination of multiple expressive forms—the very forms, one may recall, denied to Sula—Consolata becomes Morrison's performance artist of the soul. Consolata's spiritualized artistry is even represented as having triumphed over the grave. Visiting their families after their own deaths, the spirits of the Convent women continue to enjoy food and sex. Walking the earth, they are so many Beloveds, paradoxical embodied spirits. But although Consolata represents the most transcendent embodiment of artistic possibility in all of Morrison's fiction—one able to overleap even the horizon of death itself—the flight of the artist is grounded by the presence of another artist figure, Patricia Best, who perhaps more directly figures Morrison's own subject position; Patricia, like Morrison herself, writes the story of Ruby. This character seems to register Morrison's recognition that Consolata's expressive forms—body painting and the dance—are not her media. Though she writes of such expression, she still writes. As a writer within the novel, Patricia (known to the community more androgynously as "Pat") metafictionally represents Morrison in the act of authoring both her best and worst selves. In a sense, Morrison's Best returns us to the anxieties of authorship that Soaphead Church represents in *The Bluest Eye.*

"Patricia" is the sixth section of *Paradise,* and the widowed schoolteacher serves (except for a few brief moments) as the focalizer throughout the chapter.[22] At times, when we have direct access to her writing, she serves as the narrator. The matter in time present of this section (December 1974) is the preparation for and performance of the town's apparently conventional annual Christmas pageant, as well as Pat's ongoing work on a history of Ruby. In the space between these two texts—Patricia's writing and the children's play—emerges her troubled understanding of the unconscious sexual politics of Ruby's fetishized blackness. Patricia's history is conceived of "as a gift to the citizens of Ruby—a collection of family trees; the genealogies of each of the fifteen families" (187). Having completed the family trees, she decides to supplement them with interesting facts about the origin of people's names. At this point, her project, begun in innocence, immediately meets a certain resistance when she talks to her fellow townspeople and asks, for research purposes, to see family bibles, letters, and marriage certificates. In the face of this resistance, Pat's interest in her supplemental notes grows. In her text, the logic of the supplement takes over, and the unspeakable of the community's sexual politics becomes spoken. In large part, what is unspeakable is the identity that Pat labels in her charts as "8-rock"; this geological metaphor refers to a pure African genealogy that can be traced back to these families' arrival in America in the eighteenth century.

So what began as a gift becomes Pat's attempt to read between the lines of the entries in the family bibles, to get at the meaning of the names that have been struck through. As her writing turns from celebration to critical inquiry of the "town's official story," Pat believes that she is the only one capable of the task since she has the "keen imagination and the persistence of a mind uncomfortable with oral histories" (188). But in order to fashion her history, she realizes that she cannot rely exclusively on what is officially documented and so must move into the realm of speculation: "she interpreted—freely but, she thought, insightfully because she alone had the required emotional distance" (188). Her emotional distance derives from her sense of difference. But it is precisely this emotional distance that we see collapse in her writing because she and her family are so directly impacted by the town's racial and sexual ideology.

As her section unfolds, Pat arrives at a clearer understanding of her doubled otherness. Given Ruby's color code, her outsider status is primarily a function of her lighter complexion, but this exclusion on the basis of racial identity is doubled by her identity as a writer. As Morrison's artist figures—Soaphead Church, Sula, Pilate, Baby Suggs, and the narrator of *Jazz*—repeatedly suggest, to be the artist or writer may necessarily entail one's marginality in the very community that one constitutes through the attempt to interpret and represent it.

Pat's inquiry turns deeply personal when she includes her own family history in the larger history of the community. All pretense of emotional distance drops out as she addresses her father, Roger Best, yet by turning to what is intensely personal she begins to inscribe the unspeakable things of Ruby. Referring to one of her father's business interests, his work as the town's mortician, she writes, "Daddy, they don't hate us because Mama was your first customer. They hate us because she looked like a cracker and was bound to have cracker-looking children like me, and although I married Billy Cato, who was an 8-rock like you, like them, I passed the skin on to my daughter, as you and everybody knew I would" (196). Making connections between and among the genealogies, Pat realizes the semi-incestuous nature of her community and that certain unrecorded unions of men and women have occurred outside the sanction of marriage in order to keep the racial bloodline pure.

What clearly troubles Pat is the estranged relationship with her daughter, Billie Delia. Mother and daughter have fallen out over Billie's love for two brothers of one of the 8-rock families, the Pooles. But rather than address this immediately, Pat's manuscript shifts from an address to her father to a letter to her dead mother. Pat believes the town is implicated in her mother's (as well as her stillborn sister's) death during childbirth, interpreting the men's slowness to act on the midwives request to get help as a passive-aggressive sign of the men's desire to get rid of those with lighter skins.

Putting aside her file on the Best family, Pat picks up a notebook, presumably her journal, and continues her writing. With her focus on the trouble with her daughter, Pat's writing becomes confessional. The previous October, their fight over Billie's relation with the Poole boys turned violent, and Pat nearly killed her daughter with an electric iron. Pat writes:

> "I didn't mean to hit her so hard. I didn't know I had. I just meant to stop her lying mouth telling me she didn't do anything. I saw them. All three of

them back behind the Oven and she was in the middle. Plus I am the one who washes sheets around here."

Pat stopped, put down her pen and, covering her eyes with her hand, tried to separate what she had seen from what she feared to see. And what did the sheets have to do with it? Was there blood where there should not have been or no blood where there should have been? (202)

Pat's instinctive question of the role that the sheets play points to a crucial metafictional turn. Three pages earlier, the narrator interrupts Pat's address to her dead mother to note: "The words had long ago covered the back of the page, so she was using fresh sheets" (199). The space thus collapses between what the pen inscribes on the manuscript sheets and the blood traces (whether they mark phallic penetration or the absence of menstrual blood) on the sheets of the bedding. Therefore, the (paper) sheets—which decode the racial blood laws of Ruby—have everything to do with Pat's anger directed toward her daughter. Interestingly Morrison herself has spoken of her anger in relation to this mother-daughter relationship: "Now, I did get angry recently, about this daughter [Billie Delia]. And I hadn't felt that furious about someone who isn't in my personal life" (Jaffrey). This interesting conjunction of the author's and her character's anger reminds us of the doubled role Toni and Pat share: they both are engaged in writing the history of Ruby, a writing that maps the abuses of patriarchal cultural.

Unconsciously connecting her textual pleasure (her work on Ruby's history) with what she imagines to be her daughter's sexual pleasure, Pat begins to realize that she too is implicated in the communal judgment of her daughter as sexually promiscuous, a judgment that turns out to be untrue. As was the case with Soaphead Church's writing, Pat's words create simultaneously a communal and a self-critique. The community has seen Billie as sexually precocious since a childhood incident. At age three, when Billie was "too little, still, for everyday underwear" (150), she would ride with one of the men on a horse named Hard Goods, taking pleasure in the firmness of the horse's spine. One Sunday, when offered the ride, she "pulled down her Sunday panties before raising her arms to be lifted" (151). For this, she received a whipping from Pat and a sense of shame. Despite being relegated to promiscuity by both the community and her mother, Billie has remained a virgin.

Patricia's troubled confrontation with genealogy, I think, needs to be read against Milkman's triumphant interpretation of his family's genealogy that is coded in the song sung by the children of Shalimar. Like Milkman, who is suddenly able to interpret the hidden meaning of a coded genealogical text—the iterated children's song—Pat finds the final key to decoding the meaning of her genealogies in the annual play that the children perform. Having returned home from the pageant, Pat understands that the multiple Marys and Josephs stand for the founding families of Ruby. Originally the pageant had represented all nine of the founding families, but that number had dropped to eight and finally seven in the most recent production. She realizes that yet another family has been disallowed for violating the community's rigid rule of blood.

Patricia's epiphany, which allows her a full recognition of her complicity with the community in creating its other (even to the point of making her own daughter an other), leads to a final act that oddly comments on Morrison's own very personal relationship to fire. Overwhelmed by her sense that she has decoded the meaning of the family genealogies—that the purity of the all-African blood lines depends on the men's ownership of their women's sexuality—she understands the threat posed by the Convent women, who agressively claim their sexual potential, and Billie Delia and herself, who are light-complexioned. Although the fire that destroyed Morrison's beloved home on the Hudson River was entirely accidental, Patricia's relation to the fire is ambiguous. It appears initially that she is fully conscious of what she is doing, standing in front of a fire that she started in an oil drum out in her garden and methodically dropping file after file into the flames. Yet her final words point to a sense of love's labor lost: "'Dear God,' she murmured, 'Dear, dear God. I burned the papers'" (217), words that suggest the destruction is accidental (or at least not fully conscious) and that record her sense of loss. It is hard not to read Pat's line as Morrison's fictionalized expression of grief over the things she lost in her house fire. Not long after the fire, Morrison says in a piece that appeared in the *New York Times Magazine,* "When I think about the fire, I think I may not ever, ever, ever get over it. And it isn't even about the *things.* It's about the photographs, plants I nurtured for 20 years, about the view of the Hudson River, my children's report cards, my manuscripts" (Dreifus 74). In 1998 Morrison speaks of her initial sense of loss: "And I lost . . . I write by hand . . . I was able to save some books, but I had all my manuscripts, notes from old books, in my bedroom on the second floor, in a little trundle underneath the bed, where there was some storage space. It went up first. I said to somebody later, 'Why did I think that having those things near me was safer than having them in the basement?'" (Jaffrey).[23] These holographic manuscript pages were, as I have argued, the very site and thus the visible traces of the emergence of Morrison's class, racial, gendered, and authorial identities.

Early in this study I suggested that one might locate the Morrison who wrote *The Bluest Eye* in the space between Pecola Breedlove and Maureen Peal, because in terms of class origin Morrison was closer to Pecola but in terms of childhood appearance, the author more closely approximated

Maureen. I would like to conclude with a different pair—the two author figures of *Paradise*—because I think they help measure the distance Morrison has traveled in her career to date, and I believe they provide a point of departure for future consideration of this Nobel prize-winning author. Morrison hopes that her art performs the same healing that the gifts of Consolata enact but simultaneously fears that her writing, like Pat Best's, may only be able to diagnose the disease of American racialized discourse. Locatable neither exclusively in the realm of spiritual transcendence nor in the throes of authorial doubt, Morrison continues to write her best thing, which since *The Bluest Eye* has been her identity as an African-American woman novelist.

Having come to the end of what I wish to say about how one might discern the reflexive presence of Morrison within her fiction, a presence that suggests that all writing—much like Consolata's body art with the Convent women—serves as a tracing of the self, I am aware that what I have written can only be a harbinger for a project to come, one fashioned by a different critic. This study will be informed by the as yet unwritten authorized biography of Toni Morrison. But despite that valuable authorization, I hope that this future scholar will take whatever new stories become available to her or him and read them not as the revealed truth, but instead as subsequent chapters in the identifying fictions of Toni Morrison.

Notes

Chapter 1

1. I particularly want to thank Jeff Williams, director of the department's concentration in African-American literature, for risking the displeasure of other African-American faculty members by arguing that I should be allowed to teach Morrison.

2. No one can escape the contradictions of capitalism, but some instances seem stranger than others. Morrison is currently in vogue in the university, but in 1981 she was literally in *Vogue*, promoting her new book *Tar Baby*. Given her critique of hegemonic notions of female beauty, there is something jarring about seeing her comments on sex and beauty, love, and female friendship sandwiched among advertisements for cellulite removal and Victoria's Secret (Medwick 330–32).

3. Elizabeth Renker argues this thesis.

4. Her exact figure is of a woman riding naked on a subway. The extremity of this hypothetical example—I do not imagine too many readers have seen or ridden with naked women in public transportation—makes it difficult to accept her logic.

5. Morrison may in time prove correct but one may wish to base social policy on more than her reported conversation with an unnamed oncologist.

6. Two recent studies have noted competing strains of modernism and postmodernism in Morrison. Kimberly Chabot Davis, focusing on *Beloved*, says that the novel "exhibits a postmodern skepticism of sweeping historical narratives" but "retains an African American and modernist political commitment to the crucial importance of deep cultural memory" (242). Michael Nowlin, writing about *Jazz*, sees in the figure of Wild "[t]he two poles of black identity—authenticity derived from the connection to the ancestors and deracination paradoxically derived from race consciousness [. . .]" (167). Nowlin also hears "a confessional, autobiographical voice" (154) in *Jazz*. My study, however, locates this autobiographical voice much earlier in Morrison's writing, finding the autobiographical to be a constitutive feature of her writing.

7. Wilfred D. Samuels and Clenora Hudson-Weems productively use the existentialism of Jean-Paul Sartre and the language of modernist authenticity

to examine Morrison's fiction. See particularly the section "The Sartrean Influence" (17–18) for their rationale. What I hope to demonstrate is that such notions of authenticity are in tension with postmodern conceptions of identity.

8. Page is not alone in recognizing such parallels. For example, Patricia McKee, though not equating the two writing practices, notes that "like deconstructionists, Morrison identifies spacing as a means of producing meaning" (4). Barbara Johnson's work, which I discuss in chapter 3, also reads Morrison deconstructively.

9. It is not, however, my intention to read Morrison through Barthes's dispersal of everything into textuality. In fact, rather than the death of the author, what my study charts paradoxically is the birth of Morrison's artistic identity as it emerges through language.

10. Doreatha Drummond Mbalia is the first to focus attention exclusively on class. See her comments on how Morrison's sense of class may have been focused by her experiences as an instructor at Howard University in the late 1950s and early 1960s (*Toni* 105–06). See also Linden Peach's study, which in a number of instances draws attention to class issues.

11. Other statements, however, suggest Morrison did experience racism as a child, most notably her comments about white teenaged boys throwing rocks at her and her friends when she was six. (Kramer 15).

12. Dwight McBride, in examining Morrison's use of essentializing rhetoric in her essay "Unspeakable Things Unspoken," argues that "a strategic essentialism becomes an almost indispensable tool" for an oppressed "people whose individual lives may be markedly different, but who nonetheless suffer from a common form of racial hegemony" (150).

13. This is not to say that an institutional affirmative action does not still have an important cultural work to perform.

14. See, for example, Hutcheon's comments on *Tar Baby* (*Poetics* 68–69) and *Song of Solomon* (*Poetics* 151–52).

15. Homi Bhabha has identified Morrison's *Beloved* as exemplary of postcoloniality's "salutary reminder of the persistent 'neo-colonial' relations within the 'new' world order and the multinational division of labour"; for Bhabha, perspectives such as Morrison's allow for "the authentication of histories of exploitation and the evolution of strategies of resistance" (6). And on the cover of *The Location of Culture,* Morrison provides the following endorsement: "Any serious discussion of post-colonial/postmodern scholarship is inconceivable without referencing Mr. Bhabha."

Satya Mohanty has also identified Morrison with postcolonialism. His attempt to designate what he calls a realist position on identity that mediates the essentialism of identity politics and the social constructionist views of identity is not unrelated to my sense of the tension in Morrison's work between modernist authenticity and postmodern subjectivity; the difference is that, while Mohanty uses Morrison to theorize his alternative third position, I am less certain that these tensions ever quite resolve themselves.

16. Philip Weinstein briefly notes Morrison's debt to Said (xx).

17. Martin Kreiswirth, writing about William Faulkner, has termed such revision "auto-intertextuality."

Chapter 2

1. In "Rootedness," Morrison comments that Ellison serves as an ancestor, a kind of grandfather to more contemporary African-American writers. (343).

2. Melvin Dixon sees Church as a figure whose alienation doubles Pecola's. (147). Chickwenye Okonjo Ogunyemi admits that Church's letter "is powerful and arouses pathos" but argues finally that the letter "is an unnecessary diversion" (115). Jan Furman's judgment is that Church "does little more than use [Pecola] in his own schemes of revenge against God" (22). Gurleen Grewal usefully reads Church in a postcolonial context, though she is not interested in his act of writing: "His biting letter to God shows him bound to the master's imperial power; after all, his nationalist rhetoric notwithstanding, it is a small piece of this power he desires, not revolution" (29). Denise Heinze correctly notes the self-reflexivity of the letter as a "moment in which the reader is faced with ambivalence, uncertainty, conflict, and guilt" in which both readerly and authorial implication in Pecola's fate emerge (157). I argue that the letter is more intensely self-reflexive than Heinze's useful description indicates.

3. Linda Dittmar, for example, has written intelligently about the "disparate modes of narration" in *The Bluest Eye* that point to the "insufficiency of any one voice" (143) and has much to say about Claudia and the power of different voices in the novel; however, her discussion does not consider Church's authorial voice.

4. In 1981 Morrison comments, "I went to school with white children—they were my friends. There was no awe, no fear. Only later, when things got . . . sexual . . . did I see how clear the lines really were. But when I was in first grade nobody thought I was inferior" (Strouse 54).

5. My introduction of Hawthorne into the discussion is not unmotivated. In the chapter on Virginia Woolf in her M.A. thesis, Morrison, writing about *Mrs. Dalloway,* speaks of Clarissa Dalloway and Septimus Warren Smith in terms of "the unpardonable sin" ("Virginia" 9), language that suggests Morrison's awareness of Hawthorne's obsession.

6. Morrison has even suggested that, like Church, she was celibate at the time of writing. Speaking of her move to Syracuse, Morrison says, "In those days I didn't even know any men" (Dowling 52).

7. Recognizing the disjunction between names and identity in Church's letter, Shelley Wong argues that by "refusing the fixed identity of word and object, Morrison begins the work of decentering the logos itself. Through Soaphead's address to God, Morrison reveals the inanity at the center of the authoritarian word" (478). But the moment may not be as deconstructive

as Wong sees it since the letter simultaneously reinscribes a new authorial identity that is unwilling to abdicate this newly constituted authority.

8. Grewal suggests V. S. Naipaul's *The Mimic Men* as a different intertextual possibility arising out of Church's added middle name (28).

9. This story is repeated in Douglas Century's biography aimed at adolescent readers (33).

10. In 1948, The Gillette Company acquired The Toni Company and its line of home permanents and brought the Toni brand to national prominence in the 1950s. Morrison's 1953 Howard University yearbook picture suggests she has had a permanent. In a historical irony, given Morrison's critique of standards of beauty in *The Bluest Eye*, Gillette licensed in 1958 a ten-inch-tall white fashion doll, Toni, a precursor to Mattel's more famous Barbie. Historical information about Gillette can be found on the company's Web page <www.GILETTE.com>. (Note the address's spelling with only one "l.")

11. The Toni brand's emphasis on the secret twin neatly fits into Alan Nadel's notion of the doubled space of political and gender representation in Cold War America (117–32). Inexpensive sexual allure (the inexpensive home permanent) that could pass for the effect of conspicuous consumption (an expensive salon treatment) constituted the Toni user as a secret agent.

12. Morrison, for example, is identified as Chloe Anthony Wofford in Henry Louis Gates, Jr.'s Preface (ix) to *Toni Morrison: Critical Perspectives Past and Present* and in Nellie Y. McKay's Introduction (3) to her edited collection *Critical Essays on Toni Morrison*. Gates and McKay merely repeat a presumably reliable fact from numerous other sources, such as *Current Biography Yearbook 1979* and *Contemporary Authors*, vol. 29–32 (1972). Morrison herself publishes her birth name as Chloe Anthony Wofford in *Who's Who in America* from the 1984–85 edition through the 1999 edition.

13. I first became aware of a possible discrepancy regarding Morrison's name when I read her 1955 Cornell master's thesis, "Virginia Woolf's and William Faulkner's Treatment of the Alienated"; the title page of the thesis employs "Ardellia" [*sic*] as her middle name. Morrison's birth certificate is part of the public record at the Lorain Department of Health, 205 W. 14th St., Lorain, Ohio 44052.

Chapter 3

1. Morrison has warned of the dangers of seeking the white intertexts in African-American literature: "Finding or imposing Western influences in/on Afro-American literature has value, but when its sole purpose is to *place* value only where that influence is located it is pernicious." She is particularly concerned about what such comparisons make of black "work's own canvas"; nevertheless, Morrison imagines an "alternative utility" to such comparative study if it, rather than using the white canonical writer to "rank and grade" the African-American writer, can find "ways in which

the author combats and confronts received prejudices and even creates *other terms* in which to rethink one's attachment to or intolerance of the material of these works." My reading of *Sula* seeks precisely to use Morrison's metaphor, to examine the novel's "paint, its frame, its framelessness, its spaces" ("Unspeakable" 10).

2. Despite this summary of the ethical content of the novel, Nissen is more interested in developing an ethics of narrative form and uses a close analysis of issues of focalization and narration to argue that Eva is perhaps closest the novel's ethical center (283).

3. The very notion of center is one that the novel makes problematic, as a number of readings have suggested. See particularly Deborah McDowell's reading, which emphasizes "[t]he novel's fragmentary, episodic, elliptical quality" that frustrates "totalized interpretation." (68).

4. Eileen Barrett has commented on the Septimus-Shadrack connection, noting particularly how both writers figure their character's relation to post-traumatic stress through a troubled relation to their hands ("Septimus" 27); Christian more briefly notes the relation between Septimus and Shadrack (25).

5. Barbara Christian notes "an instance of serendipity" in Woolf's use "of the name Chloe" in *A Room of One's Own* and wonders how that might impinge on Morrison's decision to change her name "from Chloe (a name in America associated with blacks) to Toni (an androgynous name)" (20–21).

6. Gurleen Grewal begins to explore this topic when she suggests: "*Sula*, as if drawing out the subtext of Woolf's novel [*Mrs. Dalloway*], is an interrogation of all that makes women's friendships with other women secondary to their relationships with men" (58). While quite correctly noting that "the early relationship between Clarissa and her girlhood friend Sally Seton is comparable to the friendship of Sula and Nel," Grewal carefully demarcates what she sees as the shared matter of the two novels: "Representing female friendship, heterosexual love, and marriage, both novels raise the issue of women's alienation" (57). This articulation, however, leaves the boundaries between same-sex friendship and sexual identity rather rigid, and as Woolf scholars are aware, a character's (such as Mrs. Dalloway's) or author's (such as Woolf's) public performance of heterosexual identity may not exhaust the matter of sexual identity.

7. Eileen Barrett's "Unmasking Lesbian Passion: The Inverted World of *Mrs. Dalloway*," for example, traces an awareness of the novel's representation of lesbianism to the 1950s (151).

8. Barbara Rigney (92), for example, seems to want to follow up on Smith's reading but appears blocked by Morrison's declaration and readings that emphasize Sula's heterosexual acts.

9. In Morrison's most recent novel, *Paradise,* there is lesbianism both in the narrow sense that she means (women who have had sex with another woman) and the broader sense that Smith uses (women-centered women who challenge patriarchal social organization).

10. I am using "queer" in this instance as Sedgwick has delineated one of its meanings: "the open mesh of possibilities, gaps, overlaps, dissonances and resonances, lapses and excesses of meaning when the constituent elements of anyone's gender, of anyone's sexuality aren't made (or *can't be* made) to signify monolithically" (*Tendencies* 8).

11. For this definition I draw on Johnson's discussion of the relation between interest and Kant's notion of aesthetic disinterest, which Johnson likens to Freud's *heimlich* and *unheimlich* as "almost impossible to tell apart" (171). Also drawing on Johnson, Philip Novak, noting Sula's relation to her mother's death, has spoken of her attitude as "disinterested interest" (186). What I hope to add to Johnson's and Novak's discussion is an elaboration of the way that Morrison reflexively represents her anxieties regarding her own developing artistic identity and the problem of disinterested interest.

12. In Johnson's formulation, Eva accuses Sula and Nel of privileging "aesthetics over rapport" (171).

13. To think in the collapsed space of text and sex has been a standard trope since Roland Barthes's erotics of textuality, *The Pleasure of the Text*. Feminist scholars have also deployed this figure to think about the cultural scripts of sexual identity, perhaps nowhere more plainly that Toril Moi's *Sexual/Textual Politics.*

14. McDowell notes that for Sula, "[n]ot only is sexual expression an act of self-exploration, but it is also associated throughout the narrative with creativity, as seen in the long prose poem she creates while making love to Ajax" (64).

15. For a useful introduction to the psychoanalytic conception, see "Narcissism" and "Narcissistic Object Choice" in Laplanche and Pontalis. Working from Otto Rank's concept of the double, John Irwin, in his discussion of narcissistic figuration in Faulkner, usefully underscores how the myth represents the instability of identity:

> In the myth, Narcissus sees his image reflected in the water; he recognizes the image as himself, yet sees that it is shadowed on a medium whose fluidity, whose lack of differentiation, whose anarchy continually threaten to dissolve the unity of that image at the very moment that the medium itself seems to supply the force to sustain that image. What Narcissus sees is that unified image of his conscious life buoyed up from moment to moment by a medium whose very constitution, in relation to the ego, seems, paradoxically, to be dissolution and death. (33)

16. For Julia Kristeva in *Powers of Horror,* abjection—what the body refuses—figures identity formation. Identity emerges only by denying parts of oneself, as the body does in the process of evacuation. In the problematic space, then, of the "me" and the "not-me," what is inside and outside the body represent the problematic definition of subject and object (4). For

Shadrack, his identification with blackness (what the dominant culture finds abject) emerges at precisely the site of bodily evacuation.

17. Kathryn Bond Stockton reads this scene as a "regression to an anal economy" in which Shadrack is "a kind of obsessional neurotic, fixed on Bottom values" (101).

18. For Rigney, the girls' play suggests "a defloration ritual, like those performed in connection with some historical matriarchal cultures" (90).

19. Stockton reads this scene specifically as an instance of women's anal eroticism, since Sula begins with Ajax's cheekbone but then moves downward; such movement links what Sula does with Ajax to Eva's penetrating Plum's rectum (111).

20. From his useful survey of previous critical readings of her concluding cry, Page rightly notes that "Nel's cry is ambiguous. In it she finally finds her voice, but her cry is wordless, void of representational meaning" (76). But this ambiguity itself may represent the text's desire to encrypt the plurality of Nel's desire.

Chapter 4

1. As Samuels and Hudson-Weems point out, in *Song of Solomon* "Morrison had obviously drawn from her personal history; the story of Solomon Willis, her grandfather, is the source of this work." (8).

2. Barbara Christian suggests that white critics who contextualize Morrison with Woolf and Faulkner do so out of an unacknowledged racism. For Christian, such critics' motivation is to demean Morrison's African-American heritage (19–20). According to Christian, what empowers her to go on and speak about the relationship of Morrison to white modernism is that Christian is "an African American woman critic" (20) and therefore better understands the importance of African-American identity to Morrison. Christian's argument is an example of the identity politics that I discussed in chapter 1 and that I return to in this chapter.

3. Although Harold Bloom's version of intertextuality, *The Anxiety of Influence,* may seem implicit in some of my thinking, I wish to distance my work from Bloom's oedipalization of anxiety. Bloom's sense of poetic misprision, however, does seem to have some utility, so that one might say the strong novelist (such as Morrison) will inevitably misread her own work's relation to the aesthetic past. Bloom's point in this regard may be suggestive in the inevitably racialized context of thinking about Morrison and Faulkner: if overidentifying with one's aesthetic precursors is a metaphorical form of slavery, then reading one's difference is creatively liberating.

4. David Cowart has explored stylistic and thematic similarities between Morrison and Faulkner. Cowart judges Morrison's fiction a success inasmuch as she performs "meaningful variations on [Joyce's and Faulkner's] themes—freedom, identity, history" (89).

5. For example, in her interview with Nellie McKay, Morrison claims:

   Black people have a story, and that story has to be heard. There was
   an articulate literature before there was print. There were griots.
   They memorized it. People heard it. It is important that there is
   sound in my books—that you can hear it, that I can hear it. . . .
        That oral quality is deliberate. (152)

   Trudier Harris's "study of the influence of oral traditions upon" (1) Morrison's fiction is the fullest treatment to date on this topic.

6. Morrison was asked again in 1994 about her student reading of American
   literature and responded, "As for Faulkner, I read him with enormous pleasure. He seemed to me the only writer who took black people seriously.
   Which is not to say he was, or was not, a bigot" (Dreifus 73).

7. Patrick O'Donnell suggests that "one of the reasons Morrison has little to
   say about Faulkner in *Playing in the Dark* is that, perhaps, she has already
   said a great deal about him in her fiction" (225).

8. Harue Minakawa briefly notes a connection between *Song of Solomon* and
   Go Down, Moses: "Milkman goes through a process similar to what Ike
   McCaslin goes through in 'The Bear.' Hunting strips one to the essentials"
   (52–53). Although not specifically addressed in Morrison's thesis, *Go
   Down, Moses* is in her bibliography, as are all of Faulkner's novels published
   prior to 1955. More recently, Lucinda MacKethan, drawing on my earlier
   work on Morrison and Faulkner, develops a reading of *Song of Solomon* and
   "The Bear" that compliments my own.

9. Two articles particularly note the subversion of Macon's teachings.
   Robert James Butler, who sees the novel growing "out of this dialectic
   between the possibilities of space and the securities of place" (63), focuses
   on Guitar's influence on Milkman. Valerie Smith, arguing that the novel
   opposes linear time (exemplified by Macon Dead) and cyclical time (as
   Pilate lives it) foregrounds Pilate's shaping hand (726).

10. Juliet Mitchell summarizes the Lacanian view: "The phallus is not identi-
    cal with the actual penis, for it is what it signifies that is important. [. . .]
    The phallus [. . .] indicates the desire of the mother (the desire for the
    phallus) into which the child is born. [. . .] The primary dyadic relation-
    ship between mother and child . . . enters immediately into the possibility
    of a dialectical relationship between three terms: mother, child, and phal-
    lus. So already, even so to speak *before,* [the child] wants to be the phallus
    for the mother [. . .]. In submitting to the completely unreal possibility of
    castration the little boy acknowledges the situation and learns that one day
    he, too, will accede to the father's function. He pays thereby his symbolic
    debt to the father he has murdered in his rivalrous thoughts. So the phal-
    lus is intimately connected both with the symbolic father and the law"
    (396–97).

11. Earlier Macon's walk is described as a strut, again linking him to the
    peacock (17).

12. Emmett Till's murder has been the occasion of other African-American writers to think in the space between history and fiction. Morrison herself has written a play, *Dreaming Emmett* (1985). Ishmael Reed even more metafictionally titles his novel *Reckless Eyeballing* (1988) which in turn is the title of the play that the novel's main character, Ian Ball, has written about Till; the novel chronicles Ball's efforts to have his play produced.

13. That the members of the Seven Days invoke the authority of monotheistic Christianity to name their organization recalls Julia Kristeva's point in *About Chinese Women* that "monotheistic unity is sustained by a radical separation of the sexes: indeed, this separation is its prerequisite. For without this gap between the sexes . . . it would be impossible, in the symbolic sphere, to isolate the principle of One Law—One, Purifying, Transcendent Guarantor of the ideal interests of the community" (19). The Seven Days, by passing judgment and telling its victims "Your day has come," aligns itself with transcendent authority and attempts to be the guarantor of the ideal interests of the African-American community, all the while reducing African-American women to property.

14. Charles Scruggs briefly comments on this scene, suggesting that when Milkman removes the bobcat's heart he "realizes that Guitar was trying to tell him how he could save his own life, that he could save it only if he bridged the gap between himself and others, between himself and the past" (322). Far from teaching Milkman how to save himself, Guitar's teachings reinscribe a significant aspect of the Dead father's ideology of possession. Weinstein much more closely reads this scene, though in a largely unironized way so that Guitar's claim that the killing of whites is done out of love for African Americans is less problematic than I see it. The very title of Weinstein's book, *What Else But Love?*, in fact is the question Guitar asks.

15. Susan Willis suggests that Morrison's "three-woman utopian households" (41) contrast with Faulkner's failure to conceive of the radical possibility represented by Judith, Clytie, and Rosa living together without men at Supten's house. The three-woman household in *Absalom,* however, is primarily concerned that they not be raped by the desperate and defeated men returning to a ravaged land. Willis of course writes prior to *Beloved,* but her sense of utopian households becomes problematic if we think of Sethe, Denver, and Beloved. Sethe's emotional and sexual longings cannot be exhausted in female bonding and in fact her very life is threatened by her obsessional attachment to Beloved.

16. That Milkman comes to a belief in ghosts as a result of his movement toward Pilate reminds us that Isaac McCaslin is similarly introduced to a world beyond the material by his mentor in "The Old People" when Sam Fathers shows the boy the spirit of the dead buck.

17. See for example the description of the ginger-smelling air prior to Guitar's and Milkman's unacknowledged encounter with the ghost of Jake (186).

18. Milkman's belief in ghosts is another sign that he has moved beyond his father's middle-class values, values that derive from the white ruling class. Morrison tells a pointed story on this matter: "Once a woman asked me 'Do you believe in ghosts?' I said, 'Yes. Do you believe in germs?' It's part of our cultural heritage" (Watkins 50).

19. Gerry Brenner's claim that the Milkman who returns to Pilate "assigns himself no culpability" (18) for Hagar's death depends on an odd interpolation of the word "it" in the line "What difference did it make?" (336). Let's look at what precedes this sentence:

> Hagar was dead. The cords of his neck tightened. How? In Guitar's room, did she . . . ?
> What difference did it make? He had hurt her, left her, and now she was dead—he was certain of it." (336).

Brenner reads the sentence as follows: "What difference did [Hagar's death] make?" The context, however, suggests a more plausible reading. Milkman starts to ask himself if Hagar killed herself as he had suggested she do in Guitar's room, but then he realizes that how she died is irrelevant: "What difference did it make [how Hagar died]?" Milkman recognizes that his treatment of her implicates him in her death no matter what the particular circumstances surrounding that death are.

20. The moment is hardly the suicidal gesture that some critics have made it out to be (Brenner 18; Butler 72). Guitar's rifle has Milkman pinned down. There are not many options for life-affirming action open to Milkman, but he does act with a knowledge of his life-long friend and stands up. Guitar's sense of fair play—there are rules good hunters follow, after all—and his love for his friend lead him to lay aside his rifle.

Although I do not wish to grant special privilege to the author's reconstruction of this scene, Morrison's comments on the novel's ending seem germane. In an interview with Pepsi Charles, Morrison calls *Song of Solomon* an "absolute triumph" since "a man learns the only important lesson there is to learn. And he wins himself, he wins himself. And the quality of his life improves immeasurably. Whether its length improves or lengthens is irrelevant" (50).

Chapter 5

1. Trudier Harris has commented on the various versions of the tar baby story Morrison may be drawing upon (116–119).

2. A number of critics have noticed this feature. For Terry Otten, the novel is "an extensive adaptation of the fall myth" (63). Lauren Lepow argues not only that "Morrison recasts the Genesis story" but also that the "version of the Genesis story she invokes most sharply is Milton's" from *Paradise Lost* (365).

3. Morrison has been quite clear about her choice to use the tar baby story as "the skeleton" of her novel: "So I just gave these characters parts, Tar Baby being a black woman and the rabbit a black man" (Ruas 102); the plot, however, problematizes the matter of who entraps whom.

4. I am indebted to Barbara Williams Lewis for pointing out that the opening page of the novel is the same as Morrison's birthday, and to Teresa Towner who noticed that, although Ruth goes into the hospital on this day, her son is not born until the following day.

5. Speaking in 1980 about her manuscript and the "contemporary woman" who is at its center, Morrison again is careful to disclaim any link between life and art: "I've never been able to get interested in writing about any event that I'd lived through. It didn't seem to have the right color. It's sort of blank. My imagination is more interesting than my life" (Koenen 82).

6. In what is probably the most probing interview conducted with Morrison, Cecil Brown returns repeatedly to the issue of who reads her fiction. At one point he asks, "Do you have many black male readers?" to which Morrison says she "would imagine so." In response to his next question—"Do you have a greater following among white female readers?"—she responds, "I don't know. I can't tell. It seems to me that [. . .] in the academy, I think I have just as many black women who read as white, if not more, but it's proportionate, because there are just more white people in the university. So how can I tell?" (459). Morrison's uncertain comments illustrate her desire to claim that her fiction speaks more to African-American than white women, but in order to do so, she limits her audience to academic readers. Even then she has to further qualify her response by speaking of the percentage of black academic women readers as opposed to that of white academic women readers.

7. Judylyn S. Ryan has made this point specifically in relation to *Tar Baby* (600). More recently, Denise Heinze has made Du Bois the jumping off point for her larger consideration of Morrison.

8. Morrison delineates Jadine's skin throughout the novel as honey-colored, a designation that itself may be another oblique self-reference since a journalistic biography described Morrison's skin as "honey-brown." See *Current Biography 1979*, p. 276.

9. Eleanor W. Traylor first drew my attention to the dedication through her suggestion that these women "are the guides to whom the narrative voice of the writer is accountable" (149).

10. This story is repeated in Douglas Century's biography aimed at adolescent readers (33).

11. Dorothy H. Lee is the first to suggests that it "is tempting to theorize that the 'house of Chloe' is Chloe Anthony Wofford Morrison's own" (356). With regard to the epigraphy, Marilyn E. Mobley also briefly notes that Morrison was "born Chloe Anthony Wofford" (762), though as I noted in chapter 2, Morrison's middle name, as recorded on her birth certificate, is

"Ardelia." Curiously, one of Milkman's sisters is named First Corinthians, the biblical book that provides Morrison her epigraph for *Tar Baby*. So it seems that Chloe is present again in coded form in *Song of Solomon*.

12. The Revised Standard version of the bible offers an alternative translation of the epigraph Morrison uses, speaking of "Chloe's people," and in one sense, all the characters in *Tar Baby* are just that—Chloe's people.

13. Morrison's treatment of rape in *Tar Baby* seems fundamentally different than the paradigm Laura E. Tanner articulates. For Tanner, the act of reading rape rhetorically implicates the reader, but in Morrison's novel how can the reader assert a right to "resist the message of the text" (103) when the text itself resists revealing the rape?

14. I do not want to reduce the representation of Son and Jadine to the relationship between Morrison and her former husband, Harold. Nevertheless, Morrison makes an intriguing comment to Karen De Witt in a newspaper piece that publicizes *Song of Solomon*. De Witt contextualizes the author's comments as follows:

But Morrison who doesn't like to talk about her Jamaican architect ex-husband, says she doesn't know a thing about love.
   "I know about passion," she says, "but not about love." She changes her mind. "Yes, I know about that," she muses, "I know these people, knew these people once."
   It is the beginning of another story, a story that Morrison is already at work on. (C3)

That story is, of course, *Tar Baby*.

15. Peter B. Erickson maintains that the "central fact about the Jadine-Son relationship is its failure" and that "the interest lies in the reasons for the failure" (21); however, quoting material from the page on which the rape has occurred says only that "Jadine's definitive decision to break with Son [. . .] is immediately preceded by her recollection of the 'mother-daughter day' at college" (21). Mobley characterizes the end of the Jadine-Son relationship as follows: "Because Son is rooted in the past, symbolized by his romantic attachment to Eloe, and because Jadine feels the key to personal and collective success is to forget the past, their relationship cannot hold itself together. The novel goes full circle in that once again a crisis causes Jadine to flee" (768–769). Other critical treatments similarly fail to see the sexual violence of this "crisis."

16. The most extreme articulation of this may be James Coleman's; he claims that "the sentiments of the reader are most likely with Son, a sensitive, warm man who possesses definite folk values and qualities [. . .]" (65). See also Evelyn Hawthorne (104).

17. Even Harris, who aptly describes Son's sexual aggressiveness, claims that Son "certainly does not rape anyone" (120). Harris, however, perhaps better than anyone has described the way in which Son as much as Jadine is figured as a tar baby (119). Missing Son's rape of Jadine leads Harris finally

to see him as the more victimized of the two; for Harris, Jadine simply leaves Son "when he proves intractable" (124–25).

18. Son's desire to reconstitute Jadine's subjectivity recalls Wallace's point about the African-American male, "particularly since the Black Movement," who wishes to "define the black woman. He is the one who tells her whether or not she is a woman and what it is to be a woman"; this woman "is the workhorse that keeps his house functioning, she is the foundation of his community, she raises his children, and she faithfully votes for him in elections, goes to his movies, reads his books, watches him on television, buys in his stores, solicits his services as doctor, lawyer, accountant" (14). Both Morrison and Wallace argue that African-American women should have greater autonomy in determining identity.

19. In passing one should note that the opening paragraph of the article in *Newsweek* with Morrison's picture on the cover identifies her, among her other identities, as a former beauty queen. See Jean Strouse (52).

20. Sandra Pouchet Paquet perceptively notes this parallel between *Song of Solomon* and *Tar Baby,* arguing that Jadine's situation is more ambiguous than Milkman's because, unlike Milkman, she cannot accept a segregated, patriarchal black rural community as the basis for identity (512).

21. Speaking with Judith Wilson, Morrison claims that Jadine "has lost the tar quality, the ability to hold something together that otherwise would fall apart—which is what I mean by the nurturing ability" (131). Morrison more explicitly positions herself with Thérèse when speaking with Charles Ruas: Jadine, she says, "does not have, as Thérèse says, her ancient properties" (104).

22. Lepow suggests that the soldier aunt queen "is a deliberately antiromantic image of solitary fecundity designed to reinforce our knowledge that Jade must be alone in her act of self-redemption" (376).

Chapter 6

1. Ashraf H. A. Rushdy has thoroughly laid out the historical documents surrounding Margaret Garner, both in the popular press and in abolitionist journals. Rushdy's central assertion, that Morrison has added "a feminist voice" to "revisionist historiography and contemporary fiction," is unassailable (568).

2. My thanks to Catherine Gunther Kodat who suggested Morrison's apparent desire to conceal the extent of her knowledge about Margaret Garner.

3. Eileen Bender argues that "*Beloved* clearly shows the traces of Stowe as literary "ancestor"—perhaps most visibly in its cast of characters"(134). The characters Bender is most interested in are Eliza and Sethe.

4. For a different reading of intertextual possibility placing the white and black texts against one another, see Moreland's discussion of *Beloved* and Mark Twain's *Huckleberry Finn* (37–63).

5. In her review of *Beloved,* Margaret Atwood, for example, suggestively notes that Sethe's escape "makes the ice-floe scene in 'Uncle Tom's Cabin' look like a stroll around the block" (1).

6. Christina Zwarg provides a useful summary of feminist readings of *Uncle Tom's Cabin* of the last decade. Her own work examines "the radical nature of Stowe's feminism" through an examination of Stowe's "treatment of fatherhood" (274). Her nuanced reading of the way the blackface George Washington hanging on the wall of Tom's cabin enters a symbolic economy with Tom's own role as black Christ and with the character of Black Sam as "politician" reveals several gaps in patriarchal authority; however, Zwarg's acknowledgement that, despite these subversions of the father, "Tom and Stowe become subsumed under the hierarchical representations of Christianity and patriarchy" corresponds much more closely to my own sense of Stowe's reinscription of a transcendent patriarchy.

   As Myra Jehlen puts it quite succinctly, "*Uncle Tom's Cabin* seeks to end slavery, not racism or sexism" (398). Jehlen sees a clear limit to Stowe's feminism and poses a particular challenge to those who would assert a matriarchy in the novel. For Jehlen, Rachel Halliday, whose kitchen is the ultimate cite of domesticity and women power, "blesses the restoration of patriarchal power to the slave [George Harris] whose manhood is inextricably a matter of self-possession and of the possession of others, of *his* wife and child" (392).

7. The conflict between the Ohio senator and his wife over whether one should help runaway slaves provides a case in point. John Bird tells Mary: "Your feelings are all quite right, dear, and interesting, and I love you for them; but then, we mustn't suffer our feelings to run away with our judgment. You must consider it's not a matter of private feeling; there are great public interests involved [. . .]" (85). John's words divide the world in sharp dichotomies that gender the public and private spheres: men and the public sphere govern by reason; women and the private sphere are the appropriate site of emotion. Yet a woman's feelings, informed by the bible, may lead reason to a higher truth that emotion has intuited. So when Eliza appears at the Birds' house, the senator eventually takes the leading role in assisting her escape. Mary's reactions to her husband's reversal is telling:

   Now, little Mrs. Bird was a discreet woman—a woman who never in her life said, "I told you so!" and, on the present occasion, though pretty well aware of the shape her husband's meditations were taking, she very prudently forebode to meddle with them, only sat very quietly in her chair, and looked quite ready to hear her liege lord's intentions, when he should think proper to utter them. (92)

   Although a touch of irony flirts in the narrator's description of Mary's role here, it is impossible to forget that the word "lord" cannot signify without nodding toward the Lord, the transcendent model for masculine earthly rule.

8. Lori Askeland has explored a similar thesis, arguing that Morrison examines and revises the ideology of *Uncle Tom's Cabin* "in a way that avoids reification of a patriarchal power structure" (787). The evidence that she uses is quite different, based on the ideology of nineteenth-century domesticity, and she does not take up intertextual possibilities between Uncle Tom and Baby Suggs.

9. Elizabeth House's closely argued case that the young woman who appears at 124 is not the ghost of Sethe's daughter "but simply a young woman who has herself suffered the horrors of slavery" (17) usefully corrects those who would take ghostliness to be a simple matter in the novel. However, House's argument overnaturalizes a novel that insists upon a realm beyond the natural. At the outset 124 is unquestionably haunted by an authentic ghost and this ghost's disappearance, occasioned by Paul D's arrival, ushers in the arrival of Beloved.

10. For Askeland, Bodwin is "the good-intentioned whiteman who still carries in him the ghosts of the patriarchal institution" (801).

11. Harryette Mullen has described this scene in terms of Kristeva's *chora,* a space prior to naming and "associated with the maternal semiotic" that parallels "Morrison's chorus of mothers unnaming the unspeakable desire that precedes language" (263). The limitation of this fictive resolution is that, while an emotionally satisfying conclusion to the narrative, it does not provide a clear guideline for overturning patriarchal language. The cry of the women is before language. Does this mean that there is no language a woman can speak that will not speak her own oppression? The ending of *Beloved* does not resolve the issue, and we are left with the implication at least that to enter the Symbolic compromisingly positions women much as Sethe is positioned in relation to a different fluid produced by her laboring body, the ink she makes. This flowing substance is appropriated by her master, schoolteacher, who writes the "scientific" treatise that authorizes his nephews' the appropriation of her milk. Still, as Morrison notes, the novel's role is to stage a problem, not to provide a "recipe" for solving it ("Rootedness" 341).

12. Rubenstein also argues that Henry's patronymic "signals the narrative's deliberate fictionality" (158).

13. One reason for thinking of the supernatural narrator of *Jazz* in this fashion comes from the representation of spirituality in *Paradise.* In Morrison's most recent novel, Consolata is visited by a god/goddess figure that alternately manifests itself as male and as female.

14. Rubenstein notes that "Morrison explicitly places in the reader's hands the responsibility for constructing the meaning of her text, affirming the imaginative collaboration between narrator and reader" (162). What needs to be underscored, though, is the profoundly sexual figuration of this collaboration.

15. For example, in chapter 3 I detail Morrison's repudiation of the lesbian reading of *Sula.*

16. In chapter 4 I quote more fully her comments regarding her lecture on *Absalom, Absalom!*

17. Philip Weinstein also uses this passage as a clue to Morrison's rewriting of Faulkner (147–48).

18. Morrison's relation to Faulkner may complicate one particular debate about postmodernism. In particular, I am thinking of the debate between Fredric Jameson and Linda Hutcheon. For Jameson, postmodern narrative is ahistorical (and hence politically dangerous), playing only with pastiched images and aesthetic forms that produce a degraded historicism (see chapter 1 of *Postmodernism*); for Hutcheon, as I discuss in my opening chapter, postmodern fiction remains historical, precisely because it problematizes history through parody, and thus retains its potential for cultural critique. Thus, Hutcheon's celebration of the power of postmodern parody to produce historical thinking stands in direct opposition to Jameson's despair over postmodernism, which for him is not an oppositional aesthetic but only the cultural logic of multinational capitalism. *Jazz*'s pastiche of Faulknerian textuality complicates Jameson's and Hutcheon's positions because Morrison's pastiche may actually perform the cultural work that Hutcheon ascribes to parody.

19. Some readers may object to my use of the word "rape," but the dynamics of master and slave make any notion of consent impossibly problematic.

20. *Beloved* in particular seems like an intervention in the critical commentary by African-American writers, such as Ishmael Reed, who were critical of the portrayal of the African-American male in the fiction of black women authors such as Alice Walker.

21. Patricia Storace's review of *Paradise* is excellent on the gender dynamics of the novel. Storace notes that the "women of Ruby [. . .]live in the mansion of freedom, a freedom granted to them, which they do not possess— they are free to live the lives whose purpose and limits are imagined for them by Ruby men [. . .]."

22. When asked by an interviewer about her sense of achievement in *Paradise,* Morrison somewhat cryptically remarks, "I wanted another kind of confrontation with Patricia, the one who kept the genealogies together" (Jaffrey).

23. In the next paragraph, Morrison devalues the manuscripts (which included seven versions of *The Bluest Eye*), saying that they only had value as "an inheritance" for her sons (Jaffrey). The fact, however, that Morrison chose to focus on them first (rather than the loss of her children's report cards) and the halting fashion in which she expresses the loss suggests that the later comments serve as a kind of cover for the deep sense of loss she feels regarding the manuscripts.

Works Cited

I. Primary Morrison Material

Novels

Beloved. New York: Knopf, 1987.
The Bluest Eye. 1970. New York: Plume, 1994.
Jazz. New York: Knopf, 1992.
Paradise. New York: Knopf, 1997.
Song of Solomon. New York: Knopf, 1977.
Sula. New York: Knopf, 1973.
Tar Baby. New York: Knopf, 1981.

Criticism and Essays

"Faulkner and Women." *Faulkner and Women.* Ed. Doreen Fowler and Ann J. Abadie. Jackson: UP of Mississippi, 1986. 295–302.
"The Official Story: Dead Man Golfing." *Birth of a Nation'hood: Gaze, Script, and Spectacle in the O.J. Simpson Case.* Ed. Toni Morrison and Claudia Brodsky Lacour. New York: Pantheon, 1997. vii–xxviii.
Playing in the Dark: Whiteness and the Literary Imagination. Cambridge: Harvard UP, 1992.
"Rootedness: The Ancestor as Foundation." Evans, 339–45.
"A Slow Walk of Trees (as Grandmother Would Say) Hopeless (as Grandfather Would Say)." *The New York Times Magazine* 4 July 1976: 104+.
"Unspeakable Things Unspoken: The Afro-American Presence in American Literature." *Michigan Quarterly Review* 28 (1989): 1–34.
[Chloe Ardellia Wofford]. "Virginia Woolf's and William Faulkner's Treatment of the Alienated." M.A. thesis. Cornell U, 1955. [Note: Morrison uses the middle name recorded on her birth certificate on the title page of her thesis, but it is spelled "Ardellia" rather than "Ardelia."]

Interviews and Profiles

Although MLA style calls for 1) listing interviews by the last name of the figure interviewed and 2) internal citations using a short title, this becomes confusing since so many of Morrison's interviews have identical or similar titles; therefore,

I cite interviews by the last name of the interviewer. Whenever the interviews have been reprinted in *Conversations with Toni Morrison* (Jackson: UP of Mississippi, 1994) edited by Danille Taylor-Guthrie, I have cited that volume. The term "profile" includes any article or review for which Morrison has supplied oral or written comments to the author.

Bakerman, Jane. "The Seams Can't Show: An Interview with Toni Morrison." Taylor-Guthrie, 30–42. Rpt. from *Black American Literature Forum* 12.2 (1978): 56–60.

Bigsby, Christopher. "Jazz Queen." *The Independent* [London]. 26 April 1992, Sunday Review Page, 28. Online. Nexis. 20 Ap. 1996.

Brown, Cecil. "Interview with Toni Morrison." *Massachusetts Review* 36 (1995): 455–73.

Charles, Pepsi. "An Interview with Toni Morrison." *Nimrod* 21.2 (1977): 43–51.

"Conversation with Alice Chidress and Toni Morrison." Taylor-Guthrie, 3–9. Rpt. from *Black Creation Annual 1974–1975*. 90–92.

DeWitt, Karen. "Song of Solomon." *Washington Post*. 30 Sept 1977: C1, C3.

Dreifus, Claudia. "Chloe Wofford Talks about Toni Morrison." *New York Times Magazine* 11 Sept. 1994: 72–75.

Gray, Paul. "Paradise Found." *Time* 19 Jan. 1998: 62–68.

Jaffrey, Zia. "The Salon Interview." *Salon* 2 Feb. 1998. 20 Oct. 1998. <http://www.salonmagazine.com/books/int/1998/02/cov_si_02int.html>.

Jones, Bessie W. and Audre Vinson. "An Interview with Toni Morrison." Taylor-Guthrie, 171–187. Rpt. from *The World of Toni Morrison* (Debuque: Kendall Hunt, 1985): 127–51.

Koenen, Anne. "The One Out of Sequence." Taylor-Guthrie, 67–83. Rpt. from *History and Tradition in Afro-American Culture,* ed. Gunther Lenz. (Frankfurt: Campus, 1984): 207–21.

LeClair, Thomas. "The Language Must Not Sweat: A Conversation with Toni Morrison." *Conversations with Toni Morrison*. Taylor-Guthrie, 119–128. Rpt. from *New Republic* 21 March 1981: 25–29.

McKay, Nellie. "An Interview with Toni Morrison." Taylor-Guthrie, 138–55. Rpt. from *Contemporary Literature* 24 (1983): 413–429.

Medwick, Cathleen. "Toni Morrison." *Vogue* April 1981: 288+.

Morales, Robert. "Toni Morrison." *The Vibe Q* May 1998. 19 Nov. 1998. <http://www.vibe.com/archive/may98/docs/toni.html>.

"Morrison, Toni." *Contemporary Authors*. Vol. 29–32. 1972.

"Morrison, Toni." *Current Biography Yearbook*. 40th ed. 1979.

Naylor, Gloria. "A Conversation: Gloria Naylor and Toni Morrison." Taylor-Guthrie, 188–217. Rpt. from *Southern Review* 21 (1985): 567–593.

Neustadt, Kathy. "The Visits of the Writers Toni Morrison and Eudora Welty." Taylor-Guthrie, 84–92. Rpt. from *Bryn Mawr Alumnae Bulletin* Spring 1980: 2–5.

Ruas, Charles. "Toni Morrison." Taylor-Guthrie 93–118. Rpt. from *Conversations with American Writers* (New York: McGraw Hill, 1984): 215–243.

Schappell, Elissa. "The Art of Fiction CXXXIV." *The Paris Review* 129 (1993): 83–125.

Stepto, Robert. "Intimate Things in Place: A Conversation with Toni Morrison." Taylor-Guthrie, 10–29. Rpt. from *Massachusetts Review* 18 (1977): 473–489.

Strouse, Jean. "Toni Morrison's Black Magic." *Newsweek* 30 March 1981: 52–56.

Tate, Claudia. "Toni Morrison." Taylor-Guthrie 156–170. Rpt. from *Black Women Writers at Work* (New York: Continuum, 1983): 117–131.

Watkins, Mel. "Talk with Toni Morrison." *New York Times Book Review* 11 Sept. 1977. 48, 50.

Wilson, Judith. "A Conversation with Toni Morrison." Taylor-Guthrie 129–37. Rpt. from *Essence* July, 1981: 84–6, 128.

II. Secondary Sources

Appiah, Kwame Anthony. "Race." *Critical Terms for Literary Study.* Ed. Frank Lentricchia and Thomas McLaughlin. Chicago: U of Chicago P, 1990. 274–87.

Althusser, Louis. *Lenin and Philosophy and Other Essays.* Trans. Ben Brewster. New York: Monthly Review, 1971.

Askeland, Lori. "Remodeling the Model Home in *Uncle Tom's Cabin* and *Beloved.*" *American Literature* 64 (1992): 785–805.

Atwood, Margaret. "Haunted by Their Nightmares." *New York Times Book Review.* 13 Sept. 1987: 1+.

Awkward, Michael. *Inspiriting Influences: Tradition, Revision, and Afro-American Women's Novels.* Gender and Culture. New York: Columbia UP, 1989.

———. "Negotiations of Power: White Critics, Black Texts, and the Self-Referential Impulse." *American Literary History* 2 (1990): 581–606.

Baker, Houston A., Jr., and Patricia Redmond. *Afro-American Literary Study in the 1990s.* Chicago: U of Chicago P, 1989.

Barrett, Eileen. "Septimus and Shadrack: Woolf and Morrison Envision the Madness of War." Hussey and Neverow, 26–32.

———. "Unmasking Lesbian Passion: The Inverted World of *Mrs. Dalloway.*" *Virginia Woolf: Lesbian Readings.* Ed. Eileen Barrett and Patricia Cramer. The Cutting Edge: Lesbian Life and Experience. New York: New York UP, 1997. 146–64.

Barthes, Roland. *The Pleasure of the Text.* 1973. Trans. Richard Miller. New York: Hill, 1975.

———. *Roland Barthes.* 1975. Trans. Richard Howard. New York: Hill, 1977.

Bender, Eileen T. "Repossessing *Uncle Tom's Cabin:* Toni Morrison's *Beloved.*" *Cultural Power/Cultural Literacy.* Ed. Bonnie Braendlin. Tallahassee: Florida State UP, 1991.

Bhabha, Homi K. *The Location of Culture.* London: Routledge, 1994.

Bloom, Harold. *The Anxiety of Influence: A Theory of Poetry.* New York: Oxford UP, 1973.

Blotner, Joseph. *Faulkner: A Biography.* One-Volume Edition. New York: Random, 1984.

Brenner, Gerry. "*Song of Solomon:* Morrison's Rejection of Rank's Monomyth and Feminism." *Studies in American Fiction* 15 (1987): 13–24.

Butler, Robert James. "Open Movement and Self-hood in Toni Morrison's *Song of Solomon.*" *Centennial Review* 28.1 (1984–85): 58–75.

Carmean, Karen. *Toni Morrison's World of Fiction.* Troy, NY: Whitston, 1993.

Century, Douglas. *Toni Morrison.* Black Americans of Achievement. New York: Chelsea, 1994.

Christian, Barbara. "Layered Rhythms: Virginia Woolf and Toni Morrison." Peterson. 19–36.

Coleman, James. "Toni Morrison's *Tar Baby.*" *Black American Literature Forum* 20 (1986): 63–73.

Cowart, David. "Faulkner and Joyce in Morrison's *Song of Solomon.*" *American Literature* 62 (1990): 87–100.

Davis, Kimberly Chabot. "'Postmodern Blackness': Toni Morrison's *Beloved* and the End of History." *Twentieth Century Literature* 44 (1998): 242–60.

Dittmar, Linda. "'Will the Circle Be Unbroken?': The Politics of Form in *The Bluest Eye.*" *Novel* 23 (1990): 137–55.

Dixon, Melvin. *Ride Out the Wilderness: Geography and Identity in Afro-American Literature.* Urbana: U of Illinois P, 1987.

Dowling, Colette. "The Song of Toni Morrison." Taylor-Guthrie 49–59. Rpt. from *The New York Times Magazine* 20 May 1979: 40+.

Du Bois, W. E. B. *The Souls of Black Folk.* 1903. Ed. Henry Louis Gates, Jr., and Terri Hume Oliver. New York: Norton, 1999.

Ellison, Ralph. "Hidden Name and Complex Fate." *Shadow and Act.* New York: Random, 1964. 144–66.

———. *Invisible Man.* 1952. New York: Random, 1972.

Erickson, Peter B. "Images of Nurturance in Toni Morrison's *Tar Baby.*" *CLA Journal* 28 (1984): 11–32.

Evans, Mari, ed. *Black Women Writers (1950–1980): A Critical Evaluation.* Garden City, NY: Anchor, 1984.

Fanon, Franz. *Black Skin, White Masks.* Trans. Charles Lam Markmann. New York: Grove, 1967.

Faulkner, William. *Absalom, Absalom!* 1936. New York: Vintage International, 1990.

———. *Go Down, Moses.* 1942. New York: Vintage International, 1990.

———. *Light in August.* 1932. New York: Vintage International, 1990.

Furman, Jan. *Toni Morrison's Fiction.* Understanding Contemporary American Literature. Columbia: U of South Carolina P, 1996.

Gates, Henry Lewis, Jr. "*Jazz* (1992)." Gates and Appiah, 52–55.

———. "Preface." Gates and Appiah ix–xiii.

———. *The Signifying Monkey: A Theory of Afro-American Literary Criticism.* New York: Oxford UP, 1988.

Gates, Henry Lewis, Jr., and K.A. Appiah, eds. *Toni Morrison: Critical Perspectives Past and Present.* New York: Amistad, 1993.

Greenblatt, Stephen. *Renaissance Self-Fashioning From Moore to Shakespeare.* Chicago: U of Chicago P, 1980.

Grewal, Gurleen. *Circles of Sorrow, Lines of Struggle: The Novels of Toni Morrison.* Baton Rouge: Louisiana State UP, 1998.

Harris, Trudier. *Fiction and Folklore: The Novels of Toni Morrison*. Knoxville: U of Tennessee P, 1991.

Harris-Wilson, Ann. "Woolf and Toni Morrison: Moments from the Critical Dialogue." Hussey and Neverow, 32–37.

Hawthorne, Evelyn. "On Gaining the Double-Vision: *Tar Baby* as Diasporean Novel." *Black American Literature Forum* 22 (1988): 97–107.

Heinze, Denise. *The Dilemma of "Double-Consciousness: Toni Morrison's Novels*. Athens: U of Georgia P, 1993.

hooks, bell. *Yearnings: Race, Gender, and Cultural Politics*. Boston: South End, 1990.

House, Elizabeth. "Toni Morrison's Ghost: The Beloved Who is Not Beloved." *Studies in American Fiction* 18 (1990): 17–26.

Hussey, Mark and Vara Neverow, eds. *Virginia Woolf: Emerging Perspectives*. New York: Pace UP, 1994.

Hutcheon, Linda. *The Poetics of Postmodernism*. New York: Routledge, 1988.

Irigaray, Luce. "Volume-Fluidity." 1974. *Speculum of the Other Woman*. Trans. Gillian C. Gill. Ithaca: Cornell UP, 1985. 227–40.

Irwin, John T. *Doubling and Incest/Repetition and Revenge: A Speculative Reading of Faulkner*. Baltimore: Johns Hopkins UP, 1975.

James, Henry. "The Art of Fiction." 1884. *Selected Literary Criticism*. Ed. Morris Shapira. New York: Horizon, 1964. 49–67.

Jameson, Fredric. *Postmodernism, or, The Cultural Logic of Late Capitalism*. Post-Contemporary Interventions. Durham: Duke UP, 1991.

Jehlen, Myra. "The Family Militant: Domesticity Versus Slavery in *Uncle Tom's Cabin*." *Criticism* 31 (1989): 383–400.

Johnson, Barbara. "'Aesthetic' and 'Rapport' in Toni Morrison's *Sula*." *Textual Practices* 7 (1993): 165–72.

Kolmerten, Carol A., Steven M. Ross and Judith Bryant Wittenberg. *Unflinching Gaze: Morrison and Faulkner Re-Envisioned*. Jackson: UP of Mississippi, 1997.

Kramer, Barbara. *Toni Morrison: Nobel Prize-Winning Author*. African-American Biographies. Sringfield, NJ: Enslow, 1996.

Kreiswirth, Martin. "'Paradoxical and Outrageous Discrepancy': Transgression, Auto-Intertextuality, and Faulkner's Yoknapatawpha." *Faulkner in Cultural Context*. Ed. Donald M. Kartiganer and Ann J. Abadie. UP of Mississippi, 1997. 161–80.

Kristeva, Julia. *About Chinese Women*. Trans. Anita Barrows. London: Marion Boyars, 1977.

———. *Powers of Horror: An Essay on Abjection*. Trans. Leon S. Roudiez. New York: Columbia UP, 1982.

Lacan, Jacques. *Écrits: A Selection*. Trans. Alan Sheridan. New York: Norton, 1977.

Laplanche, J. and J.-B. Pontalis. *The Language of Psycho-Analysis*. Tran. Donald Nicholson-Smith. New York: Norton, 1973.

Lee, Dorothy H. "The Quest for Self: Triumph in the Works of Toni Morrison." Evans, 346–60.

Lepow, Lauren. "Paradise Lost and Found: Dualism and Edenic Myth in Toni Morrison's *Tar Baby*." *Contemporary Literature* 28 (1987): 363–377.

MacKethan, Lucinda H. "The Grandfather Clause: Reading the Legacy from 'The Bear.'" Kolmerten, Ross, and Wittenberg, 99–114

Marcus, Jane. *Virginia Woolf and the Languages of Patriarchy.* Bloomington: Indiana UP, 1987.

Mbalia, Doreatha Drummond. *Toni Morrison's Developing Class Consciousness.* Selinsgrove: Susquehanna UP, 1991.

———. "Women Who Run with Wild: The Need for Sisterhoods in *Jazz*." *Modern Fiction Studies* 39 (1993): 623–46.

McBride, Dwight. A. "Speaking the Unspeakable: On Toni Morrison, African American Intellectuals and the Uses of Essentialist Rhetoric." Peterson, 131–52.

McDowell, Deborah E. "Boundaries: Or, Distant Relations and Close Kin." Baker and Redmond, 51–77. 1989.

McKay, Nellie. "Introduction." *Critical Essays on Toni Morrison.* Boston: G. K. Hall, 1988. 1–15.

McKee, Patricia. "Spacing and Placing Experience in Toni Morrison's *Sula*." *Modern Fiction Studies* 42 (1996): 1–30.

Meriwether, James B. "Faulkner and the South." *The Dilemma of the Southern Writer.* Ed. Richard Meeker. Farmville, VA: Longwood College, 1961. 143–63.

Minakawa, Harue. "The Motif of Sweetness in Toni Morrison's *Song of Solomon*." *Kyushu American Literature* 26 (1985): 47–56.

Mitchell, Juliet. *Feminism and Psychoanalysis.* New York: Random, 1975.

Mobley, Marilyn E. "Narrative Dilemma: Jadine as Cultural Orphan in Toni Morrison's *Tar Baby*." *Southern Review* NS 23 (1987): 761–770.

Mohanty, Satya P. "The Epistemic Status of Cultural Identity: On *Beloved* and the Postcolonial Condition." *Cultural Critique* 24 (1993): 41–80.

Moi, Toril. *Sexual-Textual Politics: Feminist Literary Theory.* London: Routledge, 1985.

Moreland, Richard C. *Learning from Difference: Teaching Morrison, Twain, Ellison, and Eliot.* Columbus: Ohio State UP, 1999.

Mullen, Harryette. "Runaway Tongue: Resistant Orality in *Uncle Tom's Cabin, Our Nig, Incidents in the Life of a Slave Girl,* and *Beloved*." *The Culture of Sentiment: Race, Gender, and Sentimentality in Nineteenth-Century America.* Ed. Shirley Samuels. New York: Oxford UP, 1992.

Nadel, Alan. *Containment Culture: American Narratives, Postmodernism, and the Atomic Age.* New Americanists. Durham: Duke UP, 1995.

Nielsen, Aldon L. *Writing Between the Lines: Race and Intertextuality.* Athens: U of Georgia P, 1994.

Nissen, Axel. "Form Matters: Toni Morrison's *Sula* and the Ethics of Narrative." *Contemporary Literature* 40 (1999): 263–85.

Novak, Philip. "'Circles and Circles of Sorrow'": In the Wake of Morrison's *Sula*." *PMLA* 114 (1999): 181–93.

Nowlin, Michael. "Toni Morrison's *Jazz* and the Racial Dreams of the American Writer." *American Literature* 71 (1999): 151–74.

O'Donnell, Patrick. "Faulkner in Light of Morrison." Kolmerten, Ross, and Wittenberg, 219–27.

Ogunyemi, Chikwenye Okonjo. "Order and Disorder in Toni Morrison's *The Bluest Eye.*" *Critique* 19 (1977): 112–120.

O'Keefe, Vincent A. "From 'Other' Sides of the Realist Tracks: (A)gnostic Narratives in Toni Morrison's *Jazz.*" *Centennial Review* 41 (1997): 331–49.

Otten, Terry. *The Crimes of Innocence in the Fiction of Toni Morrison.* Columbia: U of Missouri P, 1989.

Page, Philip. *Dangerous Freedom: Fusion and Fragmentation in Toni Morrison's Novels.* Jackson: UP of Mississippi, 1995.

Paquet, Sandra Pouchet. "The Ancestor as Foundation in *Their Eyes Were Watching God* and *Tar Baby.*" *Callaloo* 13 (1990): 499–515.

Peach, Linden. *Toni Morrison.* Modern Novelists. New York: St. Martin's, 1995.

Peterson, Nancy, ed. *Toni Morrison: Critical and Theoretical Approaches.* Baltimore: Johns Hopkins UP, 1997.

Rampersad, Arnold. "Psychology and Afro-American Biography." Baker and Redmond, 194–208.

Renker, Elizabeth. "Herman Melville, Wife Beating, and the Written Page." *American Literature* 66 (1994): 123–50.

Rigney, Barbara Hill. *The Voices of Toni Morrison.* Columbus: Ohio State UP, 1991.

Rodrigues, Eusebio L. "Experiencing *Jazz.*" Peterson, 245–66.

Rubenstein, Roberta. "History and Story, Sign and Design: Faulknerian and Postmodern Voices in *Jazz.*" Kolmerten, Ross, and Wittenberg, 152–64.

Rushdy, Afhraf H. A. "Daughters Signifyin(g) History: The Example of Toni Morrison's *Beloved.*" *American Literature* 64 (1992): 567–97.

Ryan, Judylyn S. "Contested Vision/Double-Vision in *Tar Baby.*" *Modern Fiction Studies* 39 (1993): 597–621.

Said, Edward. *Orientalism.* New York: Random, 1978.

Samuels, Wilfred D. and Clenora Hudson-Weems. *Toni Morrison.* Twaynes' United States Authors Series. Boston: Twayne, 1990.

Scruggs, Charles. "The Nature of Desire in Toni Morrison's *Song of Solomon.*" *Arizona Quarterly* 38 (1982): 311–35.

Sedgwick, Eve Kosofsky. *Epistemology of the Closet.* Berkeley: U of California P, 1990.

———. *Tendencies.* Durham: Duke UP, 1993.

Smith, Barbara. *Toward a Black Feminist Criticism.* Brooklyn, NY: Out and Out Books, 1980.

Smith, Valerie. "The Quest for Discovery of Identity in Toni Morrison's *Song of Solomon.*" *The Southern Review* 21 (1985): 721–32.

Stockton, Kathryn Bond. "Heaven's Bottom: Anal Economics and the Critical Debasement of Freud in Toni Morrison's *Sula.*" *Cultural Critique* 24 (1993): 81–118.

Storace, Patricia. "The Scripture of Utopia." *New York Review of Books* 11 June 1998. 21 Oct. 1998 <http://www.nybooks.com/nyrev.WWWarchdisplay.cgi?1998061164R>.

Stowe, Harriet Beecher. 1852. New York: Dutton, 1909.

Tanner, Laura E. *Intimate Violence: Reading Rape and Torture in Twentieth Century Fiction*. Bloomington: Indiana UP, 1994.

Tate, Claudia. *Psychoanalysis and Black Novels: Desire and the Protocols of Race*. New York: Oxford UP, 1998.

Traylor, Eleanor W. "The Fabulous World of Toni Morrison's *Tar Baby*." In *Critical Essays on Toni Morrison*. Ed. Nellie Y. McKay. Boston: G. K. Hall, 1988. 135–150.

Wallace, Michele. *Black Macho and the Myth of the Superwoman*. New York: Dial, 1978.

Weinstein, Philip. *What Else But Love?: The Ordeal of Race in Faulkner and Morrison*. New York: Columbia UP, 1996.

Willis, Susan. "Eruptions of Funk: Historicizing Toni Morrison." *Black American Literature Forum* 16 (1982): 34–42.

Wittenberg, Judith Bryant. *Faulkner: The Transfiguration of Biography*. Lincoln: U of Nebraska P, 1979.

Wong, Shelley. "Transgression as Poesis in *The Bluest Eye*." *Callaloo* 13 (1990): 471–48.

Woolf, Virginia. *Mrs. Dalloway*. New York: Harcourt, 1925.

———. *A Room of One's Own*. 1929. New York: Harcourt, 1957.

Zwarg, Christina. "Fathering and Blackface in *Uncle Tom's Cabin*." *Novel* 22 (1989): 275–87.

Index